BYE
FOR
NOW

Thank you for ordering
my trilogy. I hope you
enjoy them as much as
I enjoyed writing them ♡

Bye for now,
Cindy

BYE
FOR
NOW

CINDY LYNCH

My Three Sons Publishing

Gramp's Camp

Published in the United States by
My Three Sons Publishing, LLC

mythreesonspublishing.com

ISBN: 978-0-9864476-0-0

Book cover design by: Ivan Terzic

Interior design by: Katie Mullaly, Faceted Press

Author's photo by: Sharisse Coulter

To Jack, Ian and Michael,

Dream big, believe in yourself and never give up.

You can achieve anything you set your mind to.

PROLOGUE

December 14, 2012

"Callie, it's been a long time since you've been in; have you been cheating on us?" Jenny asks with a smile as she takes my shoes and socks off my feet. "This water feel okay? Too hot, too cold?"

Gingerly, I submerge my feet in the tub. "Feels perfect, thanks."

I'd forgotten how nice this is. Beginning to relax now, I close my eyes, my head resting on the back of the plush salon chair. The TV is on for the patrons, but no one seems to take notice. Like the white noise played in a nursery to lull children to sleep, the drone of the TV begins to have the same effect on me. Lazily, I open one eye to have a look at what is being touted as breaking news. I glance at the screen, watching tragedy unfold.

There is something vaguely familiar about this scene, something that captivates, enthralls. As they break for commercials, I am confronted by the haunting image of a little girl staring at the camera. Her face is stained with tears streaming from haunting green eyes open wide with terror. I watch her curly, chestnut hair bounce at her shoulders as she is shepherded past century-old trees into a church. I feel as though I'm looking at a younger version of myself—right down to the freckles scattered across the bridge of her nose.

Then I see it. After a feeling of déjà vu, I realize that this is happening in my hometown. I can't breathe. "Sandy Hook

School Shooting" scrolls across the bottom of the screen. My stomach rolls and my hands begin to shake as my phone rings to life.

School shooting in Sandy Hook Elementary. Gunman Dead. The text is from my husband.

"Jenny, can you turn up the volume, please?" I can feel the panic rising in my voice. She uses the remote control to turn up the volume. I continue to sit and stare at the TV. On the screen: a police officer holding the hand of a confused first-grader and her frantic mother as he rushes them to safety. I recognize the parking lot and the school. Horror paralyzes me as the newscaster proclaims that twenty first-graders, along with six educators, were killed. Unable to contain my emotions, I weep openly. Jenny gazes with concern as I listen intently to the report.

"Police have set up a staging area at the Methodist church in Sandy Hook for parents to wait for word on their children..."

This is the church I attended through college. Pockets of time encapsulated in warmth, in love. Now, this place I hold so dear in my heart is a place of horrific sadness and uncertainty. My phone rings and my hands are shaking so badly that I can't seem to unlock it. I swipe at it frantically, to no avail, as it continues to ring. Seeing my frustration, Jenny discards her pedicure tools and reaches for my phone; she slides her finger across the screen so that I can answer the call.

"Hello?"

"Callie? It's Sandy." Her voice is fuzzy through the receiver, but calm. "Have you heard the news? How're you holding up, dear?"

"I'm not sure ... I'm in shock ... I just got a text from my husband. I need to get in touch with some friends." Annoyed with her disruption, I end the call without waiting for a response.

My family and friends who still live in Newtown, so close to the … what do you call it? Tragedy? Disaster? Multiple murder? None of these are adequate. I begin to text them.

Please tell me Prue is safe? I text my brother, Jimmy.

As I wait to hear word, I continue to text friends while thinking to myself, *No. No, no, no. God, please let Prue be safe. How can this be happening? And what about Mrs. Canfield?* A mental picture of her standing in front of a classroom of first-graders asserts itself, stark and full of horror.

The first text comes in from my high school friend, Sheilah, but still no word from Jimmy. *Hi, Cal. Kids are OK. Not the school my kids go to, but all schools were in a lockdown that has been lifted. So upsetting.*

Oh my God, I can't believe this. The place I called home is now on national news, not because of its New England beauty and style, but for this unimaginable tragedy. I'm caught in an undertow of emotion, flooded with memories of growing up in this quaint, Rockwellian town. I remember moving into the area with the babbling brook that ran through a town dotted with colonial style homes. I remember the ever-present Town Hall with the enormous flagpole smack-dab in the center of town. Directions would always begin with sayings like, "At the flagpole, make a left," or "You know where the flagpole is? Go past it and make a right."

There I was, meeting new friends while attending Newtown High School, joining the swim team, going to college and becoming an adult, doing normal things, living a normal life—something these beautiful babies and educators can no longer have. I feel a crushing sadness that I can't shake. The pain is so real, so intense my bones ache. A place deep in my soul begins to unravel. How does one move forward from this?

I continue to watch the images of children scrambling to safety past the beautiful white and green ash trees that stand as sentinels, offering shade in the summer months and coloring the town with their crimson and gold leaves in the fall. Seeing the magnificent landscape instantly floods my thoughts with memories of driving to Vermont with my family as a young girl to visit relatives. Watching the flagpole from the center of town recede in the distance would wash the stress of school away.

My fondest memories growing up were those times walking through the Black Forest with my dad, where rows of evergreens would greet us as we entered, and the perfume of pine would penetrate our sinuses. The canopy of trees shading us from the summer sun, yet through the filter, the sunlight would dance along the bark and on the carpet of needles shed by the trees. *Something these children will never experience.* As I sit here, anxiety ridden, numb, thirteen hundred miles from my hometown, I catch a glimpse of a turquoise shed as the camera sweeps across the scenery. I'm comforted by this image and how it connects me to my childhood. It instantly brings me back to a simpler time when my biggest concern was how I would spend my summer vacation in Franklin, Vermont with its sweeping pastures and friendly red barns on the countryside. We would drive to Gramp's camp past properties that grew fewer and farther between as the great expanse of farmland took over the landscape.

This familiarity seems to obscure the darkness of the day as I am bathed in the security of the past. In a fleeting instant, I felt that familiar rush of butterflies in my belly at the sight of the turquoise shed. It seems like an eternity ago…

CHAPTER 1

June 24, 1982

Seven hours. Four hundred and twenty minutes, really. Twenty-five thousand two hundred seconds, to be exact. That's how long it took us to get to my grandparents' cabin on Lake Carmi in Vermont, otherwise known as Gramp's camp. This was their home for the summer months, and during the winter, they stayed at their home in Franklin, Vermont. Navigating the windy Camp Road in the snow proved to be too difficult for my aging grandparents. Maybe next year, once I've had a year of driving under my belt, I could drive the family and cut that time to six hours thirty minutes. Humph.

"Callista Lamply, stop sighing. It's not going to get us there any faster," my mom chided while suppressing a yawn. I could tell she felt the same way that I did.

For years we'd been coming up here for family reunions and vacations. It seemed pretty fun most of the time. Meeting up with all the cousins and playing on the lake could be a trip. Many of them were at least ten years older than me. It felt strange; even though we were years apart in age, we almost always had a good time together.

My mind had wandered, and unlike most rides up here in the past, time had been flying until my thoughts were interrupted.

"Home again, home again, jiggity jog. I wonder who's home at the Lamplys' house?" my eternally optimistic mom chirped from the front seat.

We made our final right, descending onto the gravel, serpentine road. I saw the vast lake, little cabins dotting the shore like patches of fern and mahogany. The sun continued shining without a hint of humidity and the air felt crisp and clear. I rolled the window down and inhaled deeply—expanding my lungs with that fresh, clean Vermont air. I felt at peace.

We made a left at the water pump and pulled in behind Gramp's camp. My hand was on the door handle; I was just aching to get out to stretch my legs. Across the lawn, I saw Nanny and Gramp sitting on weathered lawn chairs next to the dilapidated swing set we used to play on many years ago. They waved and walked over. My brother and I jumped out simultaneously, without closing the car doors, and Stubby, our Chinese pug, jumped out after us, barking.

"Well, James, look how you've grown!" Nanny exclaimed. She examined him from head to toe and pinched his cheek. "You need to eat. Hungry?" This she said as if examining a patient in her office back when she worked as a nurse. She guided him inside the cabin as Gramp gave me a big, gentle hug and a scruffy kiss on my cheek.

"Well, Callie, it's good to see you again." The smell of Listerine wafted past my nose. Mom and Dad were close behind, and we all walked into the cabin as Dad scooped up Stubby.

It was past noon when I realized I was famished. We feasted on salad with fresh peppers, tomatoes, and cucumbers, and each of us inhaled the cheeseburgers that Gramp had grilled. Delicious.

After the dishes were done, we all discussed the water sport in which we were going to partake. Jimmy decided this happened to be a great opportunity to shake my confidence.

"You think you can master drop skiing this year? It didn't go so well for you last time you tried." He snickered.

"I would have done just fine if you hadn't yelled, 'Look out!' and pointed at the water in front of me," I said, jabbing him in the side. I resolved at that moment to conquer drop skiing.

We got the equipment ready and piled into the boat. My dad and mom served as captain and co-captain. My brother remained in the back with me. Dad backed the boat out and away from the dock, and with a wave of his hand, we were off.

When the boat came to a stop, my brother jumped into the lake with the skis floating at his side. He placed both skis on his feet. His plan was to make one pass around Rock Island and then to drop a ski, which he had perfected with little difficulty. He made a full sweep of the lake, going in and out of the wake gracefully. Eventually, he made the hand signal to stop.

"Great job! That was really good!" I enthused as he grinned from ear to ear.

"Your turn," he said, as I jumped in. The cold water caught me off guard, causing me to take several full breaths. Finally acclimating to the temperature, I slid both skis on and gave the go-ahead signal. The engine carried the boat and lifted me up and over into a graceful face-plant. *Ugh.* This appeared harder than I remembered. I looked up just in time to see my brother laughing heartily.

"James, don't laugh at your sister. She's trying her hardest to get up," my mom warned. Jimmy rolled his eyes.

I managed to swim back to the skis and put them on for round two, bound and determined to drop one ski successfully.

I had a wobbly start and managed to get up and around Rock Island, but as I made my approach for a ski drop, I could feel the death wobble coming on. I dropped the ski, but this time, instead of falling forward, I managed to fall right on my backside. Imagine having a fire hose aimed right at your bum while turned on maximum velocity—years later, my brother and I would refer to this as a lake enema—and you'll have an idea what it felt like. Persistent pain. Not only was I fishing out a major wedgie, I was also emptying lake water from my bowels. With a glance toward the boat, I realized my brother knew exactly what had happened. His shoulders were bouncing with laughter, like he'd just heard the most inappropriate joke.

I slowly ventured back to the boat. *Put a fork in me, I'm done.* My mom grabbed the skis and dropped the ladder into the water for me to climb aboard. I carefully sat next to my brother.

"Nice one. How's that water treating you?" he said, with uncontrollable laughter. At first I gave him the evil eye, but eventually, I just laughed at myself. As we came to the shore, my grandparents were hooting and hollering about how well *I* did. They were clapping and cheering for me and made no mention of how well my brother did. I loved the attention, but Jimmy looked at me and said, "What am I, chopped liver?"

CHAPTER 2

"Psst…Hey…Callie…wake up…"

I vaguely recognized the voice calling me. "Wha—Jimmy, it's like six o'clock in the morning. Wake me up in about three more hours."

"Hey…wake up. Come on. You gotta see this."

I stumbled out of bed and slugged my brother in the arm. "What is it?"

We went outside. At first I thought Jimmy wanted me to see the beautiful sunrise—vibrant yellow, red, and orange streaked across the sky—but then I looked over my left shoulder and saw Gramp sitting very still in his Adirondack chair. He had a bag of ballpark-style peanuts in his lap, and on his right arm sat a chipmunk. I quietly approached and whispered, "Gramp, what are you doing?"

"This is Chip, and Dale is too afraid to come close just yet, but don't worry; I'll get him over here."

He continued to roll a peanut around between his forefinger and thumb. Eventually, I saw Dale's head pop out from under the chair. He scampered toward Gramp and hopped on his left leg. He climbed into Gramp's lap and took the peanut from his fingers and proceeded to jam the nut, shell and all, into his cheek.

I'd never seen a chipmunk do that before. Astonished, I took a peanut from the bag to try for myself. Dale approached and grabbed the nut from my hand, and again, jammed the nut into his cheek. This little game went on for about forty-five minutes until Mom came out with a tray of breakfast food and coffee, scaring Chip and Dale away. Dad followed close behind, wearing his faded T-shirt and pajama bottoms, carrying two coffees. Handing one coffee to Gramp, Dad turned to me and asked, "So what's the plan for today, Cal?"

"I think I'll go for a run and check out the area, see if anything has changed around here. Maybe I'll go down the gravel road and stop in to see Aunt Doris."

ભ ભ ભ

I started my run slowly and took a left just past the water pump, turning toward Aunt Doris and Uncle Oscar's house. Big, fat, beautiful blackberries at the peak of ripeness dotted the vegetation along the side of the road. I made a mental note to go back that afternoon to pick some for a blackberry pie. Once I saw the familiar wooden DORIS & OSCAR'S CAMP sign nailed to a pine, I decided to run past Aunt Doris's house and continued down the road until it ended. Making a U-turn back to Gramp's camp, I spotted Aunt Marilyn out filling her bucket with blackberries and seemingly having a conversation with the berries. "... of course I can. She'll be open to it eventually, just not at the moment. These things take time."

"Aunt Marilyn? Everything all right?" Startled, she dropped her bucket and yelped, "Farfegnugen!"

"Oh man, I'm so sorry. I didn't mean to startle you. Here, let me help you pick those up."

"Callie, my girl, you gave my heart quite the start! Thank you, but it's not necessary. Come here. Put that bucket down and come give your favorite aunt a hug!"

Instantly, I put the berries in the bucket and set it back on the ground, walking into her welcoming arms. She smelled of baby powder, licorice, and patchouli—such a comforting smell, bringing on fond memories and warm feelings. "Well my goodness, you've gone and grown up on me."

"Well, it has been about a year. We just got in, and I needed to stretch my legs. Thought I would come down this way to see if anything had changed …who were you talking to just then?"

"Ha, oh, Callista, you know your aunt, she talks to everything," not giving me any information at all. "You should go finish your run before you start to cramp up. I'll see you real soon." She sent me off with a hug. Just out of earshot, her conversation resumed.

Once I passed Gramp's decades-long neighbor, Mr. Silk, my pace slowed to a walk and I waved. He waved back from his position on his dock, reading the paper with his trusty companion, Freckles.

At the end of the gravel road, behind Gramp's camp, stood the Black Forest. Over the years, this had been one of my favorite places to walk. Long ago, my dad had carved our initials in a tree with the date, and every year after that I had located the tree and carved the date under the one before.

The intoxicating perfume of pine relaxed me as I drew near. I walked past the Wilsons' house on my left. They lived in a huge, blue saltbox home with a large yard for five kids to play in. The Wilsons lived here year-round. Time and again I would enviously watch them all play volleyball in their front yard, laughing and hollering. Year after year I secretly wished they would come over and invite my brother and me to play. They never did.

I walked past the end of their property and climbed into the forest. Though it remained sunny outside of the forest, the pines choked out the light and enveloped me in darkness. I slowly walked past the first row of trees, touching the rough, damp bark, searching for my tree. Up ahead, a deer munched on the vegetation. As I got closer, I realized the deer was standing a short distance from my tree.

As my fingertips brushed over the splintered surface of the letters and numbers that had been left behind, I made a mental note to come back with my dad and carve in this year's date. The grace and beauty of the deer was captivating. Suddenly, she snapped her head up and seemed startled. As I turned to see the cause of the sound, a shadow quickly ran behind a tree. *Probably just Freckles coming to see what I'm up to.* Unfortunately, when I turned back, the deer was gone.

I continued to walk, now cooled off from my run, and managed to catch up to the deer again. She was ahead of me on the left, away from the lake, and I watched as she tenderly approached her fawn. *Breathtaking.*

A twig snapped behind me and startled the doe and fawn. They scampered. I was all alone now, in the middle of the forest. *I feel eyes on me.* Instantly, the hair on the back of my neck stood on end. This was fight or flight. I quickly made my way to the opening where I'd entered the forest. Not far from the Wilsons' home, the sounds of Freckles barking, splashing, and chasing after his beloved water toy reached me through the trees. As I left the forest and neared the Wilsons' yard, I surveyed my surroundings and once again glimpsed the shadow, disappearing behind a tree. *Okay, I'm outta here.* My pace picked up quickly; soon I was sprinting into the side yard of Gramp's camp. There my brother stood, just returning from the store with a brown bag stamped **Stewart's** on the front. That bag meant he bought live bait. It was precariously balanced on top of the tackle box that he had tucked under his left arm. The fishing rods were see-sawing in his right hand while he carefully closed the pump house door with his foot. "Ready for some fishing?" he hollered to me.

ભ ભ ભ

Using worms as bait, we managed to bring in a hefty load of fish: eleven perch, three bass, and of course, "the one that got away was thiiiis big." My favorite part of fishing was cleaning the fish: cutting into the base of the head and popping the air pocket with my thumb, pulling the skin back. Gross, yes, and bloody, but for some reason, I loved it. While I cleaned, my thoughts went back to the shadow I saw in the forest that morning.

I was lost in thought when my brother asked, "Where are you? You look like you're a million miles away."

"It's nothing," I said with a laugh. "I was just thinking about this place, that's all. Nanny and Gramp have owned this place for a long time. It seems weird that I'm really just now starting to like it here."

"Okay…that's deep," Jimmy said sarcastically.

"You're such a dork," I said, throwing a fish eye in his direction. Jimmy artfully dodged the projectile with a chuckle. The unfortunate move led Dad to fish out the eyeball from his ear, putting an end to our fun. With only one word, "Enough", we knew we had to start wiping up all the blood and guts and wrap the entrails in newspaper to deposit in a metal trash can specifically kept for this job. I brought the fourteen fish fillets in to Nanny, already heating oil in a pan on the stove. She put each fillet into cornmeal and gently placed them in the oil. In minutes, they were golden brown and, voilà, fried fish for lunch.

"Who's hungry?" I called out.

Nanny said, "You are!"

After lunch, Mom, Jimmy, and I decided to go blackberry picking. We brought along buckets and empty one-gallon milk jugs. We walked down the gravel road I had just run that morning and made a left at the water pump.

"Oh, Jimmy," Mom said in a singsong voice as she placed the milk jugs next to the pump. "Don't forget to fill these up with water on the way back to camp."

"Hey Mom, have you ever noticed anything weird about Aunt Marilyn?" I questioned tentatively.

"Other than her being a little eccentric, nothing comes to mind. Why do you ask?"

"Well, I saw her picking berries and... well, she was talking to them."

"Oh, that. Well, she's been talking to 'things' for years. She used to say that she would hear voices and those voices would communicate with her. It used to be quite shocking to encounter. Once Uncle Fred was so concerned, he said he was going to bring her to see a doctor. That frightened her, so she stopped. I'm surprised you saw that. She doesn't do that in front of people anymore."

We walked back down the driveway, our footsteps soft on the pine needles. We were about to place the blackberries on the ground near Aunt Doris's door when Uncle Oscar came out.

"Fred and Shirley are here and they brought Justa, so you prolly should put those buckets up high so as Justa won't get into 'em."

We moved the buckets to the top of his car in the driveway.

"Come on in. I'd ask if you want something to eat, but by the looks of it, you've had your share of blackberries already."

Happily, we walked through the screen door. Entering the cabin was like stepping back in time. The cabin hadn't changed over the past twenty years—exactly the reason why I loved coming here. Warmth emanated from this place, with the kitschy, eclectic knickknacks that seemed to give the room a friendly glow. Over the back of the old patchwork couch stretched an afghan that Aunt Doris had made. Next to the bathroom sat a miniature outhouse, about the size of a shoebox, made from colorful plywood, with a slot on top. On it, a sign read, PLEASE DEPOSIT FIVE CENTS. PAY TOILET. A large oil landscape painting with forest animals walking among pine trees occupied the wall above the couch.

Uncle Oscar brought us each a Dr. Pepper, and we drank them gratefully. When Mom excused herself to use the bathroom, Uncle Oscar brought over foot-long ropes of bubble gum.

"Quick. Put this somewhere for later." With a wink, he handed each of us a rope. I tried to stuff mine in a pocket, to no avail, and as Mom walked out of the bathroom, she just shook her head.

Our enjoyable visit with the aunts and uncles was winding down, and as I exited the cabin, I turned to Uncle Fred, "Why exactly did you name your dog Justa anyway?"

Characteristically, Uncle Fred responded with a shrug, "Because he's justa dog." I guffawed as we left the cabin.

Mom, Jimmy, and I picked up the buckets of blackberries and continued down the gravel road to the water pump. We were at Gramp's driveway when Mom gestured with her head, "Jimmy, water jugs."

"It's Callie's turn. I do it all the time," he whined.

"Fine," I said, exasperated. "Take my bucket, and you can help Nanny make blackberry pie."

He smiled and walked to the cabin with both buckets.

"Well, James, look how many berries you collected," I could hear Nanny exclaim through the screen door.

"Yep, it was all me," he said smugly, louder than necessary.

"Typical," I huffed under my breath. I went to the water pump, and right as I picked up the first jug, a red streak of light dashed behind Gramp's garage. *What the heck?*

After what I learned from my conversation with Mom and the uneasy feeling of being watched, my senses were on full alert. Slowly, I primed the pump, one eye on Gramp's garage. There were windows on the front and back of the structure, and when I looked in, I could see all the way through to the field behind. As the water started to flow, I placed one jug under the pump and noticed a crimson flurry in my peripheral vision. *There it is again.* But this time, I saw sandy blond hair attached to the light. This hide-and-seek continued as I filled the second jug and walked back to the cabin. Glancing in the direction of the garage, I could see someone smiling from behind my grandfather's beloved Cadillac.

CHAPTER 3

"Hey, Gramp. Do you ever have any of the Wilson kids get into your garage and…I don't know…work on your Cadillac or something?" I asked as I entered the camp.

"Oh, yeah. I have one of the Wilson boys take the riding mower out and cut down the tall grass around the garage and field. Every coupla weeks or so he'll do that, or when it's needed."

As if on cue, the riding mower started up and began to run back and forth across the tall grass. I went to the dining room in the back of the cabin, the room Gramp added on twenty years ago. It was a little off-kilter, but it had charm all the same. A wall of windows stretched across the back of the cabin, allowing for a great view of the field behind Gramp's camp and the Wilsons' yard.

As I set the table for dinner, I glanced outside and saw this blond kid, shirtless, riding the lawn mower. It must have been hot out there, because many times he took his shirt from where he tucked it in his waistband and wiped himself down. *Cute*, I thought. He looked to be about sixteen and pretty fit. I hadn't realized it, but I had stopped in the middle of setting the table.

I stood there, plate hovering over the table.

"Take a picture; it lasts longer," Jimmy quipped. He had come in with the bread and butter and caught me staring out the window. I felt my face flush, slammed the plate down and ignored him.

After dinner, Mom removed the blackberry pie from the oven and brought it, with dessert plates, to the table. The delicious aroma wafted through the room. We ate dessert and played cards, part of our summertime routine here at camp. Spades, rummy, spoons, it didn't matter which game; we were all involved, creating opportunity for great fun to laugh and play together.

The evening ended with coffee for the adults and dishes, once again, for the kids. I went outside after finishing the dishes, sat on one of the dilapidated lawn chairs and looked up to see the glow of a full moon. I loved the cast of moonlight across the lake in the evening.

The gravel crunched as footsteps approached, which surprised me, given the time. I watched as five teenagers walked by with towels in hand. They were all laughing and talking at once, walking toward the water pump. From the side yard, I could make out that one of them was the blond boy from earlier. They turned left as though heading down to Aunt Doris's house, but then made an immediate left. Soon after they made the turn, I heard a splash, followed by peals of laughter.

I got off the chair, thinking about the kids, when a figure sprang toward me. "BLAHHHH!!" I screamed, and my brother laughed so hard that he doubled over. I'd been so intent on seeing who was in the group that I hadn't noticed Jimmy sneaking up on me from the other side of the cabin.

"Holy crap, you idiot! You scared the crap outta me!"

"Yeah, that's the point," he said, still laughing. "What're you doing out here?"

"Nothing, just looking at the stars and stuff." I heard a splash and more laughter.

"Who's that?" Jimmy asked, heading toward the sound.

"Not sure. I think maybe some of the Wilsons are going for a night swim." I acted uninterested and began walking back inside. "Really? You don't wanna check it out?" He continued to walk toward the pump house that held our water skis, extra gas cans, and fishing gear at the top of Gramp's dock. I turned to follow. We walked down the rickety wooden steps and sat on the dock watching the teenagers swing over and into the lake from a long rope three camps down.

"I never noticed that before," I exclaimed, yet I felt the tug of a distant memory: my mom mentioning something about a rope swing years ago.

"Me either. Wonder how long that's been there?"

We watched for about twenty minutes, then decided we'd seen enough and walked back to the cabin.

"Night, Jimmy." Exhausted, I went to bed.

My bedroom was situated in the back, just off the dining room on the left-hand side. It held a twin bed, too small for my growing body, shoved against the wall. When not slept in, the bed doubled as a sofa. The stiff bedspread, flanked by a bed-length pleather wedge that leaned against the wall, maintained its shape when you lifted it up to get into bed.

The room felt stuffy, so I propped the window open using a stick from outside (our high-tech way of allowing fresh air into the room). Trying to read my V.C. Andrews book in the lamplight, I quickly realized that my eyes weren't going to cooperate. Unable to stay awake, I turned the light off and dozed. Just about to fall into a deep sleep, I heard footsteps approaching outside. People were talking softly as they walked by, and I could make out some of the conversation.

"… I don't know who she is, but I saw her earlier today while out mowing for Mr. Lamply. Must be his granddaughter. She's definitely not from around here."

Oh my God. They're talking about me.

"I think she has a brother, too. It looked like they just got here the other day."

"Come on, Earp, really? You don't know who she is? Don't you remember little "Callie-flower?"

"What are you talking about? Callie-flower?" Earp asked, annoyed.

"Yeah, you used to call her that when she was like five. A few times we had cookouts in the yard and the Lamply and Silk families came by. One particular cookout, someone brought over a tray of veggies and she was all over the cauliflower, dipping it in ranch dressing. At one point, she had dressing all over her face and someone said, 'She looks just like a piece of cauliflower!' and you started giggling, shouting 'Callie-flower!, Callie-flower!' You must have been six-ish at the time."

"Geez, I don't remember that at all. No wonder she acts like she doesn't see me."

Laughing, Earp's sister said, "Yeah, I wouldn't be the first person to acknowledge that memory either."

As the voices trailed off, I let the air out of my lungs. My mind was racing now. How embarrassing. I truly did not remember that nickname, or the blond-haired boy, for that matter. *How could I have blocked that from my mind?*

CHAPTER 4

I woke up on the later side of morning to the sound of a lawn mower. I knelt on my bed and looked out the side window to see Earp at it again. *Earp, was it? What kind of name is that? I wondered.*

Following the same routine as I had the last few lazy days—a whole lot of nothing—I put my running shoes on and ran down the gravel road past the water pump. I felt eyes on me as I neared the pump. My heart was racing, not from the running, but because I knew this Earp character was watching me. Without turning my head, I looked at him up in the field. He sat on the now-idling mower, looking in my direction as I ran past about two hundred yards below him. He took a drink from a water bottle as I ran toward my aunt's house.

Finally, my heartbeat slowed and my breathing began to sync with my run. Justa ran up to greet me with some kisses as I neared my aunt's cabin. I slowed briefly to give him a friendly scratch behind the ears before heading for home. At the crossroad, I noticed the rope swing swaying in the breeze. It behaved like it wanted me to investigate. Slowing to a trot, I walked between two camps to see the remnants of a fire—stones placed in a circle near the rope swing. The swing seemed quite a distance from the water and would make for a scary jump, especially at night.

Back on the gravel road, I prepared to finish my run in hopes of seeing 'Earp' again. At the end of the road, I stepped from gravel onto pine needles, and, as I approached my tree, I saw a carving I hadn't noticed before, "WW."

Well, certainly I have the wrong tree, I thought. Then I looked more thoroughly and found that our initials and dates from years past were on the other side. I circled around the tree again to place my fingers on the *WW* carving. I could smell sap running from the wounded trunk. As I came around the tree a second time, with my back to the lake, I could see Earp quickly approaching—walking into the forest with a blonde girl. She looked like she could be his sister.

Crap, where do I go now? Feeling embarrassed from overhearing their conversation about me last night, I moved to a tree closer to the lake and froze, watching.

"See, this is the tree I was telling you about. She comes here every day and looks at this thing."

"Well, maybe she has some weird connection with the tree." The girl placed her fingers over the two Ws and said, "Wyatt Wilson. Come on, Earp. Leave the tree alone. What's your next move? Why don't you just go over to the camp and say 'Hey Callie-flower, remember me?' That seems like as good an icebreaker as any."

"Ha, yeah. Just stop it. It's not that simple. She won't even look my way." They rounded the tree and saw our initials, *RL, BL, JL, CL.*

"It is that simple. You're just being a big chicken. Come on, Earp. I'm heading back." She got a head start and had almost made it back to the house when he yelled, "You know I really hate when you call me that!"

I smiled, listening to the banter between the two of them.

"Callie-flower…you certainly have grown up," he whispered to himself as he touched each of the initials. When Wyatt was nearly back on his property, I decided to leave my hiding spot. Apparently I left too soon, because he spotted me from his perch on the deck of his house, looking like he'd seen a ghost.

ભ   ભ   ભ

My heart was pounding. *Get it together.* Lunch preparations were being made as I entered the cabin, and there was talk of going to the state park. After lunch, my brother and I packed ourselves into my grandfather's Cadillac, while my mom and dad followed in Dad's Impala. The twenty-minute drive around the lake led us past many of our relatives' homes. Nanny pointed out the house her mother, my great-grandmother Julia, was born and raised in and told us how the house had burned down many years ago. She continued with another story about Aunt Marilyn's best friend, Elizabeth, who lived on that road. "She lived right here. Funny sort. Had a real funny way of talking. Obviously not from these parts; Scottish, I think she was."

At the park, we broke out our beach paraphernalia and set up our spot. The roped-off swimming area collected many of us as we floated and lounged for a few hours. Several groups of young people played nearby with their families, but not the young person I wanted to see.

Nanny looked at her watch, declared, "It's happy hour!" and pulled out her shaker, gin, vermouth, maraschino cherries, and martini glass. How and when she packed all of this amazed me. She shook up her concoction and poured it into her favorite martini glass. My parents each opened beers, and Jimmy and I had sodas. "Cheers! Here's to summer!" We enjoyed the beach and each other's company awhile longer and soon we began to pack up. I could see Gramp's camp from the beach and thought, *that doesn't seem so far away.* "Hey, Jimmy, I bet we could swim to this beach from camp."

"Yeah, probably. It looks like it's about a mile away. You should try it."

"What do you mean *me*?"

"I haven't been in swimming shape in years. Nobody wants to see all this in a Speedo. I'll take the canoe out if you want to try it."

Hmmm. That sounded like a good challenge for tomorrow.

Later in the evening, Dad took Mom, Jimmy, Nanny, Gramp, and me for a sunset cruise around the lake at dusk—my favorite time for cruising.

"You know, they never did catch the Lake Carmi monster," Gramp said with a twinkle in his eye.

I played along. "Oh yeah, is that so?"

"Many have reported seeing her spiky spine above the surface of the water. Over the years, there have been multiple sightings, but only one caught on film. Some say she's over a hundred feet long with a massive head the size of a VW bus."

I'd heard this story for as long as I could remember. The familiarity made me smile, yet still, even after all these years, I felt slightly uneasy as I looked out over the rippling water.

We continued to boat around past Aunt Doris and Uncle Oscar's cabin. They waved from their dock, out enjoying the night, as well. We took a spin past the state park and continued on until we got to the end of the lake. We docked the boat at a family-owned ice cream shop/convenience store called Stewart's. The Stewart family had owned this place for decades.

The bell on the door rang as we stepped inside. The smell inside was musty and stale, but the ice cream was cool and refreshing, same as ever. Behind the counter, a girl who looked to be a little older than Jimmy, greeted us with a smile.

"Hi, can I help you?" She asked everyone, though she was only looking at Jimmy. "I'll have a chocolate chip cone, please." Jimmy said, blushing in awe of the girl.

We enjoyed our sweet treats on our ride back to camp, and during the ride, I asked Dad about the girl behind the counter. He told me about the Stewart family.

"Her name is Riley Stewart. She lives with her grandmother and her younger sister, Megan. Together they run the family business."

"Why aren't her parents running the store if it's a family business?" I quizzed.

At this point, Jimmy began listening with intent.

"Well, tragically, both Riley's parents have passed away. Riley's paternal grandmother, Margaret Stewart, now has custody of the two girls. Even though Riley is eighteen and legally able to live on her own, she chooses to live in her grandmother's cabin down by Aunt Doris and Uncle Oscar."

As the boat pulled into Gramp's dock, Dad slowed the engine and instructed Jimmy on how to dock the boat, which Jimmy did by raising the lift. Although a little rusty, he managed to get it done, and Dad smiled at his accomplishment.

CHAPTER 5

Exhausted from the day's activities, I called it a night. I dreamed of dragons and sea monsters and a certain blond-haired boy…

I woke with a start; my heart pounding, my breath ragged. Darkness filtered in through the window, but feeling clammy and as though I couldn't breathe, I ventured outside for some air. The view from the dock stairs was magnificent; the moon bright and the lake calm. A luxurious, cool breeze flitted off the lake as I lay down on the dock and breathed deeply.

I heard a splash to my right and noticed a young couple jumping into the water. As I turned my head to the sound, I recognized the girl from behind the counter at Stewart's. She was a pretty girl with blue eyes, freckles, and wavy brunette hair down her back.

They didn't see me lying on the dock. I tried to remain as still as possible so they wouldn't notice me, fascinated by the way they were playfully swimming around each other. Going under, the boy pretended that something had ahold of his leg, and then popped up laughing. She giggled. The water lapped at his waist as he pulled her into his arms. They began to kiss, slowly at first. Then her hands moved down his back and around his waist, lingering at his waistband.

I shouldn't be watching this…

He reached for the bottom of her tank top, and with one fell swoop, pulled it up and over her head, tossing it to shore. With one hand, he masterfully unhooked her bra and flung it aside. He gently moved her back away from him, as if to drink her in. She smiled shyly and reached for his belt loop, using it to yank him forward and causing them to fall back into shallow water. He steadied himself above her, one arm stabilizing him and the other working to remove her shorts.

I can't believe what I'm watching. It was getting pretty heated, and I decided they needed privacy, so I quietly got up off the dock and headed for the stairs. Apparently being stealthy isn't my forte. I had almost reached the steps before I realized the splashing had stopped. I stood still, moving only my eyes left to see two sets of eyes staring back at me. No need to be stealthy anymore. I ran up the stairs and into the camp. Quickly moving to the back of the cabin, leaping from the entrance of my room, I hopped into bed and covered my head. *I really hope they didn't recognize my face.* I closed my eyes; visions of their bodies floating on the lake filled my mind.

I woke up anxious and needed to run. Without thinking, I put on my running clothes. Too anxious to perform the run-of-the-mill morning routine around the cabin, I decided to run up the gravel road to the top of the hill, making a right onto the six-mile loop through Franklin. I ran past the dairy farm, inhaled the smell of cow...cow everything. *The joys of staying in the country.* I tried to hold my breath past the stench as I continued onto the main road.

My head was still swimming with what I'd witnessed last night. *What if they saw me? They did. I know they did. What if they call me out, confront me?*

I ran a little faster along the road through Franklin, past what must have been the most ramshackle building in the country, and wondered how it could possibly still be standing. At the fork, I turned left onto Lake Road when a red pickup came up from behind me and slowed to make the same turn. I looked at the people in the truck and saw familiar faces staring back at me. The vision of them in the lake came to mind as they continued to stare me down while driving slowly past.

My face reddened. *Sheesh. What have I gotten myself into?* I rounded the corner, passed the vegetable farm and turned right at the top of Camp Road. Partway down the hill, I made a left at the pump and continued all the way to my tree. I saw the red pickup truck parked at the Wilsons' as I slowly walked past to my tree and stretched. Leaning with one hand on my tree, I pulled my left foot up to stretch my hamstring. The lake was "working" today. The algae slithered its way to the surface, and unless you wanted to be covered in green goo, it wasn't ideal for swimming.

"Um…hey," I heard from behind me.

Startled, I nearly fell over. "Uh, hi," I said, looking directly at the most amazing blue eyes I had ever seen in my life. Earp stood wearing athletic shorts, flip-flops, and a well-loved T-shirt with holes sporadically scattered throughout. His clothes were covered with dirt. He wore work gloves, and he carried brush and twigs that had been cut from the ground. Only then did I notice that the undergrowth around my tree had been cleared.

"What are you doing with all that?" I asked curiously.

His face flushed, his cheeks taking on an adorable shade of pink just below the cheekbones.

"Um, well…I noticed you come here just about every day, and I thought it must be hard to get to the tree with all this to climb over. I just thought I'd clear it out a bit…I had to do some clearing out here for my pop anyway, so it was no big deal."

"Thanks."

"Don't mention it. My name is Wyatt," he smiled uncomfortably, while removing his glove and extending his hand. I took his hand and felt his rough and callused skin.

"Callie. Nice to meet you." I stepped back and took my right ankle into my hand to stretch my hamstring. I reached out, looking at the tree, and placed my left hand on my family's initials. I could feel his eyes on me in the uncomfortable silence.

"Well, I should take care of this and let you finish up. See you 'round… Callie-flower," he said with a fond snicker.

I lifted my eyes, unsure if I'd heard him correctly. Embarrassed with the reference to my childhood nickname, I decide to retaliate. "Thanks again … Earp"

Looking up at me in disbelief, he said, "Ha, touché! Don't mention it … really … if my sister gets wind of this, she'll never let me live it down. She's relentless."

With an armload of brush, he walked off and left me smiling. He dumped it into the barrel-fire he had smoldering in his backyard. That's what folks around here did with anything they wanted to get rid of. A comfortable sigh escaped me. *My how you've grown up, Earp.*

CHAPTER 6

When I got back to the cabin, everyone had just begun getting up for the day. No need for a watch—we were in vacation mode, or as I like to call it, Vermont time. The only person that got up earlier was Gramp. He had settled into his Adirondack chair with a bag of peanuts, and judging by the number of peanut shells on the ground, he'd been up for several hours.

"Morning, Gramp."

"Mornin."

I walked past him; saw Nanny sitting in her lawn chair a few feet away.

"Morning, Callie. How was your run?"

"It was good. Where is everyone?"

"Oh, your mom and dad went into town, and Jimmy is out fishing with Aunt Marilyn already. They wanted to get an early start. Jimmy said that if you want to swim later on, he'll have the canoe ready." I smiled at the thought of Aunt Marilyn being here for the day. Aunt Marilyn is, by far, my favorite relative.

"Okay, cool. Thanks. I think I'm gonna float on the lake awhile."

"Are you sure that's such a good idea, young lady? The lake is working," warned Gramp.

"Yeah, I noticed that. I'm willing to take my chances."

I changed into my swimsuit, grabbed a large float, and began to blow it up. The sandy slope between Mr. Silk's and Gramp's camps appeared to be thinning; eroding over time. When Jimmy and I were little, Gramp used to bring in several loads of sand every summer to create a beach for us. Sadly, as Jimmy and I grew, we didn't really have a use for a beach anymore. Over the years, it had eroded away, exposing the rocks beneath.

I tried my best to climb onto the float without collecting too much algae on my skin. With a firm hold on the end of the dock, I lay still in the lake. The sun shone brightly, the water was cool. I closed my eyes. I was startled by a sudden splash as Stubby jumped from the dock and dog paddled toward my raft. I grabbed him, helped him up, and we floated happily together.

After my soak in the water and sun, I climbed out of the lake and sat outside the cabin, watching the day go by with Stubby by my side. His head rested on my lap as I pet his velvety, soft black ears and removed green residue from his fur. Across the lake, I could see cars filing in, indicating a busy day at the state park. With a contented sigh, Mom came to sit with me. "Soooo, what's the plan today?"

"I think when Jimmy gets back, I'm going to swim, and he's going to canoe next to me, to the state park."

"Hmmm. Please be careful. Stay close to the canoe. Some of these people on the lake just don't pay any attention to what's going on around them." She leaned over and pulled a long strand of green goo off my shoulder.

"I know, Mom. It'll be fine," I said, pulling more slime from my legs. If she had her way, my brother would be canoeing with a PA system to announce my arrival. We watched many boats go by; some with water skiers, some with tubes.

Hours passed. Finally, Aunt Marilyn and Jimmy returned, and by the looks on their faces, we weren't going to be having a fish fry for dinner. I stood and climbed down the stairs to the dock to help Jimmy tie up the boat. Aunt Marilyn took my hand and stepped out of the boat with her fishing rod as Jimmy cleaned up. I grabbed the fish bucket and saw that there were only two fish; one was a good sized bass and the other a tiny perch. Nothing to write home about.

"Wow, good thing we didn't rely on you guys for dinner," I winked at Aunt Marilyn.

"You just never know what you're going to get out there," Aunt Marilyn complained.

Jimmy just grumbled.

"You ready to canoe?" I asked.

"Are you kidding? I just spent six hours in this boat trying to catch something, anything! Those two fish you see, I didn't catch either one. So, no. No, I don't want to go out in another boat. Maybe tomorrow."

Grumble, grumble. *He's such a crab.* I turned to walk inside just in time for happy hour. Nanny had her concoction poured, then made one for Aunt Marilyn. All the adults sat outside and enjoyed their drinks. Jimmy sat in his chair in a funk. *Looks like I won't be swimming across the lake today.* I opted for a shower instead.

When I returned, happy hour was in full swing. I brought out the lawn darts from the hall closet and set up the game. "Hey, Jimmy, come over here," I hollered.

He sulked over, still bummed about the failed fishing trip. Blue lawn darts in hand, he played without saying a word. I sent curious glances his way several times before I finally spoke.

"How about that rope swing down the road past the pump? It's funny, I remember Mom and Dad talking about it, but I never went down to check it out."

In mid-throw he replied, "Yeah."

"Do you know any of those Wilson kids?"

"No."

Sheesh. This was going to be harder than I thought. It was my turn, and I threw my red dart right in the middle of the hoop for the win. Jimmy glared and collected his darts, eager to restart the game. He was not going to give up until he won. That could take a while, so I attempted to continue my one-sided conversation.

"The other night, I couldn't sleep; I went down to the dock to cool off. Lying on the dock, I heard some people jump into the lake." I finally had his attention.

"And?" He turned to look at me, his dart frozen in mid-throw.

"Well, I think it was the oldest Wilson boy. He was with that Riley girl who works at the ice cream shop."

Now I had his *full* attention. He put the darts down. "What do you mean, they were *together*? What were they doing?"

Blushing, I tried to continue with the game, but Jimmy wanted details.

"What were they *doing*?" he repeated.

"Well, it was dark. I couldn't see very well."

"Callie, just tell me what they were doing."

"I was sitting on the dock about fifty yards away, but in the dark, it looked like they really liked each other. It was so dark, I don't know. They started making out. Clothing was tossed aside. Did I mention it was *really* dark?"

Dead silence. He dropped the darts, walked away. I started after him. "Hey, what's going on?" He didn't answer; just kept walking. I stopped at our property line and watched as he marched down the gravel road, making a left at the water pump and disappearing.

CHAPTER 7

"Hey, Cal, could you walk Aunt Marilyn back to Aunt Doris and Uncle Oscar's cabin for me?" Mom whispered out of Aunt Marilyn's earshot, "She got a little too happy during happy hour and needs some assistance walking."

Aunt Marilyn stumbled across the yard. I grabbed her arm and started walking with her, arm in arm, in the direction of the cabin she occasionally shared with Uncle Oscar and Aunt Doris.

"Aunt Marilyn, what did you and Jimmy talk about on the boat all day? Did he mention anything about a girl?"

"Ahh, Riley. Yep, he did mention her today. He told me he was having girl trouble with a cute little thing who works at Stewart's. He really likes her and thought they were starting to hit it off, but he's been seeing that Wilson boy around the shop a lot lately. That's really bothering your brother." Teetering, nearly falling to the ground, she mumbled to herself, "God bless America, I can't seem to walk in a straight line…"

Ignoring her comment, I continued, "Wow, that's some conversation. No wonder he was such a grump when you guys returned." I hugged Aunt Marilyn at her cabin door.

Opening the screen door, she turned with a far-away look in her eye. Looking just over my head, she spoke softly. As sober as a judge, she said, "I know, but now's not the time." "Not time for what?" I nervously questioned. As if coming out of a trance, our eyes met, and between hiccups, she said, "Oh, just Travis putting a bug in my ear. Next time remind me to stick to beer." The hair on the back of my neck stood up.

Leaving Aunt Marilyn, I racked my brain trying to come up with whom she might be speaking. *Herself? Dare I say a spirit? Sheesh, knock it off.* Then, as I approached Riley's driveway, I heard Jimmy's voice and stopped to listen. He stood holding her screen door open. "Really, Riley? I thought you said you liked me! Is that how you show someone you like them? Go and get all hot and heavy with another guy? *REALLY?*"

Riley tried to calm him down. "Jimmy, I *do* like you, but I like Tyler, too. You and your family only come up here during the summer, and Tyler lives here year-round. How can I really get involved if you're never here? I see Tyler all year. How can you expect me to wait for your visit?"

"I just thought I meant more to you. Obviously not." He slammed the screen door, and as he marched down the driveway, he halted when he spotted me.

"Jimmy—"

He cut me off. "I don't want to talk about it," and charged past me toward the water pump.

ରେ ରେ ରେ

In the morning, I got up and walked into the kitchen to the tapping of rain on the roof. No one else had arisen yet. I walked past my parents' room and heard my dad snoring. Through the curtain that served as their bedroom door, I noticed that Mom was awake and reading in bed. I popped my head in. "Mornin," I whispered. She smiled and waved me into the room, patting the bed next to her. I was a little girl all over again, hopping into bed with my parents. We sat there quietly listening to the rainfall. I looked up at the shoe prints on the ceiling. Mom followed the direction of my gaze.

"Do you remember when you were a little girl and Dad used to tell you stories about a man who would come to the cabin while we were sleeping and walk on the ceiling?" I quietly laughed. "Yeah, I totally believed him. Not once did I ever think that those were the footprints of the workers who built the cabin." I felt so content sitting there, laughing with my mom.

From the other side of the bed, my dad emitted a sleepy chuckle. As he rolled onto his back, he chided, "You believed me hook, line, and sinker." Surrounded by the love of my parents in this minute bubble of happiness, I didn't want it to end ... but then mister grumpy pants got up.

The morning slowly rolled along, the rain periodically heavy, then tapering off after lunch. Jimmy got the canoe out and went down to the lake. I followed him outside and watched as he slid the canoe into the water.

"Cal, you wanna swim today? Canoe's ready."

"Sure," I replied as I ran back inside. Suit, cap, goggles; I was ready in an instant.

I tucked my hair under my cap and jumped off the end of the dock as Jimmy steadied himself in the canoe. My body felt stiff from sitting around the cabin all morning, and stretching, I tried to work out the kinks. The sun broke through the clouds and warmed my back as I swam toward Rock Island. My muscles warmed, and just past the island, I felt myself getting into a groove. Every twenty-five strokes or so, I lifted my head to make sure I stayed on course. Jimmy paddled diligently beside me, keeping me safe from harm. Halfway, my fingers brushed something that slithered, and I froze. I surfaced, scanning the surrounding lake for trouble.

"Aaaah, what's that?" I screamed.

Jimmy just laughed. "Oh yeah, didn't you hear? They spotted that Lake Carmi monster out here today."

Even though I knew he was joking with me, I couldn't help but think about a gigantic aquatic monster swimming beneath me. Dark tentacles. Strange layers of teeth. I picked up my pace until I could see the state park clearly. One hundred more strokes and I would reach the swimming buoy and rope. I ducked under as Jimmy continued to shore, since the swimming area remained empty, thanks to the rain. Tired but pleased with myself for making the mile swim, I helped Jimmy drag the canoe onto the beach. We grabbed the towels from the boat and lounged on the damp sand.

"Thanks," I offered, "for coming with me today."

"No problem. It was fun."

Content, we sat in silence for a bit. But I had to ask, "So, what are you going to do about Riley?"

"Boy, you just don't give up, do you?" he half joked. "Not much to do. She's obviously chosen the guy she wants." He got up and sort of ambled toward the shoreline, stooping to gather smooth rocks. Smiling, I started collecting rocks, as well. The first one I threw skipped three times over the water. He threw next, and it skipped six times. We continued for a while; picking up a few rocks, skimming them across the water and repeat— one of our favorite lake activities.

"Well, her loss," I said as I walked back to my towel. He continued skipping rocks as people started to crowd the beach.

"Hey, I don't really feel up to swimming back. Mind if I get in the canoe? Either you can strip down to your skivvies and swim back or we can paddle back together."

As we were getting the canoe back into the lake, I heard a familiar voice behind me.

"Leaving so soon?"

I put my end of the canoe down and turned to look into those crystal blue eyes. "Uh, yeah, we gotta get back."

"Too bad…we were just gonna get a game of volleyball going. Later on we're gonna have a bonfire with some friends. If you don't have anything going on tonight, you should come by."

I glanced at my brother, who looked my way suspiciously.

"Oh, hey, Wyatt, this is my brother, Jimmy."

"Hey, man, good to meet you," he said, extending his hand toward my brother.

"Hey," Jimmy said, and picked up the canoe again.

"See you later?" Wyatt said to me.

"Yeah, I don't think I can, but thanks." Paddling away, I glanced over my shoulder to see Wyatt waving as he picked up the volleyball at his feet.

"So when did you start hanging out with that Wilson kid?"

"I'm not *hanging out* with him. I just met him a few days ago."

"Just be careful; those Wilson kids are no good." Still sore about Wyatt's brother stealing Riley's attention, he continued with his advice, "If I were you, I'd just keep my distance from him."

CHAPTER 8

"Who's up for an evening ride on the boat?" Dad asked later in the evening; immediately I jumped up. Tonight it was my dad, Gramp, and me on the boat. We rode around Rock Island, past Aunt Doris's house and around the state park.

The sun had begun to set, but I could see people on the beach stacking logs in the twilight. Excited cheers accompanied an eruption of flames as they lit the first fire of the night. About fifteen people were on the beach, and several more cars were coming down the path. That little green head of envy began to emerge in me.

Wyatt's blond hair glowed in the firelight as he stacked more wood to start the next bonfire. He looked up, hearing the sound of our boat, but turned away when a tall brunette ran up to him and gave him a giant bear hug. Before I could see what happened next, we were off. We made a few more turns before reaching camp. Deep in thought, I didn't listen to Gramp and Dad talking. Dad docked the boat and they continued their conversation as I got out and went up the stairs to sit and look out across the lake. I watched the flames continue to burn and listened to the soft music carrying across the lake. *He has a girlfriend.* I drew my legs in and rested my chin on my knees. *Humph.*

The next morning, I got up early and stretched my legs before my run through Franklin. Coming up to the left turn onto Lake Road, a cramp developed in my left calf, and I slowed to a walk in order to stretch. Once I'd worked it out, I continued the remainder of my run. Just past the vegetable garden, I landed precariously on a loose rock and turned my left ankle. *Crap, I still have about a mile to go.* I sat on the side of the road and assessed the damage. My ankle had already turned purple and begun to swell. Getting up, I tried to hobble home, but every step hurt worse than the last. The hum of an engine approached from behind me. I moved to the side of the road and noticed the truck slowing.

"You okay?" It was Wyatt's older brother, Tyler, by himself in his red pickup.

"I'm fine," I said nervously, really not wanting help from my brother's nemesis.

"You don't look fine; you look like you have a purple softball stuck to the side of your leg."

"It's not that bad. I'm good, thanks."

"Suit yourself." And he took off down the road.

I continued to hobble toward the turn up ahead. After what seemed like an eternity, I finally started to descend Camp Road. The familiar hum of the lawn mower greeted me, and down the road, Wyatt stood talking to Tyler through the truck window. The truck moved on, as did the lawn mower, but to my surprise and delight, the mower proceeded up the field toward me. Wyatt pulled the riding mower onto the gravel road, stopped, jumped off, and quickly came to my aid.

"Come on. Let me give you a lift the rest of the way." He put his arm around me and helped me get on the mower. He drove through the field, making a beeline toward camp.

"What happened to you? Tyler said your ankle looked pretty bad to him, but you were being stubborn and refused a ride. He asked me to come up here and get you."

"It's nothing. I twisted my ankle on a rock. No biggie."

We reached Gramp's drive, where Wyatt stopped the mower to help me off and into a lawn chair. Gramp came out to investigate, and Wyatt explained what happened.

"Thanks for helping, Wyatt," Gramp said, dismissing him. Gramp called Nanny out to examine my ankle, and just as I thought, it was only a sprain. I sat in the rickety lawn chair with my foot resting on a bag of ice wrapped with an ace bandage to keep it in place. The lawn mower started up again, and I turned to see that Wyatt had gone back to finishing up the field.

I remained out of commission for the next few days, and I spent my time icing my foot, reading, and floating in the lake with my loyal companion, Stubby. By day three, I realized that the next day was the Fourth of July, the date of our annual family reunion with the big fireworks display. *All that and I'm stuck with a purple ankle. Great,* I thought.

The cabin exuded excitement. My grandparents prepared the food while my parents cleaned the cabin to make it presentable. I, on the other hand, remained useless; I sat with a dark cloud over my head, watching the excitement unfold around me. I decided, in my funk, to pass up my evening ride on the lake due to my throbbing ankle. I hobbled from room to room, and eventually, at the end of the day, exhaustion set in. Frankly, I felt frustrated and just plain angry with myself, so I sulked into my room to continue my personal pity party.

Suddenly, I woke with a bang. Literally. Firecrackers were going off in the field behind the cabin, and as I scrambled to look out the back window, I noted Tyler was the one setting them off, with Riley next to him, laughing. Not cool! It wasn't even ten in the morning.

I swung my legs off the side of the bed and found, to my delight, that my ankle didn't hurt as badly. I could actually walk with a normal gait. Woo-hoo! One small victory helped to elevate my mood. Grabbing a leash to take Stubby for a walk, I hollered, "Here, boy! Stubby! Master Stubbing." He snorted over on his tiny legs, his curly tail bouncing behind him. Our beloved, aging Stubby belonged to Dad. I swear my dad loved that dog more than life itself, and from what I could tell, the feeling was mutual.

I put the leash on Stubby and we set out. To my surprise, it was after ten, and it was a warm, sunny day. We traveled in the usual direction down past Aunt Doris's and then turned back. I took Stubby into the Black Forest, walking easily now that the area had been cleared. As we walked up to my tree, I saw something protruding from it. Closer examination revealed a piece of paper rolled up and stuck into the knot of the tree.

Hi Callie,

I hope your ankle is healing and you're feeling better. I haven't seen you out in several days, and I knew that if you were out, you'd come here. Since I never know when that'll be, I thought I'd leave a note. I'm going to the Fourth of July fireworks at the state park and was wondering if you'd come with me. If you can't come with me, maybe you and your family will be there.

Either way, I hope I see you at the beach.

Wyatt

Huh. That was a first. I'd never had anyone leave a note for me, let alone in a tree. I folded the note and put it in my pocket. "So, Stubby, whatdaya think? Should I go to the beach tonight?" He looked up at me and cocked his head to the left with a whimper. I stared back, butterflies bouncing around in my belly.

The cars started to arrive. Aunt Shirley and Uncle Fred were the first to show up, with Aunt Shirley's famous desserts. She exited the car, and while walking into the throng of family, she reminded us that we needed to come to her house for a dessert night before we left to head back home.

In the next car were my cousins with Stubby's buddy, Justa. Aunt Marilyn, Uncle Oscar, and Aunt Doris were rounding the corner at the pump with a pot of beans and beer. Grammie, my mom's mom, and Uncle Dick were driving down Camp Road in his Z28. This always made me chuckle, as Grammie did not find any sports cars exciting.

Everyone arrived within minutes of each other, except my dad's brother and wife, who were driving from Lake Champlain forty-five minutes away. People were scurrying around with food and drink, and laughter could be heard from all corners of the cabin. Watching my family made me smile, and today we had an added bonus: a little surprise anniversary party for Nanny and Gramp.

When everyone had arrived, we had our big meal for the day. Knowing that Aunt Shirley had made an anniversary cake for Nanny and Gramp, I made sure to save some room. Gramp walked over to the cake with his arm around Nanny to say a few words before he cut into it.

"I just want to thank you all for coming out here today. Who would have thought this beautiful lady would end up with a schlub like me. She's just as beautiful today as she was the day I met her sixty years ago. I'm so thankful that her father opened his barn door that fateful day."

We all chuckled. "I'll drink to that!" Aunt Marilyn exclaimed, with raised glass. Bringing the glass to her lips, eager for a sip, she spilled down the front of her blouse. Standing there, staring down at the wetness soaking in, she exclaimed, "Shii ..." before she could finish her thought, she glanced around, remembering there were young ones about and continued with her exclamation, "tak-e mushrooms."

This family folklore had endured decades, yet still we enjoyed listening. Gramp used to drive over the Canadian border to buy alcohol and drive back to Vermont to bootleg it during Prohibition. By the time he turned eighteen, he had been doing this for months without any problem. That particular night, he hadn't been so lucky. The cops got wind that he was coming across the border, and when border patrol asked to search his car, he put the pedal to the metal and took off, with the cops in hot pursuit. He raced through winding farm roads, far enough ahead that he could no longer see the flashing lights. He knew they were still hot on his trail, so he frantically looked for a farm with a large barn. He found one. This particular barn had a gentleman closing up the barn doors when Gramp peeled into the barnyard. He pleaded with the gentleman to allow him to hide his car in the barn. After Gramp handed him a bottle of whiskey, the man allowed it. That man was Nanny's father, and the rest is history.

After the dishes had been cleaned and the food cleared, my cousin got the kids together and announced that we were going to have a volleyball game against the Silks. All the cousins walked to Mr. Silk's and knocked on the door where Kitty, Mr. Silk's daughter, answered.

"Hi, fellas. Is it really that time of year again? Oh, it's on! Give us twenty minutes to clean up."

So in twenty minutes, we were all out at the Wilsons' volleyball net, Silks on one side and Lamplys on the other. The game began with a spike to Kitty. She dove for it but missed, and the Lamplys took the lead. The score went back and forth before tying up. Now I had to serve. I carefully aimed for Mr. Silk's youngest niece. She was about a year younger than me, and when she hit the ball with all her might, it went out of bounds. We hooted and hollered, congratulating ourselves for winning game one, but we decided we needed to play best out of three.

The second game began with Kitty diving for the ball and hurting her shoulder, causing her to leave the game. As she walked off the court, a figure emerged, leaning on the garage, watching the game. Wyatt had just put the yard tools away in Gramp's garage. With no subs to take her place, we were at a standstill. "Hey, Wyatt, why don't you help us out," Kitty called. With a nod, Wyatt took her spot on the Silks' side and play continued. They played hard and fought to win game two.

Now it was getting tough to concentrate. We served first for game three, and it went back and forth for several sets. Jimmy served next, and I crossed my fingers that he had brought his A game. He served, and it hit the net. The second serve was good. One hit, two, three … *Game over!* We ended victoriously, and our side went crazy, with high fives all around. The cousins ended up carrying Jimmy to the lake, and in a celebratory move, threw him in. Wyatt looked uncomfortable, retreating to his house before we could ask him to join us for dinner.

We brought out all the leftovers from the afternoon feast, and both families dined together outside. There were more laughs and great conversation about years past, like the time we forgot to bring beer and had to make the drive back from the state park and pay the extra entry fee to get back inside.

The deal was that if you lost the annual volleyball match, you had to bring the beer and pay for the cars of both families to get into the state park for the fireworks later in the evening.

Time had come to fill the coolers with ice, chilling the beverages before the big display. Around dusk, we drove to the state park in a large caravan for the fireworks, with the Silks in the lead to pay the way. The long line of traffic snaked down the road. We waited patiently to get in, and once inside, we found a spot on the grass and brought out the blankets to sit on. We set up our spot with the Silks.

All the while, I was searching the crowd for Wyatt, but I didn't recognize any faces. The fireworks colorfully burst above us, and I forgot all about him until I felt a tap on my shoulder. I turned around right as a giant, golden firework went off in every direction, illuminating his youthful face.

"You made it!" he said happily, as though he'd been searching for me all night. "I didn't think you'd come."

"I came with my entire extended family and the Silks. It's a tradition we started many years ago. Where are you sitting?" I asked, standing.

"We're up by the concession stand. Wanna come up?" he asked hopefully.

"Thanks, but I better hang down here with the family. Have fun," I said, dejected.

"Okay. Well, maybe I'll see you back at the camp later on."

"Yeah, maybe," I said as I sat back down on the blanket next to Jimmy. I thought that he'd been watching me, but as I sat, I realized it wasn't me he'd been watching but Riley. She sat behind us by the concession stand and talked to Wyatt as he approached her. She looked over at Jimmy and smiled. In that instant, I realized that the girl that had hugged Wyatt on the beach the other night had been Riley. Jimmy turned around to face the lake and continued watching the fireworks as if he didn't see her.

"You know she's watching you," I said to Jimmy.

"Who?"

"Don't play like that. You know who."

I grabbed a soda from the cooler and sat silently next to him. Two seats down from Jimmy sat Gramp.

"Happy Fourth, Wyatt," Gramp offered.

"Thanks, Mr. Lamply. Mind if I sit with you guys for the rest of the show?" he said as he walked toward me.

Gramp smiled and winked at me. "Not at all. Maybe this way Callie will pay attention to the show in front of her and not the one behind her." I blushed uncontrollably.

Wyatt squished in between Jimmy and I. "Hey, man, s'cuse me. You mind if I take this spot?"

Jimmy moved over with a grunt, saying something under his breath that I couldn't quite make out. Nervously I sat, unable to concentrate on the fireworks. I could feel the warmth radiating from him, and I breathed him in … He smelled like summer, like my idea of summer: the tang of pine needles and the coconut perfume of sunscreen.

I could see in my periphery that Wyatt was peeking at me out of the corner of his eye. His legs were outstretched, as were mine, and we both had our arms by our sides. He sat so close to me that our shoulders were almost touching. He leaned in to say, "So all these people around us are part of your family?"

"Mmhmmm."

"That's a lot," he said.

"It is," I returned.

"You're not big on conversation, are you?"

"Nope," I smiled.

We continued to watch the stunning display above us. He leaned in again and whispered in my ear, "Did you get my note?"

I smiled and nodded my head.

"That may be my only way to communicate with you." He sat with his thoughts for a minute and then said, "And I'm cool with that." Without turning, I smiled again. When the fireworks ended, we folded the blankets and got our things gathered. Wyatt smiled and said, "So I guess that was like, our first date?"

I giggled. *Who says that?*

"See ya 'round. If not, you know how I'll reach you," he said with a wink.

Gramp teased, "I do believe that boy fancies you."

For the hundredth time, I could feel heat radiating from my cheeks. Jimmy walked to the car and said, "Gross," under his breath.

It's funny how things turned out. Who would have thought I would be crushing on a boy that lived just a few doors down from Gramp's camp. Unfortunately, our stays at camp were short-lived, only lasting two months, and time was flying by.

Gramp's lead foot got him home way before the rest of us. "Lead Foot Lamply," Dad would say under his breath, all the while worrying about Gramp's safety. Watching the man peel out of a parking lot definitely provided a cause for worry. We happened to be the second-to-last car, and upon returning, we witnessed a large commotion back at camp. All the lights in the cabin were on, and people were screaming and running from room to room. *What on earth is going on?*

Nanny stood on a chair with a badminton racket in her hand, waving it around as if competing with an invisible opponent. Gramp yelled, "Open the door!!" so we did, and Gramp, with a racket in his hand, swung wildly at a black thing that eventually found the door and flew out. Oh. My. God. It was a bat. Over the winter they tended to find the nooks and crannies of the cabin to reside in while we were all away. Now that it had warmed outside and we'd been here for two weeks, the bat wanted out. That bat prevailed. It must have been his lucky day! I remembered one year Dad had opened the camp with Gramp and killed two bats that were holed up for the winter. I'd just screamed and hidden in the bathroom.

"Mother, get down from the chair; it's gone now," Dad said to Nanny. She laughed, grabbed Dad's outstretched hand, and climbed down from her roost. We all calmed down and went to bed.

CHAPTER 9

Several days passed without any craziness. I didn't see Wyatt around, which left me feeling disappointed. I went to my tree every day, hoping for a note. On the third day, I saw paper sticking out of the knot.

Callie,

I'm sure you've been wondering where I've been. Or maybe not...in any case, I had to go to Burlington for a few days with my family to visit relatives and take Tyler to the Marine recruiting office (he's been recruited), which has my mom a bit shaken and my dad as proud as a peacock. He is so proud of Tyler for taking this on. Tyler gets his orders on Saturday, and that's when we find out when and where he goes. I'm not sure why I'm telling you all this. I just feel like I can talk to you. I hope to see you soon.

-W

I folded the paper, tucked it in my pocket and walked out of the Black Forest with Stubby by my side. Knowing that Wyatt wasn't around made me want to see him all the more.

After dinner, Mom and I drove up to Franklin to do some laundry, and we spent the rest of the evening folding clothes and putting the beds back together. As I settled in with my book, Jimmy appeared.

"Hey, what's this all about?" Jimmy said, holding a piece of paper. Immediately I felt for the note in my pocket and realized it had fallen out when I made the beds earlier.

"Tyler's being shipped out of here? That's the best news I've heard all week. Is this yours?" he asked excitedly.

"Uh, yeah. Yep, that's mine. I got it from Wyatt."

"Why wouldn't he just tell you this in person?"

How do I explain this to him? "It's just a thing he does. He started this about a week ago."

"That's weird, but whatever. He can write you all he wants as long as it's news like this." As Jimmy left my room, he crumpled the note up and tossed it over his shoulder, whistling.

From the open window I could smell cigarette smoke, and I knelt to look outside. I could see the amber glow at the end of two cigarettes and listened intently as two older girls walked by, in quiet conversation.

"Hang in there, Sam. I'm sure Tyler will be fine. He's a strong kid." I saw the girls consoling each other. From what I gathered, Sam was Wyatt's sister, and she was talking to Kitty Silk. They each took a long drag from their cigarettes and continued walking slowly down the gravel road.

I'd imagine Tyler's enlistment created a lot of tension for the Wilson family. Lying my head on the pillow, I closed my eyes and said a quick prayer for Tyler.

In the morning, the sun shined brightly, giving me reason to take on the day. Whistling, Jimmy drifted through the kitchen. As I walked past the counter, I grabbed a box of cereal, milk from the fridge, a bowl, and a spoon.

"So what are you gonna do today?" I asked Jimmy as I poured the milk into my bowl at the table.

"Mom says Grammie is coming down and wants to go fishing, so I'm going to take her out. What are you doing today? No, wait. Lemme guess. You're gonna write love notes to your boyfriend and then go for a run."

I picked up some cereal with my spoon and proceeded to flick it in his direction. "Yeah, you're funny. As a matter of fact, I *am* going to go for a run. My ankle is feeling much better," I said, flexing and pointing my foot.

"Look out for lover boy. Since you've been out of commission, I've seen him running the stretch of gravel road early in the morning. What do you suppose he's doing that for?" he said, smiling.

"Whatever do you mean?" I feigned ignorance. I washed out the bowl and spoon and put them on the drying rack, since there was no dishwasher in this place. "That's what kids are for," Gramp always said. I got changed, tied my shoes, and started slowly down the path toward Aunt Doris's.

I hadn't noticed when I started, but Wyatt was in the field on the riding mower. An unusual quiet had moved in, but as I was cresting the hill, I heard heavy breathing coming up behind me. Shirtless and in cutoff denim shorts, Wyatt caught up and ran alongside me for a few hundred yards. At that point, his breathing came fast and hard, so I slowed to a trot.

"You okay?" I asked, amused.

He stopped and put his hands on his knees and lowered his head, holding one finger up.

"Dang! Didn't you...hear me...coming up...the hill?" he said in short spurts.

"I did," I laughed. "You gonna finish the run with me or just stand there panting?"

He continued to gasp, and his breathing slowly returned to normal. "I'm gonna stand here panting. You finish on your own, but before you go, just say yes for me."

"Huh? To what?"

"Just say it."

"Okay...yes," I said warily.

He spun on his heels, trotting down the hill back toward the mower. "This is so much easier going downhill!" he said, running backward, smiling from ear to ear.

"Tell me what I said yes to!" I hollered.

"I will later. Go get 'em, Callie-flower!" he yelled as he climbed back on the mower and started it up. Then, oddly, he just sat there idling, staring into the sky for at least a minute before moving on.

I continued running up to the farm and took the long way around through Franklin. My ankle felt great, so I decided to make a pit stop at Aunt Marilyn's house, which she seemed happy about. We sat in the screened-in porch for a bit.

"Are you guys going to Aunt Shirley's for her dessert extravaganza tonight?" Aunt Marilyn asked.

"I didn't know it was tonight, but I'm pretty sure we'll be there. When have we ever missed dessert night?"

"You'll have to have Uncle Fred take you out to the barn and show you the new kittens. Five were born last weekend, and they are the cutest little things. Lemonade?"

"Yes, please."

She brought me lemonade as we talked about her beloved Boston Red Sox team and how she used to like a ballplayer when she was younger.

"You know, rumor has it you're sweet on a certain Wilson boy. I used to have a sweetheart back in the day. When I worked at the general store for my dad, there was a boy that used to come in pretending he needed to buy things for his mother. His name was Travis Metcalf. Really, he was just coming in to see me. Pretty soon he was in every day, and he finally asked me to go steady with him. I really liked him. We dated for years, and wouldn't you know it, he wanted to marry me?" she said, amused. She looked as though she were miles away. "My father's health was failing, and my guy wanted to move out of state," she continued, "so you see, I had to turn him down. It was the hardest decision I ever had to make. Travis was in such a fragile state when I said no to his proposal, I worried for his well-being, but it was up to me to help my mother tend to the store. As it was, my father wasn't long for this world. I still miss him."

At this point, I wasn't sure if she was talking about her father or her beau. She'd never married and never had a family of her own. Instead, she was like a second mother to her sister Shirley's kids.

"I so enjoy when you and James come up for visits. I always look forward to fishing and boating with you kids."

"Can I ask you something?"

"Anything."

"Who do you talk to?"

"What on earth do you mean?"

"I've seen you many times having conversations with … nobody."

Embarrassed, she replied, "Ah yes, that. It's my guardian angel. Travis died years ago, but I still feel him around me. His body was found in Lake Carmi by one of those 'Cookie Cutter' handlers. It was the worst day of my life. Now he comes to me frequently to guide me along my path." Matter-of-factly, she said, "You have the gift."

"The what?"

"The ability to sense the other side. I can see it in your eyes and your aura."

Making a circular motion with my head to try to get a glimpse of what she was talking about, I saw nothing. "Well … what does that mean exactly? I don't get it."

Her eyes twinkled as she spoke, "Oh, I think you do."

"No, not really," I confessed, feeling a bit wigged out.

"You're just not paying attention," she winked.

The small hairs on my arms stood on end.

I finished my lemonade and stood to leave. She followed me to the door and enveloped me in her arms.

"I'll be there tonight," I told her. "Thanks for the lemonade. I should be getting back before they call out the search party." She thanked me for stopping by, and I left feeling content yet slightly alarmed.

Back at camp I had not gotten a glimpse of Wyatt. Disappointed, I walked through the door and realized that no one was inside. In front of the cabin, I found my mom and Nanny sitting at the picnic table watching the lake.

"Where is everyone?"

Mom pointed out to a boat not far offshore. "Dad, Jimmy, Gramp, and Grammie went fishing."

At that exact moment, we heard a scream and could see that Grammie had one foot on the side of the boat about to jump ship. Jimmy stood, holding a fishing rod with something long and black wiggling on the end of it.

"RICHARD, GET THAT OUT OF THIS BOAT!" Grammie screamed. I could hear Dad's hearty belly laugh as he dangled the thing in front of my grandmother. "I MEAN IT! EITHER IT GOES OR I'M JUMPING OVERBOARD!" She sounded terrified, on the verge of tears. My brother continued to howl.

Gramp grabbed some pliers, put a glove on and wrangled the hook out of the eel. Then he just couldn't help himself; he wiggled the eel in front of my grandmother one last time, causing another wail to escape her lips. Gramp finally released the eel into the water.

That pretty much ended the fishing excursion. They brought the boat in, and before they cut the motor, my grandmother had one foot out on the dock. I didn't think I'd ever seen her move so fast. We were all laughing as they raised the boat and brought in the bucket of fish. It was a fish-fry night.

Jimmy and I took the bucket to the side of the pump house and started cleaning the fish as Nanny got the batter ready inside. Dad supervised as we worked and brought the cleaned fillets to Nanny in the kitchen. He came out with his swimsuit on and a bar of soap. "Time to shower," he said to no one in particular as he walked down the eroding embankment to the lake.

The water used inside the cabin came directly from the lake, hence the well water we pumped into gallon jugs for drinking and cleaning dishes. Since the temperature of the shower water was the only difference, we'd just bring a bar of soap into the lake and clean up there.

As he cleaned up, we saw another fishing boat off the shore in front of the cabin. It looked like the person standing in the middle of the boat was trying to bring in the big one, but we discovered he was just trying to relieve himself off the side of the boat. He pulled his pants down around his ankles, and though he tried to steady himself, we were shocked to see the man fall overboard. We heard a lot of thrashing, yet no one emerged.

Throwing the bar of soap aside, Dad dove forward into the deep water and swam to the boat. He dove under the boat once and came up empty-handed. On his second attempt, he popped to the surface with a man under his arm. Dad managed to drag the man to shore, and at this point, I realized it was Tyler. He was sputtering, and when they reached shore, Tyler managed to pull up his shorts before leaning over to vomit. From the stench, we could tell he'd been drinking.

"You all right, Tyler?" Dad asked, concerned.

"Yeah, man, I'm all right," he slurred.

Dad helped Tyler up the embankment with an arm around his waist and walked him back to his house. Jimmy and I took the canoe to retrieve the fishing boat that Tyler left behind. Jimmy paddled our canoe as I held on to Tyler's boat. We tied the canoe to the dock and tied the fishing boat to the canoe so it didn't float away.

Nanny continued to fry up the fish while we were waiting, and I set the table. From the back wall of windows, I could see Dad returning to our cabin. As we sat down for dinner, Dad told us that Tyler went on a bender and took the boat out for one last ride. He'd received his orders earlier in the week, which meant leaving for boot camp the next morning. As we were eating, we saw Tommy Wilson, one of the Wilson boys, and Mr. Wilson walk around the camp to retrieve the fishing boat from our dock. Dad excused himself to help. We could hear their conversation through the screen door.

"Thanks for your help, Rit. He's having a hard time with this decision. He'll be fine once he gets there."

"Well, tell him we wish him well, Sam. Have a good night."
Dad came back in, and the Wilsons untied the boat and rode it
down to their dock. I felt bad for Tyler; that had to be a tough
decision for someone to make.

We finished our dinner with some small talk but ate mostly
in silence. We cleaned up the kitchen; I got to wash the dishes,
while Jimmy dried.

"So what do you think will happen to him?" I asked.

"Well, I know he's gonna be ripped when he comes back to
visit his family. Boot camp will whip him into shape."

I gently patted his belly and said, "Maybe that's what
you need."

My brother had always been in good shape from all the years
of swimming; I just wanted to give him a hard time.

He wound the dish towel up and snapped it at me several
times. I yipped and moved out of the way. As I tried to continue
washing, he snapped the towel a few more times.

ؑ ؑ ؑ

That evening we drove to Aunt Shirley's for a delicious spread
of cookies, homemade fruit pies, fresh lemonade, and coffee.

"Shirley, you've outdone yourself again," Dad said. Aunt
Shirley hugged everyone as we scoped out what kinds of dessert
were being offered.

Aunt Shirley asked me to go get Uncle Fred from the barn,
and as I walked there, my senses were assaulted by the smell
of cows. Oddly enough, it didn't seem like a foul smell to me
anymore, and in a strange way, I found it comforting. I entered
the barn and saw Uncle Fred kneeling next to something.

"Come see," Uncle Fred called to me. I walked over and saw
a barn cat nursing her five brand-new kittens, three calicos, one

gray, and one black, and they were beautiful. Uncle Fred took a seat at the stool next to them and started milking a cow. He took the cow's teat and sprayed the mother cat with milk. She proceeded to lick her whiskers clean, so Uncle Fred sprayed her a few more times.

"She needs some TLC, too," he said with a smile.

"Uncle Fred, Aunt Shirley says it's time to come in for dessert."

"A-yup," he answered and whistled for Justa to follow. When we walked in, everyone already had their plates full of goodies. Uncle Fred and I dug in, as well, and as usual, everything was delicious. As we chatted, more cousins walked in and took part in the desserts. Seconds on coffee and lemonade were passed around, and soon the long goodbyes began. It was getting dark, and with each drawn out goodbye, Dad grew more agitated knowing that 'Lead Foot Lamply' still had a drive ahead of him. Fortunately, the evening ended safely back at Gramp's camp.

Everyone took their spot in the living room: Gramp in the maroon leather chair, Nanny in the rocking chair, Mom and Dad on the love seat, and Jimmy and I on the floor with pillows. The one TV we had in the cabin was turned on, which was a rare event. We watched an episode of *Hollywood Squares* and called it a night.

Forget about reading; I'm too tired. I'd closed my eyes for what seemed like two minutes, when a rap at my window woke me. On the second rap, I knelt up on my bed and looked out to see blond hair shimmering in the moonlight.

CHAPTER 10

Through the screen window, I whispered, "What are you doing here?"

"Come outside," Wyatt urged, smiling at me.

"I, I can't...It's like...what...midnight?" I stammered.

"You said yes, remember?"

What is he talking abou...oh, yeah. "I did, but you never told me what I was saying yes to."

"Come on. I have something to show you. You won't regret it. I promise!" he said, all giddy.

"Hang on. Let me throw some clothes on."

"You're going to miss it. HURRY UP!" he whispered urgently.

I quickly threw on some shorts and a sweatshirt over my pajamas. Entering the kitchen, I hurriedly trotted to the front of camp and carefully opened the heavy wooden door, unlocked the screen door, and went outside. The grass felt slick with heavy dew on my bare feet. The light seemed oddly beautiful, but I couldn't figure out what was different. Wyatt grabbed my hand, and we started jogging to the field that he had mowed the day before. As we crossed the gravel road, I could see a blanket outstretched in the field. I shot him a worried glance.

"Come on. I want to show you something." Gently tugging on my hand, he guided me to the blanket. "Come here. You gotta see this," he said as he lay down on the blanket.

Feeling my heart skip a beat as I lay down next to him, I looked up at the sky. It took my breath away. There were unusually beautiful lights wavering in the sky, thick bands of green and glowing amber. It was the most magnificent thing I'd ever seen. The lights were moving through the air like waves of color vibrating in the sky. The beauty stunned me into silence.

"See," he said, still holding my hand. "I told you you wouldn't want to miss it."

Slowly I ventured, "It's amazing ... I've never seen the northern lights before." The beauty hit me, and I could feel tears forming in the corners of my eyes. I whispered, "Thank you."

We lay there in silence for what seemed like hours. The rays of dawn were just about to break over the horizon, and the light show would end. We stood, stretched our legs and gathered the blanket as we walked back to the cabin door.

"I'm glad you liked that," he said shyly.

"I LOVED it!" and without thinking, I leaned in and kissed his cheek. I surprised myself, so I backed off immediately and ran to the door. "Bye, Wyatt." He waved and headed home. I quietly reentered the cabin and closed the door, but before I turned around, I could smell coffee.

"Whath outhide for you to thee at thith hour?" Gramp said without his dentures, stirring coffee.

"I just saw the most amazing thing!" I sat at the counter and recapped the night for my grandfather. I felt flushed when I finished, and Gramp was smiling.

"It ith magnifithent. I'm glad you enjoyed the 'danthe.' Now get thome thleep, young lady," he said teasingly. I was asleep before my head hit the pillow.

CR   CR   CR

"Wakey, wakey," Jimmy said as he tickled my feet.

"Hey, cut it out," I said groggily. "You're such a jerk sometimes." I sat up and threw a pillow at his head.

"Saw your boyfriend this morning, running again. Saw him go into the woods. Thought you'd want to know that. 'Course, it's been hours now since I saw him. You sick or something?"

"No, I just didn't sleep much last night," I said as I got out of bed. I walked into the kitchen, hoping my brother would back off since I was feeling grumpy from lack of sleep. Then I realized what he said. *He went to the woods.* I quickly walked out of the kitchen and changed into some shorts and a T-shirt. Slipping on my flip-flops, I walked out the door. I walked past a slumbering Stubby stretched out in the sun at the back of camp, and passed Freckles, who was rolling in the grass outside of Mr. Silk's. At the Wilsons' house, the red pickup truck was loaded with two large green duffel bags and a large backpack. It looked like Tyler was all packed and ready to go. I reached my tree and saw a note hanging out of the knot.

Thank you. Thanks for saying yes. Thanks for being such a good sport about the early wake-up call. I'm leaving today to take Tyler to Burlington, and we'll be spending the night there with the family one last time before he leaves tomorrow morning. It's not a huge send-off—just our family. So I guess that's it...I'll see you sometime later in the week. -W

Again, I folded the note and placed it in my pocket. I sat down next to the tree and watched as the Wilsons filed out of their house, first Mr. and Mrs. Wilson, then Samantha with her arm around Tyler, then Thomas and Sarah, and finally Wyatt. Samantha and Tyler got into the truck, and the rest of the family climbed into their Suburban. As Wyatt slowly entered the Suburban, I could see him looking toward Gramp's camp, and then to the woods. I knew he couldn't see me because I was beneath the trees, but somehow I felt he knew I was there. He smiled and closed the door behind him.

I watched as the vehicles drove out of sight; only then did I leave my spot. I went back to camp and straight to my room, feeling pretty melancholy, just wanting to be alone.

I put my suit on to swim to Rock Island—not a far swim, probably about five hundred yards. Once I reached the rocky shoreline, I climbed up to sit on a boulder. The wildlife on this island was breathtaking, and for a while, I sat still and watched as a heron and other prehistoric looking cranes took flight overhead. Walking around the small island took me all of five minutes.

That's odd, I thought, as I approached a fishing boat tied to an outstretched tree limb. It wasn't just anyone's fishing boat; it was the Wilsons'. There was an explosion of butterflies in my belly thinking that maybe Wyatt had stayed home. Someone sat sobbing nearby, so I followed the sound to find Riley, up in an old and rickety tree stand looking like a lost child.

"Riley?" I startled her. She wiped her tears quickly and turned away from me.

"What do *you* want?" she managed in a shaky voice.

"Nothing. I was just trying to find a place to get away from my family and thought I'd come here for the peace and quiet, and here you are. You okay?" I asked her quietly.

"No. Would you be if your heart was being torn apart?" she sniffed.

"If it's Tyler you're worried about, he'll be back soon. You know that he's going to be okay."

Her face started to flush as she turned to me. "Really? You think that's it? I didn't even get to say goodbye! I was too late. He had already left by the time I got off work. He might be fine for now, but who knows what's going to happen to him once he finishes boot camp. Everything is changing. He's not going to be the same Tyler!"

She began to cry again. We sat in silence for a few minutes until her crying subsided. Staring out at the lake, she said, "I saw you."

The comment didn't register immediately.

"We both did. You told Jimmy, and now, thanks to you, I don't have a chance with him either. Hope you're happy."

I didn't know what to say to that. I knew she was hurting, and obviously, nothing I could say was going to help. "Well, good luck. I hope it turns out the way you want it to … with whoever."

On with the goggles, hair tucked in—I tackled the five hundred yards back. When my toes sunk into the slimy bottom, I walked up the eroded slope, grabbed my towel, and sat down at the picnic table to watch the island for movement. Eventually, Riley got into the fishing boat and navigated back to the Wilsons' dock.

I listened to her gravelly footsteps recede. A glance over my shoulder revealed Jimmy lazing in the hammock next to the old swing set. He set his book down in his lap to watch Riley walk past. He didn't call out to her; he just let her pass. Lost in her thoughts, she didn't even notice him. As she rounded the corner, Jimmy picked up his book and continued to read.

CHAPTER 11

Later in the afternoon, Jimmy and I brought the jugs to the water pump. I primed the pump, and Jimmy placed the jugs under the clean water.

"I saw Riley today," I said to him in passing.

"Oh?" he said nonchalantly.

"Yeah, she was at Rock Island by herself. She seems pretty bummed out, confused, and very emotional. She *did not* want to talk to me. I was the last person she wanted around."

"Hmmm." He moved the full gallon out of the way and placed the second empty jug under the water.

"Maybe you should talk to her again," I suggested.

"Pfft, yeah, I think that ship has sailed."

"Hmmm." I picked up one jug and he carried the other as we walked back to the cabin in silence.

❧ ❧ ❧

I looked forward to tonight's distraction: the big band in the town square. As we exited the car, the number of people milling about amazed me. They carried fried dough and other delicious treats. It is such a quaint town, with the church in the center of the courtyard, where people were gathering around, and near the gazebo, where the band always set up.

Soon the music was in full swing with a lot of oldies. Mom and Dad were cutting a rug, dancing the jitterbug. I enjoyed watching them boogie across the makeshift dance floor in front of the gazebo. They were grinning from ear to ear, delight dancing in their eyes.

The dance ... that's what Gramp called the northern lights. I leaned against a light post on the edge of the courtyard and watched the action quietly, thinking about my adventure with Wyatt. That had been such an unexpected experience. I wanted more of that, more spontaneous fun, more playfulness, and more Wyatt.

Dad pulled me out of my trance and onto the dance floor, while Mom looked on laughing. She grabbed my brother, and within seconds, the four of us were dancing with my grandparents looking on.

After the second song had ended, I told Dad I needed a break and went to get some lemonade. I spotted Riley sitting along a rock wall with her family, listening to the music. She was dressed in a pretty white eyelet sundress and flip-flops, with her hair tied up in a high ponytail.

After stumbling upon her today on the island, I really didn't want to make eye contact. She had a distant look in her eyes as her grandmother tried to talk with her, offering lemonade and a candied apple, both of which Riley turned down. I watched her grandmother walk away in frustration leaving Riley and her sister, Megan, at the wall.

After trying a few times to have a conversation, Megan gave up and walked away to talk with some friends. As Megan bounced by, Jimmy caught my attention. He was watching Riley intently from his spot near the gazebo, and I was curious to see how this would play out. She was obviously very upset about Tyler leaving, but I thought deep down she remained confused.

The music slowed, and a girl I didn't recognize stumbled awkwardly in front of Jimmy. The two giggling friends behind her revealed that she had been pushed. Shyly, she asked Jimmy if he wanted to dance. He took hold of her hand and led her to the dance floor, but he never took his eyes off of Riley. They swayed to the music, dancing a circle that encompassed the dance floor. Riley looked up as the two passed by, staring at Jimmy in surprise and disbelief. He locked eyes with her, and before long the song ended. Jimmy relinquished his current partner back to her anxiously awaiting friends and laughed as the girl giggled and pranced off the dance floor.

Jimmy shook his head and smiled at the girl and her friends, then he looked up to find Riley staring back at him. Her smile appeared weak as she moved toward the church steps. Jimmy watched her go, and for a second, I didn't think he would follow, but he soon stood in front of her, shoving his hands in his pockets uncomfortably. By the way his shoulders were shrugging, I could tell he was asking her a question. She gestured with her hand, and they sat side by side. Jimmy fidgeted with his hands, cracking every last knuckle. He was doing most of the talking while she listened intently. She wiped at her eyes a few times, as if they had sprung a leak.

Oh, man, is he making her cry? Then, for whatever reason, her shoulders were shaking, and she started giggling. Soon she was bent over laughing so hard that she wasn't making a sound. I never really thought my brother was all that funny. I mean, he's my brother, and brothers are annoying, but he was like George Carlin over there.

I felt my dad's hand on my shoulder. "Come on, Cal. It's time to head back to camp." We started walking to the car, and I could see Jimmy wrapping up his conversation with Riley. Nanny and Gramp had already started the Cadillac and were down the street before we climbed into Dad's car. I didn't mention anything about Riley to Jimmy in the car, but as soon as we were back at camp, I turned to my brother and said, "Smooth move, ex-lax," as only a sister could.

CHAPTER 12

The morning was gorgeous when I rose. Jimmy's whistling reached my ears all the way from the kitchen.

As I walked in wearing my pajamas, I asked, "Dad up? I want to go zip sledding today."

"Yeah, he's up and out already. He went into town to get coffee and the newspaper. Should be home soon. He's been gone for about half an hour."

Waiting for my dad to return, I decided to get ready for zip sledding. I donned a swimming suit, brushed my teeth, and ventured out to the pump house. Beyond the rickety, faded, red pump-house door, the scent of rotten fish, worms, and lake water was pungent. I lugged the turquoise monstrosity of a sled out as quickly as possible and dragged it down to the dock. Dad's Impala was driving into the garage as I walked back up the steps. He parked and walked back to camp with the newspaper under his arm, carrying a box of what I guessed were donuts. A cup of coffee rested precariously on top.

We entered the kitchen at the same time—I through the creaky screen door, and he through the front. I perched on the barstool at the kitchen counter and watched him set the donuts down and grab his coffee. "Have at it." He opened the box and stepped away as my brother and I dove in and grabbed our favorites: a bear claw for Jimmy and a blueberry glazed for me.

Feeling the effects of the sugar rushing through my veins, I was ready to get out on the lake. "Dad, you wanna take me for a ride on the zip sled?"

"Sure. Let me hit the little boys' room, and I'll be ready."

Jimmy bellowed, "If it's yellow, let it mellow; if it's brown, flush it down."

Laughing, Dad closed the bathroom door saying, "Words to live by."

Back at the dock, I sat on the heavy plastic sled, waiting patiently. Dad finally emerged, with Stubby and Jimmy following closely behind. Dad got in the boat, and Jimmy rotated the wheel to lower it into the water. Once the boat was lowered, I handed Stubby off to Dad and climbed in. We were off.

Just past the island, Dad tied the water-skiing rope through the hole in the top of the sled and attached the other end to the hook inside the boat. He proceeded to throw the sled out behind the boat. With my life jacket clipped on, I jumped in. I climbed on the sled and lay on my belly, holding tightly to the thick, bristly, white rope. "Hit it," I yelled, and Dad gunned it.

My brother sat in the back facing me so that he could be Dad's eyes while Dad made a large figure eight and I fought to stay on. Aunt Marilyn appeared on the shoreline, distracting me. She seemed to be talking to the tree in Aunt Doris's yard when water splashed into my eyes. I hit the wake, and it sent me careening through the air. Jimmy yelled for Dad to kill the engine. Dad quickly spun the boat around to check on me. Giving a thumbs-up, I climbed on again, reminded immediately just how hard that zip sled was as the firm plastic dug into my hipbones, beginning to form bruises.

A few more rides, a few more tosses, and I finally made it over the wake and back, laughing the whole way. Dad made one last attempt to toss me and succeeded; I was done. He swung the boat around and dropped the ladder down. During Jimmy's turn, Dad showed no mercy, tossing Jimmy almost immediately.

"Geez, at least give me a chance to hang on before you gun it," Jimmy complained as he climbed back on the sled. He smoothly made several trips outside the wake. We needed a break, and lunch was a good reason to take one.

After lunch, I took my fishing pole and tackle box down to the boat, while Jimmy grabbed the fish bucket and worms. Dad started the boat up, and we backed away from the dock for an afternoon of fishing. We seemed to have good luck off the shore from Aunt Doris's camp. While patiently waiting for the fish to bite, I watched two large machines at the end of the lake. One was the "Cookie Cutter," which was used to chop up thick vegetation in lakes, causing me to involuntarily shiver, and the other was a mechanical harvester that would scoop up the ground-up bits. We saw these machines working endless hours chopping and scooping the vegetation all summer long. *I wonder what the operator thought when he pulled Travis from the water.*

A pulling sensation on my line pulled me from my reverie.

"I swear, if either of you catch an eel, I'm swimming back," I said as I got another nibble on the end of my line.

Dad laughed. "I have never seen your grandmother move so fast in my life."

The fish were taunting us, jumping just beyond our fishing poles and nibbling away at all our worms. Finally, I got a bite that bent the reel. The fish put up a good fight, and as I reeled it in, out popped a little sunfish. Disappointed, I tossed the thing in the bucket. Dad had a strike and started to reel it in. The fish jumped and thrashed, putting up a fight like a northern pike. As it got closer to the boat, fighting the whole way, Dad yelled for someone to grab the net.

"Hurry up, guys!"

Jimmy and I stared at each other, and without breaking eye contact, I said quickly, "Jimmy forgot the net."

His eyes bulged. "I did not! No one told me to grab it. You forgot it!"

As we continued to argue, Dad's pole bent deeper into the water, and then the line went slack, and the fish was gone. He reeled it in and saw that the fish had managed to take the hook, line, and sinker. Now Dad would have to put everything back on his rod all over again for us to continue. By the look on his face, he wasn't willing to start fresh, so without saying another word, he put the pole down, pulled up anchor, and drove at a fast clip back to camp.

There was nothing worse than getting the silent treatment from Dad. As we were cleaning out the boat, I handed Dad the bucket and started to giggle. "Better tell Nanny to fire up the oil." Jimmy began laughing. Dad saw no humor in this and continued to wipe down the boat, but by the time we got to the top of the stairs, a smile had formed on his lips.

CHAPTER 13

After dinner, I decided to take Stubby for a walk down into the Black Forest. Suddenly, he ran off in the opposite direction, barking. I chased after him trying to catch up.

"Stubby, STOP!" I shouted. The barking stopped as I approached the water pump. I found Wyatt in the middle of the road with Stubby in his arms, and water jugs on the ground at his feet.

"Thanks for catching him," I panted. "He's probably after Freckles. Those two just can't seem to get along."

He smiled.

"So you're back, I see. How did the send-off go with your brother?" I asked as I took Stubby from his arms.

"Pretty smoothly, aside from my mom sobbing in the car all the way home. Man, that was rough. No matter how many times we tell her he'll be fine, she won't listen. She keeps saying she has a bad feeling about him leaving. The way she says it gives me the willies."

"She's just worried about her son," I said.

"Yeah, I suppose so. It's just that she sounds so believable when she says it." He picked up the water jugs, signaling the end of our conversation. "Well, I'm gonna head back with these," he said, raising the jugs.

"Okay. See ya tomorrow?" I asked hopefully.

"Sure. Tomorrow is laundry day, but I should be around after noon if you want to hang out then."

"Sounds like a plan. See you tomorrow, and thanks again for catching my dog."

I carried Stubby inside and placed him on the floor next to where my dad was napping on the couch. Mom was reading, Nanny and Gramp were watching *Wheel of Fortune*, and Jimmy worked out front, fixing Dad's fishing pole. I opened the screen door and sat at the picnic table, listening to the bug zapper snap each time it claimed another victim.

"Hey," Jimmy said without lifting his eyes.

"Just saw Wyatt. He said Tyler left this morning. I hope he comes back home in one piece," I said cautiously.

Knotting the final hook onto the fishing line, Jimmy said, "Yeah, he will. He's tough enough to handle anything that comes his way...but if he doesn't come back...well, then my life gets a whole lot easier."

"That's terrible! Take that back."

"You started it," he said nonchalantly.

"You can be so awful sometimes," I said as I went back inside.

I started looking for my book, trying to shake the ominous feeling I had about Tyler. I had a fitful night's sleep, waking many times to a recurring nightmare. In it, I found myself walking toward Tyler's sprawled body that lay face-up on the ground. From above him, I noticed the shocked expression on his face, as if something unexpected had just happened. As I looked into his frozen, lifeless eyes, the smell of blood permeated my senses. Standing in a pool of blood, with his lifeless limbs floating around me, I tried to scream, but the pool had begun to rise, covering my feet and rising until it submerged my mouth. I could taste it; I was drowning in his blood.

છ્ર   છ્ર   છ્ર

I woke exhausted, with the taste of blood lingering in my mouth. *Maybe a run would shake this nightmare.* I took a different route: up Camp Road, right onto Lake Road, then toward Stewart's and back. I was finally feeling better, and when I returned, I "showered" in the lake. As I walked back into the cabin, my mom said, "let's go get lunch at The Abbey today. It's a pretty day, and it'd be nice to take a drive." So we drove to Enosburg to a great restaurant on the Missisquoi Valley Rail Trail and River—home of the best french fries I had ever eaten. On the way back, Nanny and Gramp wanted to stop at our family plot at the graveyard.

I have always enjoyed going to graveyards, the older the better. There were stories about many of our relatives buried there. When we got to the gate, my grandmother walked up to a metal post, flipped open the lid to a metal clipboard and signed us in. Reading through that clipboard was like reading a piece of living history. As I walked, I read the tombstones and saw that many dated back to the 1700s. Running my hand along the sturdy wrought-iron fence as I walked, I noticed several tiny headstones. I pointed to the tombstones on the outside of the graveyard and said, "Hey, Mom, what's that all about?"

"From what I can recall, churchyards were laid out rather like the churches themselves. They were often arranged with respect to the cardinal locations. The altar was generally located at the east end of the church. North would be the left-hand side of the altar, while the south would be the right-hand side of the altar. In many churchyards, you may see that the markers are concentrated on the south, east, and west sides of the church and that there are no headstones to be seen on the north side. The north part of the yard is usually reserved for unbaptized children, children born to mothers out of wedlock, the excommunicated, the insane, criminals, or people who committed suicide. Actors were also included in this category of undesirables during some eras."

Without realizing, I had been drawn to the location outside the graveyard and stood staring at the tiniest of tombstones. The area was overgrown with weeds and twisted, thorny vines. Carefully peeling back the undergrowth, I unearthed a name on the limestone: Lilian Julia Metcalf. Recognition sparked in my periphery, just out of reach. A breeze whispered through the leaves of nearby weeping willows. The noise made goose bumps rise on my arms. I moved on to another part of the graveyard and admired the "tablet stones," as Mom called them. According to Mom, limestone was used because it was a soft stone and more easily carved.

As I followed her around the graveyard, I noticed that she seemed to be walking toward a specific spot, and then I realized what it was: two flat markers, each with one of my parents' names and birth dates on it, and blank spots for their end dates. *Now that's downright creepy.*

"Really?" I looked at her; she smiled broadly.

"Your dad and I got a great deal on a plot. We bought four spaces for the price of two; a twofer," she said, elated.

"I think that's disgusting." Then it sunk in. "Wait. You mean the other two are for Jimmy and me? What if we have other plans?"

Not letting my mood affect hers, she fairly sang, "Well, we'll just have to cross that bridge when that time comes." *Ugh.*

My grandparents showed us a few more resting places of long-lost relatives before we walked to our cars. Back at camp, I looked for the Wilsons' truck in the driveway, and much to my chagrin, it was not there. *Wyatt must still be out helping his mom with the laundry.* I decided to grab my suit, along with a float, and enjoy the lake awhile.

Dad carried Stubby down the sandy embankment to the lake for a bath. The last thing Stubby wanted was a bath, and he kept trying to swim away. I watched the comedy unfold as Dad tried his best to soap up our dog. Stubby made a quick getaway up the embankment, suds and all. Dad tried grabbing his collar but tripped over a rock and slid back down the embankment on his belly. At the top of the hill, as if to get back at Dad, Stubby violently shook the suds and excess water off his coat in Dad's direction and ran, barking, toward Freckles. As usual, Freckles wasn't the least bit interested and remained by Mr. Silk's side on the porch. Resigned to the fact that there wouldn't be a battle, Stubby found a shady spot under the swing set and circled three times before curling up in a ball and falling fast asleep.

I grabbed a towel and decided to dry off on the chaise lounge in the side yard. While getting comfortable, I noticed the Wilsons returning, carrying loads of laundry to the house. Wyatt carried one laundry basket full of damp clothes from the car, and one by one, clipped them to the clothesline to dry. As soon as he finished hanging the laundry, he walked over to me and said, "Hey, you doing anything later on today?"

"Nope, just more of what I'm doing now. Enjoying this beautiful day."

"Yes, you are," he agreed, looking me slowly over from head to toe and back up again. A little self-conscious, I pulled the sides of the towel over my midsection. Wyatt just smiled.

"You wanna see a movie this afternoon?" he offered.

"I'll have to ask. Hang on. I'll be right back." I went into the cabin and asked Mom if I could go. She said I could if Jimmy agreed to take us. Let the begging begin...

"Please do this for me. Please, please, please!" I said with my hands clasped together.

"Oh, all right. What dumb movie does Romeo want to take you to?"

I haven't a clue. I went outside to tell Wyatt that I could go under one circumstance: my brother had to take us.

"That's fine. Tell him it's a four o'clock movie. I'll meet you back here at three fifteen." He sauntered back to his yard to take the empty laundry basket inside.

CHAPTER 14

"You ready yet?" Jimmy called. I came out of the back room into the kitchen and saw Mom cleaning string beans for dinner. *Am I ready? Seriously? I've been pacing the cabin since Wyatt asked me to go.*

Mom placed the cleaned beans into a bowl next to Nanny, who gathered the dinner dishes. Nanny made the best creamed-beans with milk, butter, salt, and pepper.

"Hurry up and wait," Mom commented as I paced the floor. Jimmy grabbed the Cadillac keys, and we left the cabin.

"You be careful with my car!" Gramp hollered from his leather chair.

From the corner of my eye, I saw Wyatt walking to the car, and I yelled, "Shotgun!" Wyatt showed no sign of protest: I sat in the front with Jimmy, and he sat in the back. He leaned his arms over the front seat and said we were going to see *Rocky III.* Jimmy rolled his eyes.

"You kids have fun," Jimmy teased. "I can't stand Sylvester Stallone. I'm going to some supernatural, freaky movie called *Poltergeist,* something I'm sure you guys wouldn't want to see anyway. I called to check movie times, and *Poltergeist* starts at four twenty. When your movie is over, just meet me in front of the theater. Just don't tell Mom I didn't sit with you; she'll freak. Deal?"

"Deal," Wyatt and I agreed simultaneously.

At three forty-five, we parked the car and had just enough time to get popcorn and a soda to share. We took a seat at the back of the theater, where it wasn't very crowded. I placed a handful of popcorn on a napkin in my lap, and we shared a soda with two straws. We endured the previews, and as I waited for the movie to begin, I reached for the popcorn just as Wyatt did the same. My hand tingled just from his touch. I jerked my hand back out and grabbed the soda instead.

Halfway through the movie, (which, frankly, I found boring) Wyatt stretched his arms in front of him and placed his left hand on my right knee. My hands began to perspire and I casually wiped my palms on my jeans. We sat like this for about fifteen minutes before he reached for my hand and our fingers became entwined. Wyatt leaned in and whispered, "Are you enjoying the movie?"

I whispered back, "Mmmm, it's okay. I'm not a huge action-movie fan."

He leaned in closer, as I continued watching the film facing straight ahead. I could feel his breath on my neck as he suggested, "Then you won't mind missing a little bit of it?"

I turned to look at him just as he leaned towards me and we bumped foreheads. I giggled, but he was unfazed. His eyes didn't stray from mine as he closed in. Hoping for a kiss, I closed my eyes. His full lips closed on mine, kissing gently at first, then pressing harder. My right hand was still clasped in his when he let go, simultaneously releasing my lips, pressing his forehead into mine. His hand found my cheek, gently tucked a wisp of hair behind my ear. He moved in on my neck with soft kisses that gave me goose bumps. His hand glided behind my head and pulled me closer for a more passionate kiss. This time his lips parted and his tongue explored mine.

I was stunned. I didn't know what to do. The only time I had ever kissed a boy was in the sixth grade, underwater. I had been waiting for my mom to pick me up from swim practice. There were six of us, the last to be picked up. To pass the time, we decided to play truth or dare. When it was my turn, I chose dare. I had to dive in the deep end with Robby Pruitt and kiss him for fifteen seconds while the others watched. Wasting no time, I ran to the deep end and jumped in, with Robby close behind. We finished the dare, hopped out, and walked to our respective cars without a word. That kiss didn't hold a candle to this. Again, I had no idea what I was doing, but, unlike last time, I liked it.

Feeling breathless from our encounter, we finally came up for air. Disappointment set in as the theater lights came on. I didn't want this date to end.

"We should get going," he conceded, reaching for my hand. I could still feel his lips on mine as we walked outside the theater, hand in hand. We found a bench on which to wait for my brother. I watched the theater empty, and soon Jimmy emerged. I let go of Wyatt's hand as he leaned in and whispered, "Rocky won."

"That was the scariest movie I have ever seen." Jimmy rambled on about *Poltergeist* while we walked to the car. "The scariest part of the whole movie was this stupid clown! I swear someday when I'm on my deathbed saying goodbye to my family, I'll be looking over my shoulder for that clown. Someday he's going to get me, and when he's done with me, he's coming for you. The stupid thing doesn't talk and shows up all over the movie in different places!" he said, shivering at the memory.

Few things in this world scared my brother, but clowns topped the list. I wasn't sure what happened to him as a kid, but clowns made him very uncomfortable.

On the ride home, Wyatt told Jimmy about our movie, and I interjected that Rocky won. We pulled into the garage, and Wyatt climbed out of the car. Jimmy and Wyatt exchanged goodbyes, and we lingered by the car as Jimmy walked back to the cabin.

"Thanks for the movie tonight. That was fun," I said, feeling self-conscious.

"Next time you choose. I could tell you were bored halfway through, because you kept checking your watch."

I was checking my watch because I didn't want the movie to end. "Like I said, action movies aren't really my thing."

He smiled and said, "I think you liked the action *in* the movie theater."

I blushed and started to back away, feeling vulnerable.

With a look of confusion, he said, "Uh, I was just teasing. Callie, wait. Don't leave. Come on."

I kept walking. "Thanks again, Wyatt. I'll see you later." I turned and walked inside. I could see through the back window that he remained standing still by the garage. He ran his hand through his wavy blond hair, turned to kick the side of the garage, and then walked back home.

"How was the movie?" Mom asked.

"It was pretty good. Rocky won. It seems like in all action movies, the good guy always wins."

"I saved some dinner for you. It's on the counter."

I took the foil off the plate and dug into delicious beans, a fresh-baked roll, and barbecued chicken.

I joined Jimmy at the dining-room table and watched the rest of the family play spoons. This silly game started with spoons centered on the table, with one less spoon than there were people playing. One person dealt four cards to each person.

The object was to collect four of the same cards. Players passed the rest of the deck, one card at a time, around the table as fast as they could. When a player had four of the same cards, they'd stealthily drag one spoon to their lap. If you saw someone pull a spoon, then you could pull one, even if you didn't have four of a kind; the last person left without a spoon was out. The play continued until the one person remaining was declared the winner.

After Jimmy and I finished eating, we joined the game. It was my turn to shuffle, and I took the cards into my lap, which drove my grandfather crazy. "Just put them on the table. On the table...no, on the table." Looking at my grandfather rebelliously, I continued to shuffle in my lap and slowly dealt the cards one by one. The round sped up, but I was just going through the motions. My mind was still in the movie theater. His hand on my knee, warm lips on mine, the goose bumps he gave me when kissing my neck...

"Aha! Young lady, you must pay closer attention. Victory is mine!" Gramp said with the spoon raised above his head. He had a devilish grin on his face and a twinkle in his eye. Play continued as Jimmy shuffled and dealt the cards. The cards went around the table like wildfire, and I tried to keep track of them, but I couldn't concentrate. The cards continued to stack up in front of me.

"Callie, come on. Pass the cards!" Jimmy shrieked.

"Oh, yeah. Right," I said, quickly picking up the pile that had accumulated in front of me and plopping it down in front of the person on my right.

"Geez, Cal, if you're not gonna play the right way, then don't play at all. One card at a time, you know that!" *Who declared him the play boss?*

Shaking my head, I announced I was out and tossed my cards to Jimmy. He looked up, confused.

"Ah, come on, Cal. That means I have to start the round all over."

"I can't compete with Gramp. He's just too quick for me." I walked away from the table to brush my teeth and go to bed. They continued playing as I climbed into bed and thought about Wyatt's kisses until I fell asleep.

CHAPTER 15

I woke up to an overcast morning and reached for my sweatshirt. I lay back in bed, not wanting to get up just yet. While listening to the soft raindrops hitting the roof of the cabin, my mind drifted to Wyatt. *I wonder if I'll see him today.* He'd had me so flustered yesterday that I couldn't think straight.

I heard footsteps walking past the cabin, and I peeked out to see Riley walking under an umbrella toward the Wilsons' house. She walked up the driveway to the front door. I hoped to catch a glimpse of Wyatt, but as the door opened, disappointment set in when Tommy answered. They hugged as he let her pass through the doorway and left me wondering *-what's going on in there today?*

Feeling as though I wouldn't see Wyatt today, I decided to pick up a notepad from the desk next to the bed to write him a letter.

Wyatt,

I'm not even sure how to start this letter to you. I have had so much fun getting to know you and really love our time together. I'm sorry I ran off yesterday after the movie. I guess, even though you were joking, it made me feel very uncomfortable. I didn't know how to react, and fear got the better of me. I hope you understand.

-Callie

Before I could make any changes to the letter, I folded it up, climbed out of bed and brushed my teeth. The persistent rain soaked me pretty thoroughly as I walked towards the Black Forest. *I guess grabbing an umbrella would have been a good idea.* I could see the Wilsons sitting around the dining-room table as I walked past and hoped no one would see me as I entered the forest. At my tree, I'd hoped to see a white sheet of paper in the knot, but alas, I did not. Instead, I placed my folded sheet of paper in the tree and left before I could change my mind.

It continued pouring as I left the shelter of the trees, and I was dripping wet when I got back to camp. As I was changing into dry clothes in my room, I heard footsteps walking outside again. There was Riley: trudging slowly, dragging her umbrella behind her, not even the motivation to shield herself from the downpour. It was like watching a death march as she slowly passed the water pump; head hung low, shoulders slumped. I made a mental note to investigate later on.

The thunderstorm rolling in put a hold on any fun we were going to have on the lake, so I suggested to Mom that we go to the Highgate Shopping Plaza to ride out the storm. Mom agreed, and she and I left for a few hours. We managed to hit all the discount racks at the clothing stores and tried on all kinds of summer clothing. I was not really a shopper, but at least it was something to do. By noon, my stomach had a life of its own and began ferociously growling, so we went to the food court to pick from a plethora of restaurants. We purchased our meal in the food court, found a spot at a booth, and sat toward the middle of the building. Through the skylights above, we watched clouds break the sunlight so that it played in streams across the windowpanes. For a moment, I felt like I was lying in that field again, watching the northern lights with Wyatt, but the noise of the mall quickly dispelled my vision.

As we ate, two girls walked past and sat behind us at an adjoining booth. They looked to be about my age and they were talking about boys, summer, and how fast time was going by. I couldn't help but eavesdrop on their conversation.

"Can you believe there is only a month left of summer?"

I got a sinking feeling in the pit of my stomach.

"I know. That stinks. I was really hoping to get somewhere with Jason this summer. I didn't have much time to get in his pants," they giggled. The knowledge that my mom was listening made me squirm uncomfortably.

"Oh, hey, speaking of guys, you know what I heard today? Tyler Wilson is being shipped to Iraq after basic training. He's supposed to leave mid-October. I hear Riley is sick over it."

"Will he be home before his deployment?"

"He has to finish twelve weeks of basic training, and then I think he can come home to say goodbye to his family. It's so sad. I hope she gets a chance to say goodbye to him."

Numb, I looked at my mom with shock in my eyes. We both lost interest in our food and decided to end our shopping excursion. The rain had slowed to a drizzle as we walked back to the car, shell-shocked from the news.

"Can you believe that? What sad news," I said to my mom.

"He's a tough kid. He'll be fine, and if Tyler and Riley are meant for each other, then it'll all work out in the end. As your dad always says, this too shall pass."

We rode in silence for a few minutes, thinking about Tyler. "So you like Tyler's brother…Wyatt, is it?" Mom asked me.

"Yeah, I guess so," I admitted, not at all in the mood for where this conversation was heading.

"He's a little older than you, isn't he?"

I'd never asked him, but I thought he was a few years older. "I think so. I'm not sure."

"Hmmm," she said. "You know, I met your father when we were about your age. He lived in a house next door to Grammie's apartment in Highgate. I thought he was the most handsome guy."

As she reminisced about Dad, she looked like she had been transported back in time. "Do you know that if I stood on top of my bathtub and looked out the window, I could see right into his bedroom?" she said, giggling. "We started dating when we were in high school. I was a basketball cheerleader, and Dad was on the basketball team. We went steady for a few years. Then Dad went to college, and we broke up for a year. I just thought it was time for a break. I started dating this guy, Buck, who was quite the looker and a real rebel. He wore a white T-shirt and leather jacket and drove a motorcycle. I thought that made him so exciting. After a few months of dating him, the excitement wore off, and I missed your father. One Christmas he came home; we had a heart-to-heart and started dating again." Smiling wistfully she said, "And the rest is history."

"How did Nanny and Gramp handle you guys dating?"

"Not so well. Nanny thought I was from the wrong side of the tracks, and she wasn't far off. Grammie had been divorced from my father since I was six. She was a single mother raising two kids, which was frowned upon back in those days. She did the best she could to raise us and had help from her mother and father. As a matter of fact, my brother and I lived with them for a year; it was rough for a while. When your dad asked me to marry him, Nanny wouldn't speak to Dad for a solid week. Gramp was the one that gave his blessing, but even he took a while to come around. I was worried your grandparents weren't going to make it to our wedding. Thankfully, they did. Now here we are, still going strong twenty-plus years later."

I loved listening to Mom tell stories of her and Dad. I wondered if I would have a relationship like theirs someday.

"Home again, home again, jiggity jog," she started.

"I wonder who's home at the Lamplys' house," I finished.

Smoke billowed from the trash can as we pulled in to the driveway. *Must be trash day.* The drizzle continued unceasing as we walked through the door, and Dad said, "The fish love this weather. Let's get Aunt Marilyn—grab the net this time, Callie—and let's go catch the one that got away."

CHAPTER 16

"Thank goodness we're back," Aunt Marilyn declared as we docked at Aunt Doris's. "I need to use the little girls' room, and I don't think I can wait another minute."

"You mind if I come in to use the bathroom, too?" I said, wiggling in my seat.

"Sure thing." Turning to Dad, she said, "I'll send her right out when we're done here, Rit. Thanks for a great day!"

"No problem," Dad replied.

We disembarked from the boat and quickly walked into Aunt Doris's cabin. "You first, sweetie," she said politely.

Passing her to the right, I caught a glimpse of Aunt Marilyn. By the way she was standing with her legs glued together, it was obvious she was uncomfortable. Hesitantly, I walked into the cabin's solitary bathroom and shut the door. Noticing immediately the aromatic incense on the shelf, wanting to contemplate this discovery but not able to because I could hear her labored breathing, I asked, "You all right, Aunt Marilyn? I'll be done in just a sec." No sooner had I spoken than I heard an audible splash outside the door. As I exited the bathroom, I could see Aunt Marilyn dabbing at her pants with a paper towel, standing in a puddle of urine. She laughed it off, "Getting old is not for sissies!" but it was obvious she was embarrassed.

I'm an idiot. "I'm so sorry. You should have gone before me. I feel terrible," I said sheepishly.

"Oh, honey, don't think twice about it. It's not the first time it's happened, and I'm pretty sure it won't be the last," she said with a laugh. She walked past me to clean up in the bathroom.

Through the closed door, I spoke, "Hey, Aunt Marilyn, are you European?"

"I think so, why?" she asked curiously.

"Because you're a peeing all over Aunt Doris's floor!" There was a moment of silence, then a burst of deep, loud, hearty laughter. "Goodbye, Callista," Aunt Marilyn chuckled.

ॐ   ॐ   ॐ

The sun shone brilliantly through my bedroom window, causing beads of sweat to form on my upper lip. The rain from the previous evening had finally passed, making it an increasingly warm and muggy morning. I could hear kids jumping from the rope swing and thought, *what a great day to play in the water.* I pulled on my swimsuit and cover-up and grabbed an apple as I walked out the door.

"Where you going?" Jimmy asked.

"Rope swing," I said as I closed the screen door. The wet grass tickled my toes as I peeked through the trees to see that Tommy and Sarah were there. "Hi, guys. Mind if I join you?"

They just looked at each other and shrugged their shoulders. I took that as a yes and cast my cover-up aside on a rock.

"Sure is going to be a hot one," I said, trying to start a conversation with them.

Tommy made a mad leap, grabbed hold of the rope with both hands and swung out over the lake, letting go with a whoop and splashing into the water. He smiled and swam to the side. I figured if those two could do it, so could I. Following Tommy's lead, I bravely made a leap for the rope. I grabbed hold and swung out over the water, my heart racing, only to make a return trip back to solid ground without even attempting to jump.

"Aren't you Wyatt's girlfriend?" Sarah asked.

I shrugged while still holding the rope.

"He talks about a girl a lot around the house."

"What does he say?" I asked curiously.

"He says that she's real pretty and a fast runner. Do you run?"

"Yep, I do. My ankle was hurt for a while, but I'm back at it again."

"He says that he's never felt this way about any girl before. I get grossed out when he starts talking like that." She proceeded to make a gagging noise while pretending to put her finger down her throat.

"It can't be her; she won't even go off the rope swing. If she was really Wyatt's girlfriend, she'd be much more daring," Tommy teased with a mischievous smile.

Challenge accepted. With that, I made a leap out over the water and let go. The free-fall made my stomach flip, and soon I was thrust into the deep water below. When I surfaced, between gasps for air, I asked, "Like that?" I felt proud and exhilarated as I climbed out of the water. They just stood there frozen, wide-eyed, staring at me. Then Tommy started laughing.

"What?" I immediately thought I had something hanging from my nose and wiped at it furiously, but that didn't stop them. I looked down, and to my horror, the top half of my suit had dropped below my right breast; I was fully exposed. Mortified,

I quickly pulled up my suit. I grabbed my cover-up and made a mad dash back to the cabin. Behind me, Tommy joked, "Wyatt's right; she does run fast."

I heard their peals of laughter trail off as I ran through the yard, grabbed a towel from the back of the lawn chair, and wrapped myself in it. With tears streaming down my face, I crashed through the screen door, bounding across the floor, making a mad dash to my bed. *That was the most humiliating thing ever*! I vowed never to leave that cabin again.

CHAPTER 17

So never leaving the cabin again just wasn't in the cards for me. Not an obtainable goal. A while later, I pulled myself together and decided to go check on my tree. Thankfully, no one was around. Through the trees, I could hear that Tommy and Sarah had resumed jumping into the lake. Entering the Black Forest, I went straight to my tree and saw that the knot remained empty. It was a rough day already, but the fact that Wyatt didn't leave a note officially made it the worst day ever. On the bright side, the empty knot meant he'd gotten my note. As I slowly walked past the Wilsons', I saw Wyatt trying to carry three gallon containers full of fresh water back to the house. I picked up the pace to meet him.

"You need some help?"

Cautiously, he handed me one of the jugs and continued toward his house. "Can you help bring it in the kitchen?" he asked.

Having never been inside his house before, I wondered what I'd find behind the front door. I nodded and followed him up the stairs. He lived in a split-level house, so when you walked inside, you immediately had to choose what direction to go: upstairs or downstairs. We went up the stairs into the living room, which was adjoined by the kitchen, and placed the water jugs on the gigantic butcher-block-topped farmhouse table. I noticed immediately how immaculate the house was. Everything seemed just so.

"Want something to drink?" he asked.

I nodded, as he filled two mason jars with fresh water from the gallon jug.

"It's so quiet around here. Where is everyone?" I asked.

"I think you know where Tommy and Sarah are," he said awkwardly.

I began to feel faint from embarrassment and sat down in the chair in front of me.

"It's not a big deal. They told me because they thought it was funny. They'll forget it ever happened by the time they get back. My parents are at the store picking up supplies for Tyler. Did you hear the news? He's being deployed to Iraq after basic training. Mom's a wreck, and Riley... she can't keep it together; she's a mess. We had her over yesterday to tell her the news in person before it got around. We didn't want her to hear it from anyone else, and needless to say, she was shocked."

He sat down across from me at the kitchen table and refilled our glasses. He took a sip, set his glass down, and fumbled with something in his pocket. "I was out by your tree this morning, clearing more brush, and found this," he said, pulling out a folded piece of paper and playing with the edge of the note. "Thanks for that. I felt pretty stupid after what I said to you yesterday. I thought I was being clever, but I'm an idiot sometimes."

Feeling that uncomfortable feeling again, I didn't want to talk about it.

As he stood up, he asked, "Want to see the rest of the house?" Before I could answer him, he had begun to walk down the hall, and I followed. "Those are three of our bedrooms and my mom and dad's bedroom. Tyler and I share a room, at least when he's home; Tommy gets his own room, as does Sarah."

"Where does Samantha sleep?"

He nearly bumped into me as he walked back toward the kitchen, causing my heart to skip a beat. "She has her own space downstairs. It's kind of like an apartment. Here, I'll show ya," he said, going down the stairs to her space.

The stairs opened up into a den with a television and two couches. "Down the hall are her bedroom and bathroom, which Pop converted from the garage. He needed to create a space for her, seeing as she moved home after college."

He was full of nervous energy, and all I could think of was how much I wanted him to touch me. Every time he came close, I hoped his hand would brush mine. It was almost too much to bear. He kept rambling on and on about Samantha and how it stunk to have her home, because now he had to share a room with Tyler again.

I slowly approached him as he leaned against the back of the couch, still rambling, and kissed him square on the mouth. He stood, stunned into silence. My face was merely inches away from his as I said, "Wyatt, I did like the action in the movie theater. I liked it so much it scared me. I've never had a boyfriend before, and this is all new to me." His breathing steadily picked up. His hands found my waist and pulled me closer, so I wrapped my arms around his neck.

"I promise not to do anything you don't want to do. I'm so sorry I was such an idiot the other day," he confessed softly. He leaned in to kiss me with those soft lips I'd been longing for.

Then, a noise from the front door upstairs: footsteps mounting the stairs, bags placed on the kitchen table. "Wyatt?"

his mom called out, setting down her car keys. I instinctively tiptoed to the sliding glass door to make my exit. Quietly, I opened the door, stepped outside, and closed it. Wyatt looked disappointed that I was leaving him, and frankly, I was, too.

I walked toward the front of the house, and through the open windows, I heard his mom asking whose water glasses were on the kitchen table.

"Tommy and Sarah came in for some water and then went back out to the rope swing," he said, not missing a beat.

CHAPTER 18

I felt as though a weight had been lifted off my shoulders. I no longer cared what Tommy and Sarah thought. They could make fun of me all day if they wanted; it just didn't matter. Up ahead, Dad was tinkering with a tandem bicycle.

"Need a hand?" I offered as I got closer.

"Sure," he said, handing me a wrench. I sat down, and for the next hour, we worked side by side.

"Ready to take her for a spin?" Dad asked. "Aunt Doris and Uncle Fred have invited us for dinner, so we'll head that way and everyone else will walk down in a little bit."

We got on and peddled down the gravel road. Dad sat on the front seat, and I was on the back. We pedaled in unison to Aunt Doris's and leaned the bike against one of the pine trees. Justa came bounding out through the screen door, barking.

"Did you bring Master Stubbing with you?" Uncle Fred asked playfully.

"I think Jimmy's walking him down in a bit," Dad replied, smiling.

"Oh good! Justa could use a friend to hang out with."

Aunt Doris and Uncle Oscar's cabin had a lakeside screened-in porch running the entire length of the cabin. I could see that they'd pushed two large picnic tables together to accommodate all of us eating here tonight.

"Honey, could you give me a hand and bring out the butter dish?" Aunt Doris asked. I brought the handcrafted glass butter dish to the table. Every meal around here had to have bread and butter. It was a dietary staple of farm families in Vermont.

Stubby suddenly appeared outside. Justa immediately lay on his back and kicked his feet in the air. In the next instant, they tackled one another and chased each other around the yard. Jimmy, Mom, Nanny, and Gramp came in the screened-in porch just as Uncle Fred, Aunt Shirley, and their kids drove up. The dogs had tired themselves out, and as we were sitting down to dinner, I could see them snuggling up together under a pine tree.

"Cheers, everyone! I just wanted a chance to have everyone over before the end of summer, which is rapidly approaching," Uncle Oscar said.

My stomach turned as he spoke. *Is summer nearly over already? Has the countdown really begun?* I couldn't even concentrate on what was being said; I was too busy trying to figure out how much time I had left before I had to go back home. If I calculated correctly, I had a little less than two weeks. That wasn't good.

"Earth calling Callie."

I looked up at everyone staring back at me. "Huh?" I mumbled.

"Can you pass the bread around, please?"

I looked to my right, and Uncle Fred had the bread basket suspended in the air for me. I passed it along. *Where did the time go?* Food continued circulating around the table along with laughter and conversation—but all I could think about was Wyatt. *What happens when I leave? Next summer is an eternity away.* Suddenly I lost my appetite.

"Are you all right, dear?" Aunt Doris asked.

I shook my head. I felt like I was about to cry. "Is it all right if I walk back? I'm not feeling so well right now."

"Sure, sweetheart. If you're sure you're going to be all right, Jimmy can ride the tandem back with Dad," Mom said, looking concerned.

"Yeah. I'm sure I'll be fine in a while."

I walked down the gravel road slowly. As I approached the cabin, I saw a bundle of wildflowers held together with twine on the top step. No card, no note. I picked them up and looked around for Wyatt. They were beautiful. Inside, I put them in a glass vase, and placed them on the kitchen counter.

I sat at the counter and stared at them, touching the petals of each flower, lost in my thoughts. I rested my head on my arms, which were folded on the counter, and started to cry. The day had had so many ups and downs.

I carried the flower vase to my room and set it on my nightstand. I rolled on my side and stared at the flowers. I'm not sure when I fell asleep, but I was awoken by the sound of my mom coming into my room and placing a hand on my forehead. I lay still with my eyes closed as she pulled the blanket up and over me. I heard her move the vase of flowers and through half-closed lids watched her walk out of the room, shaking her head.

All the lights were out, but I could hear whispers. "I think our little girl is in love," Mom said to Dad. "I went to check on her and saw a vase of flowers on her nightstand. I think that boy across the street is sweet on our Callie."

Dad gave a brief laugh. "Sounds like someone I used to know."

CHAPTER 19

For the remainder of the week, I decided I wanted to spend as much time as I could with Wyatt. He was the first person I wanted to see in the morning and the last person I wanted to see at night.

My family included him in all our activities, and even Jimmy let it happen. It was apparent that Dad's approval of Wyatt wasn't completely welcomed by Jimmy. Dad would ask Wyatt's opinion on everything from sports to politics to the weather. He even asked Wyatt to help him work on the other bikes we had in the garage, which sent Jimmy's eyes a rollin'.

On our last day of the summer, we went to the bike shop in Enosburg. My dad invited Wyatt to come along and bought us each an ice cream.

"Wyatt, what are your plans when the school year starts?"

"Well, Mr. Lamply, I'm going to be a senior this year, and I'm just waiting on a college that will accept me," he said, looking at me intently.

"Oh, yeah? Where're you thinking of going?" my dad inquired.

"That's a tough one. I'm not sure. I've applied to a bunch of schools along the East Coast. We'll just have to wait and see what I hear back."

Dad said, "Yeah, it's a real crapshoot. Hey, we're going into town tonight for the last concert of the season. You and your family should join us. I've invited the Silks to come along. It should be a fun evening."

"Thanks, Mr. Lamply. I'll let my folks know."

That evening, the music was in full swing by the time we all arrived. The adults left all the kids to their own devices, as if they could sense that we needed a night to say goodbye. I jumped at the chance to slow dance with Wyatt and hold him close. I loved the feel of his arms around me and didn't care who was watching as I placed my arms around his neck and we floated across the dance floor. *I don't want to leave you*, I pleaded with my eyes, which soon began to cloud. My head swirled with emotion. Wyatt reached up and wiped away a few rogue tears from my cheek.

"We'll keep in touch. You're only a few states away, and I'm really good at writing letters," he said, smiling.

I'm in love with you. I know it, I thought.

"You have to promise to write me back."

"I promise." My voice was nothing but a whisper. The song ended, and we walked off the dance floor hand in hand. We sat with our fingers entwined, and I realized I hadn't given him my home address. I wrote in lipstick on the palm of his hand and kissed it for good luck. My parents began saying goodbye to friends, and I began to panic. I couldn't breathe. He squeezed my hand as he let go and promised to keep in touch.

As we drove away, I looked back and waved. My heart was aching. The harvest moon followed us home, glowing enormously through the back window. Mom nervously glanced back at me in the rearview mirror.

When we got home, everyone went their separate ways, leaving me in deep thought and self-pity. I couldn't sleep. Just tossed and turned. About an hour after I had crawled into bed, I heard the sound of pebbles hitting my window. My heart skipped a beat because I knew with my whole being that it was Wyatt. I threw the blankets off and jumped out of bed, not caring that I ran into the night in only my pajamas and flip-flops. I pushed the door open and jumped the last step into Wyatt's waiting arms. I wrapped my arms around his neck tightly and squeezed him.

"I don't wanna go. They can't make me go, right?" I said, nuzzling his neck. Before I could control myself, tears were rolling down my cheeks.

He grabbed my hands from around his neck and brought them down in front of him. "I wanted to spend a little more time with you."

Holding his hand, I followed him into the forest to my tree. I looked at the tree, and though we were cloaked in darkness, the orange glow of the harvest moon lit up the newest set of initials branded there. "WW + CL."

"You like it?"

I couldn't speak and just nodded my approval.

He leaned in and whispered, "I was hoping you would." He pulled me toward him, giving me a passionate kiss. Breathless when we parted, I leaned in for yet another kiss. The thrill I felt when our lips met sent me reeling. I didn't know where to grab or touch; I was on sensory overload.

Breathlessly, he asked, "What time do you leave tomorrow?"

"Eight," I squeaked. *Why is he talking? Doesn't he realize we're running out of time? Don't stop touching me!* I screamed in my head.

"I have to get you back…it's getting late. I just had to see you one more time before you left. I didn't like the way we left it at the concert tonight." He kissed me slowly one last time and took my hand to guide me back to the cabin.

We walked more slowly that night than any human ever has, ever will. At the door, we hugged tightly.

"Safe travels tomorrow," he said. "Write when you can."

"I hate goodbyes," I said.

"We won't say goodbye then." He leaned in for a peck. "It's just bye for now."

At that, he let me go. Before I reached my bed, I was in tears once again.

CHAPTER 20

Mom woke me up at seven thirty. I got dressed and met everyone at the car.

"Well, this is it," Dad said. He hugged Gramp and Nanny goodbye. They hugged each of us as we piled in the car. Through the back window, I saw a familiar figure in the upstairs window of the Wilsons' house. Wyatt waved goodbye with one hand, and I pressed my palm to the back window. I felt numb for the seven-hour drive home.

In five short days, I would be entering my junior year in high school. I had hoped that returning to a routine with homework and swim practice would keep my mind off Wyatt. *Maybe writing him will help?* The first week back, I began my correspondence.

Dear Wyatt,

The drive home was never ending. I miss you already. What a great summer! Only what? Three hundred sixty days until next summer? That's all? Ugh. I don't think I can wait that long to see you again. I really hope we come back for Christmas. I'll have to ask and let you know.

I started swim practice again, which is taking a lot of my time. School started today. My teachers are okay. I really like my math teacher. He's super nice and fun and is also the boys' soccer coach.

Jimmy heads to college after the weekend. Mom has been on a shopping frenzy getting stuff for his room. She cries a lot just thinking about him leaving, and that's just college. I can't imagine if he joined the military. She cries at just about anything, though. She always says that if she could get paid for it, she could make a living being a professional crier. Speaking of the military, have you heard from Tyler? I have made some new friends but no one like you. Write when you can.

I miss you,

Callie

I waited, and waited, and waited a little longer for a letter. Finally, in early October, I got a response.

Dear Callie,

Thanks for the letter. I miss you, too. I'm trying to keep busy with schoolwork and working on the farm up the hill when I have time. You know, the one that smells like cows? I see your grandfather in town every so often when I'm getting supplies for the farm. I have to drive right by their place each time I'm there.

Tyler came home this past weekend for a visit. Man, has he changed. He's super muscular. He lost about ten pounds during basic training. He's almost too thin, but I'd never tell him that—ha. Riley came by when he was in town, and they had a very tearful goodbye. Mom still can't talk about Tyler leaving. It upsets her too much. Tyler left Tuesday and said he's been stationed stateside in North Carolina at Camp Lejeune, temporarily. I can't imagine what he's about to endure. You couldn't pay me to join the military.

I keep thinking I see you running when I drive through Franklin. Write back soon.

-W

I reread his letter over and over again, especially the part where he said he missed me. I put the letter in a shoebox in the bottom of my closet for safekeeping, hoping to add to it in the coming months. The thought of the long months I would have to endure before seeing him again caused my heart to ache all over again.

ભ ભ ભ

Lately I'd found myself watching and reading the news whenever possible. Last thing I'd heard, troops were being sent to Iraq to beef up the manpower, and the very mention of this in the media made my stomach twist. The military conflict seemed to be taking over the news. *Please keep Tyler safe.* Thank goodness Wyatt wasn't interested in following in his brother's footsteps. I didn't think I would be able to handle that very well. Riley's broken state made so much more sense to me now. Week after week, it seemed the conflict was escalating, but I didn't dare say anything in my letters to Wyatt. I kept to my daily routine and the ins and outs of school life in my letters.

CHAPTER 21

The weeks dragged on, and Wyatt and I continued to write back and forth. At school, I kept busy with my girlfriends, swimming, homework, and knowing that fall, my favorite time of year, was right around the corner. Invitations came in to a few Halloween parties, which I declined because they didn't interest me much. It was funny; I hadn't found myself looking at any boys at school either. I was afraid if I started looking, I'd jinx myself with Wyatt. However, that didn't stop the boys at school from looking at me. In the middle of my language-arts class, a boy walked by and dropped a note on my desk. I looked at it as if it were a smoldering ember. I held the note using only my index fingers and thumbs and opened it to find a silly note: "Want to be my ghoulfriend for the Halloween dance?" On the back was his name. I smiled and folded the note up.

Later, at my locker, the boy walked up to me and asked if I had read the note. I shrugged my shoulders in response.

"I know you did. I saw you fold it up. So what do you think?" he said, sounding slightly irritated.

"I'm busy that night, but thanks anyway," I said, handing him back the note. I really didn't want to spend the time to get to know him. If he was anything like most of the boys in my grade, he only had one thing on his mind, and it wasn't bobbing for apples.

"Excuse me. I gotta get to my next class," I said to him, hoping he'd take the hint and move out of the way.

As I walked away, I heard him say, "Whatever, princess," under his breath. *What am I doing? Does it really matter if I go to a Halloween dance with someone other than Wyatt? I have no idea what Wyatt is doing with other girls at his school.*

With a change of heart, I turned around just in time to see that he'd already handed that same note to another girl. *Boys.*

One evening on the drive home from swim practice, Mom explained the family's plan for the upcoming holidays.

"Grammie is coming down for Thanksgiving and staying for a week. After your brother's birthday, we're going to head up to Vermont to have Christmas with Nanny and Gramp. What do you think about that?" she asked with a smile.

"I like that plan. I like it a lot," I said, smiling back at her from ear to ear. Excitement filled every inch of my being. When I got home, I reached for my calendar and started a countdown with a red marker. It was exactly one month between Thanksgiving and Christmas. I could hardly wait!

Dear Wyatt,

Good news! We're heading up for Christmas! I just got word from my mom today. I'm so happy I could explode! I'll be counting the days. How's school going for you? Have you heard from any colleges yet? Anything exciting going on up there?

The letter continued on about a whole lot of nothing. I mailed it the next day and waited for a response. Each day I was greeted with an empty mailbox, disappointment smacked me in the face. Finally, the week of Thanksgiving, a letter came in the mail for me. I ran back to the house and carried it to my room, closing the door behind me.

Dear Callie,

That's great news! Less than a month now! To answer your question about schools, I've heard back from several, but I've decided to go to University of Rhode Island! It's an exciting time. I heard someone say once 'How are you going to write your page?' I feel like I've started working on my rough draft, ha! But it's a start, and I'm really looking forward to this new chapter in my life.

His letter continued on about his family and how Tyler had written often about coming home for Christmas. Tyler also wrote about receiving his papers for deployment. After Christmas, he'd be leaving for Beirut.

CHAPTER 22

Thanksgiving came and went. We had a nice visit with my grandmother. She stayed for a week. When I thought of Grammie, I saw her as an old lady, not a vibrant, older woman. But during her visit, I overheard a conversation between her and my mom. Their discussion revolved around man trouble. *Wait...what?* I entered the room and sat quietly, leafing through a magazine, pretending not to listen.

"...so I tried to call him back, but he won't return my calls. I just don't know what to do about this. I thought we were hitting it off. We've met for drinks several times, and he's had 'overnight privileges,'" she said, using air quotes.

My brain couldn't process this conversation, but by listening, I began to empathize with her. She was having the same feelings of longing that I was having, and to my surprise, we had more in common than I'd thought.

Seeing this side of my grandmother summoned the memory of the first time I'd looked at my mom and dad as real people. You know, like when you see a teacher outside the context of a classroom. This particular night, I wasn't allowed to go out with friends, and my parents had dinner plans. Rather than trust me alone in the house, they'd decided to bring me along. As we sat down at our local pizza joint, my parents seemed to forget I was there and began to enjoy their time with their friends. Mom laughed and playfully hit Dad on the shoulder, listening to him tell the same silly stories she'd heard umpteen times. They were like a bunch of teenagers, and watching the evening unfold felt like an out-of-body experience. While time keeps ticking away, people may change, but the essence of who they are remains the same.

Listening to my grandmother talk about her love life, I came to appreciate that we had shared the same feelings. She was just a real person with a longing to be loved.

Grammie left December 2nd, the day after Jimmy's birthday. Twenty days. I continued marking the calendar with big red Xs at the end of each day. *Twenty long days.*

On the evening of the 21st, we packed up the car. Excitement filled the air; I even helped my brother pack.

"What is it with you?" he asked. "You've been giddy all day. Oh, wait, is lover boy waiting for you up there?"

"Maybe," I said, smiling, folding his pants and shoving them in a suitcase. "Why, aren't you excited to go?" I asked.

"Hmmm, let's see … no friends will be there, and I'll be stuck at my grandparents' house for a week with nothing to do but sit, eat, and play cards. Not my idea of a great time."

"What about Riley? She'll be up there, most likely. She's your friend."

He scoffed at my remark. "How about because Tyler will be there?"

Ah, there it is.

We left early the next morning and started our drive. Around hour three, my excitement began to wane and my eyes got heavy. We went directly to Nanny and Gramp's winter home in Franklin, unloaded our things, and placed the presents under the tree for Christmas. That particular cold December day produced snow that dusted the ground. After we said hello, I got changed into running tights, added a couple of layers on top, and put on my running shoes.

I walked out, and Mom nervously glanced at Dad. "You're going for a run now?" she asked.

"Yeah, it was a long car ride, and I need to stretch my legs," I said as I reached for the door.

"Don't be too long; the snow is supposed to pick up out there. It's going to be slippery on the road."

"I'll be careful."

Once outside, my lungs happily filled with the cold Vermont air. Slowly, I took off down the street toward camp. Butterflies began to dance wildly inside me. From the top of Camp Road, the Wilsons' house was visible below. Several cars were parked in the drive, including that familiar, faded, red pickup truck.

This place looked so different in the winter. The field that Wyatt used to cut in the summer was now covered in snow, and the lake resembled the frozen tundra. The turquoise color of Gramp's camp popped in contrast to the white snow making it seem smaller somehow.

Feeling nervous, taking those last few steps up the stairs to knock on the door, all at once I heard the talking inside stop abruptly. Tyler opened the door and looked at me with disinterest. He turned his head and hollered, "Wyatt, someone at the door for you." He opened the door wider to let me in. Around the kitchen table sat Mr. and Mrs. Wilson, Tommy, Sarah, and Riley; Samantha was in the kitchen making tea. Wyatt walked toward me with a wide grin on his face collecting me in a huge bear hug, and I began to melt; I had been starving for his affection for months now.

He grabbed my hand as we walked into the kitchen. "Everyone remember Callie?" Heads nodded.

"Hi, everyone."

"Did you run here?" Sarah asked in disbelief.

I nodded. "Am I interrupting your dinner, Mrs. Wilson?"

"No, dear, it won't be ready for hours. Come on in, and make yourself comfortable." So I did.

"Yeah…about dinner, Mom, we're gonna eat at Rye's tonight," Tyler said, holding Riley's hand. Disappointed, Mrs. Wilson said okay, and they left the house. Tommy and Sarah were bored with the conversation in the kitchen and went downstairs with Samantha. Mr. and Mrs. Wilson busied themselves with dinner preparations as we made small talk about how my school year was going and how my swim team was performing. I politely answered all of their questions, but deep down, all I wanted was to be alone with Wyatt. Eventually, they retired to the family room and turned on the TV to give us some privacy. I placed my hands on the table in front of me, and Wyatt reached out to take both of them. He looked at me with those cobalt blue eyes and whispered, "I missed you."

"I missed you, too." We talked about our plans for the next week, how I had to shop with my grandparents one day, and how he had to shovel driveways if the snow got heavy—all small talk. We made plans to meet up on the 26th at the mall in Enosburg. Somehow, I had to find a way to get there. We sat and talked for about an hour, but seeing the snow piling up along the windowsill, I had a sinking feeling that it was time to go.

"I'd better head back. My parents will be worried," I said, disappointed. We both stood up, and he held my fleece jacket out for me to slip into. He grabbed his coat and we walked together up the hill, hand in hand. At the top, he pulled me in for a kiss.

"Be careful running back, and I'll see you on the 26th," he said. "Meet me at the food court at twelve thirty?"

"All right. I'll see you then," I said, and smiled as I turned to run back to my grandparents'. Looking back, while cresting the hill, I saw him standing where I left him, waving.

The snow piled heavy, and I had a hard time getting down the road, slip-sliding my way back to my grandparents' home. Shaking the snow from my jacket, Aunt Marilyn said, "Well, look what the cat dragged in."

The cuckoo clock on the wall sprung to life. Taking note of the time, I had been out longer than expected, and seeing the disappointment in my mom's eyes, I could tell she was thinking the same thing.

CHAPTER 23

On Christmas Eve, we went to church for a magical evening service. The church looked as though Norman Rockwell had painted it: quaint and charming. As we entered, we were handed candles for later use in the service.

This stunning church was packed to the rafters. I looked from pew to pew for the Wilsons and found them toward the front of the church. Tyler, in full uniform, sat next to Riley at the end of the first pew. The rest of the Wilson clan sat behind them on the second pew with Riley's family. Wyatt glanced back, his eyes wandering the crowd until he found me and waved.

The service began with a hymn, and then the minister greeted the congregation. He spoke of the conflict in Beirut. "We're so proud of our sons overseas. We have one in our midst this evening: Tyler Wilson. Young man, we are proud to call you one of our own. May God watch over you and bless you as you begin a new chapter in your life. We wish you Godspeed as you are deployed to Beirut. Enjoy this time with your family and friends."

Someone in the back of the church clapped, and soon the whole congregation joined. The minister said, "Tyler, please stand." He did, waving to the crowd as he returned to his seat.

The service continued, and we neared my favorite part. The lights were turned down for effect, and the minister said, "When

Mary said yes to God's call, she gave birth to Christ. When we say yes to Christ, we let him into our lives, and it gives us a light that we can carry in a dark world. It's our version of Mary's answer, and it's a way to celebrate his birth. Please stand."

The minister stood with a candle, walked to the Advent wreath on the altar, and lit the center candle. "We light a candle from the Christ candle to remind us what this holiday really means and to remind us that Christ gives us light. As we light another's candle, we pass on Christ's light." He walked to the first pew and lit Tyler's candle. Tyler, in turn, lit Riley's candle while the minister turned to light the candle of the first person in the choir loft. It continued this way, from pew to pew, until the entire church was glowing. We began to softly sing Christmas carols, starting with "O Holy Night" and ending with "Silent Night." We were bathed in Christ's light; I could feel it. We all did. It was a glorious moment.

As we left the church that evening, we hugged all the families that we recognized. Tyler received a lot of attention with handshakes and hugs, loosening the arm he had tightly wrapped around Riley's waist only briefly. The minister was shaking hands at the door of the church. "Merry Christmas," he said to our family as we shook his hand and continued on to our car.

CR   CR   CR

We all dove into our presents on Christmas morning with laughter and surprise. Dad had wrapped a piece of jewelry in a small box, which was wrapped inside another box, and Mom had to open four boxes before she got to the present. She gasped as she opened a pearl ring with diamonds on either side. Mom was in tears…shocker. Later, as the gift exchange continued, Jimmy opened an unusual one: his old sneaker. We all howled with laughter and congratulated Mom for pulling this annual prank off again. We never knew what she was going to put under the tree. One year it was an old sandal, and the year after that, an old dress shoe. She used the finest wrapping paper and bow to decorate the box. She was always doing something unexpected, and we never knew who would be the recipient. She started this when we were much younger. She liked the idea of having a lot of gifts under the tree, but my parents didn't have the funds to buy a lot for my brother and me so she started wrapping objects we already owned. Our tree was always overflowing with gifts, and by the looks of old photos, we always appeared to have an extravagant Christmas. Mom started scaling back as we grew, and by this time, she only put one previously owned object under the tree; hence the old sneaker.

After half of the presents were opened, we went into the kitchen for some delicious egg strata and pecan rolls. Year after year, our menu remained the same, and there was something comforting about that. After breakfast, Mom and Dad made Bloody Marys to enjoy during the remainder of present-opening; my parents liked to stretch Christmas out as long as possible. Dad would distribute the presents one by one until we all had one in hand, and then we would open them and share what we got, hence controlling the speed of Christmas. I appreciated it now that I was old enough to understand. As a young kid, not so much.

Once the final present had been opened, we would enjoy our gifts for a while until Mom got out the Christmas puzzle, another tradition in the Lamply home. Each year, Mom would get a jigsaw puzzle, and the number of pieces increased annually. The object was to complete the puzzle before the end of the day.

Knowing we couldn't finish on our own, we would invite friends and their families over to eat leftovers and help complete the puzzle; mostly neighbors within walking distance came by.

When this year's puzzle was close to completion, I noticed some pieces were missing. "Jimmy, come on. Don't hold on to the final piece. That's so annoying."

"You're just jealous that you didn't think to do it," he said smiling, as he placed the last piece of the puzzle.

Another wonderful Christmas: we glowed with the happiness the day had brought. Secretly, though, I couldn't wait for the next day to come.

ᘓ   ᘓ   ᘓ

I woke with a start, knowing I would see Wyatt today. Trying to think of an excuse to go to the mall without having to ask permission to see Wyatt, I thought, *I could say I need to exchange a Christmas gift.* As luck would have it, the snow had other plans: about eight inches had accumulated and it showed no sign of stopping. My heart sank. To make matters worse, the power went out around lunchtime, and I couldn't call Wyatt because the phone lines were down. *Trapped. Ugh.*

Dad started a fire in the family room, and we all sat around with blankets while Mom got the transistor radio out to listen to weather updates. Mom made the most of the situation by reading a Stephen King novel, Jimmy and Gramp were playing cards, and Nanny was doing needlepoint in her rocking chair by the fire. I moved to the couch and looked longingly outside in the direction of Lake Carmi.

"How long is this storm supposed to last?" I asked no one in particular, my breath fogging up the windowpane.

Mom replied, "They said we could expect another four inches throughout the day."

I drew a *W* in the fogged glass, then wiped it away and blew on the glass again. This time I drew a tree with a *W* beside it.

We spent the afternoon waiting for the electricity to come back on and listening to the radio for weather reports. By five thirty, the power was restored, but the snow continued falling. Mom brought out the leftovers from Christmas dinner, but I had lost my appetite. As Mom and I cleaned up the dishes, she asked, "Did you have plans today?"

"Something like that," I said, a little too sharply.

"I see," she said.

The snow fell through the evening, and by bedtime, I had a feeling I wouldn't be seeing Wyatt tomorrow either. I attempted to call him before bed but encountered a constant busy signal. Disappointed, I crawled into bed in a funk.

On the 28th, we loaded our car and began our trek home. I was miserable because this vacation wasn't at all what I had planned.

As we drove through town on our way to the interstate, I saw the Wilsons' truck at the gas station. We drove slowly enough that I could see Tyler, in uniform, with his mom and dad in the front of the truck and Wyatt, Tommy, and Sarah in the back.

We merged onto the interstate into crawling traffic. The drive back home to Connecticut took nine hours, causing me extreme mental fatigue.

The week dragged on. Mom and Dad busied themselves with preparations for their New Year's Eve party, which went off without a hitch. Mom pulled out all the stops and dressed in a long, black skirt and black-sequined blouse. Dad wore a suit. Jimmy and I were exiled upstairs. We managed to spy on them all night, watching one of our neighbors get obliterated by Jim Beam. He was slurring his words and stumbling around the party. By the time midnight rolled around, he had passed out on the living-room couch. My parents weren't concerned; this wasn't the first time. With my brother preoccupied with the neighbors' antics, I slipped into my parents' room to call Wyatt.

"Sorry, dear, he's not home tonight," Mrs. Wilson said. "I'll be sure to let him know you called. Happy New Year!"

"Five, four, three, two, one…Happy New Year!" I watched as kisses were passed all around, and I couldn't help but feel envious; I wished I had someone besides my brother to ring in the New Year with.

CHAPTER 24

The remainder of the school year was pretty uneventful, especially when swim season ended. I'd finally received a letter from Wyatt the first week of January asking where I was on the 26th. He had somehow managed to make it to the mall. He said that there was no way he was going to miss out on the opportunity to see me, but that obviously, I didn't feel the same way. I tried to write him back to explain, but it didn't seem to make things better because he never replied.

One afternoon during spring break, I found myself at home with Jimmy while my parents were out running errands. We were making SpaghettiOs for me and ravioli for Jimmy. I sat at the kitchen counter with my bowl, and Jimmy sat at the table. He had just turned off the radio as I walked into the room. I thought I'd heard the reporter saying something about a suicide bomber.

"Whatever happened to you and Riley last summer when you confronted her about Tyler?" I asked with my back to him.

He didn't answer right away.

"Oh, well, that was nothing."

Really? "That didn't sound like nothing."

"I liked her, and we had been hanging out off and on through the beginning of the summer. I met her one day at Stewart's while I was running some errands for Mom and Dad. She was funny and pretty. I liked her immediately and thought she liked me back. I would have found any reason to go to the shop—from getting ice, or buying lighter fluid for the charcoal, to picking up bait for fishing. It didn't matter what it was; I just wanted an excuse to see her again. I finally got up enough nerve to ask her out to the movies. We went and saw *Rocky III*. That's why I didn't want to see it with you and Wyatt that night."

I turned around, holding my bowl, moving to sit across from him at the kitchen table and smiled.

"I had no idea she already had a boyfriend until you told me."

I blushed at the memory.

He looked uncomfortable. "Anyway, after you told me, I wanted to confront her. I didn't want to be the idiot, but I guess I was too late."

He paused for a moment and looked down at his spoon, idly pushing ravioli around his bowl. Still looking down, he continued, "She just said that it was too hard. She had been dating Tyler all year, and they were going through a rough patch until that one night they decided to make up. Naturally, I wasn't thrilled about this. I didn't take it very well. I have to say, deep down, I'm really happy he's deployed. I don't have to worry about running into him next summer." He dropped the spoon in the bowl.

"Now that he's out of the picture, for the most part, are you going to try and get back together with her?" I asked.

"I was never really with her; we were just starting to see each other. I'm not sure what'll happen. I guess we'll have to see how the summer goes. In the meantime, I'm not wasting time pining for her. As a matter of fact, I have a date tonight," he said, getting up from his chair. He cleaned out his bowl and put it in the dishwasher.

"Really?" I asked a little too loudly.

He laughed. "Don't sound so surprised. I'm not like you, putting all my eggs in one basket. You really should get out more. I'm not so sure this Wyatt kid is worth waiting for. After all, he is a Wilson. I know that Tyler isn't the best of characters, and I know that he and Wyatt are close. I just wouldn't put a lot of worth into what he says to you. Don't let him make promises that he can't keep."

This all sounds very ominous, I thought, as I stood to clean out my bowl. "Knock it off. You don't even know Wyatt. He's nothing like his brother."

"Riley told me a thing or two about Tyler. Apparently, he was dating the women's track coach at his high school when he was working there a year after graduation. He got a job interning as a physical therapist's assistant in the school's athletic department. He almost got her fired because one of the students found them in a compromising position in the women's locker room—and told people about it. He was nineteen at the time. She was thirty. Some of the kids were teasing him about it, and he beat the shit out of this one senior, putting him in the hospital. All the kids were talking about it, Riley said. It got pretty bad. The teacher ended up taking a leave of absence at the end of the year. It doesn't really speak highly of his character. He's a real hothead."

I let what he said sink in. "If I didn't know better, I'd say you were worried about your little sister. You really do like me!"

He laughed and walked out of the room. "Just be careful, you nut-job."

I sat back down at the counter in the kitchen. *What if Jimmy's right? Eesh, I hate when he's right...*

CHAPTER 25

Days melted into weeks, weeks into months, and all the while, Wyatt and I continued to write letters to each other—though not as often as I would have liked. I wanted to read more about how much he missed me, more love letters, but lately, they were just about daily activities.

Jimmy continued to dip into the dating pool at college, but school was out now, so he came home for the summer. No one special really materialized for him. Deep down, I thought he was keeping it platonic with the girls until he could see Riley again.

Finally, talk of our summer plans popped up at dinner. We discussed when we were going to go up to camp: deciding we would head up Wednesday, June 22 and stay through August 20. I wrote my last letter to Wyatt, telling him when we'd arrive, and since today was the 17th, he wouldn't have a chance to write me back. The next few days were filled with house cleaning, laundry, packing, and getting Stubby to the groomers. Mom had contacted the post office to hold our mail for the summer and put our newspapers on vacation hold. All of these chores were indicators that summer break was nearing.

ೞ   ೞ   ೞ

June 22, 1983

On the morning of the 22nd, we packed the car up early, while trying to dodge the raindrops. This wasn't a good sign. As

I got in the car, I prepared myself for the marathon drive. Seven and a half hours later, owing to a longer-than-planned pit stop for Stubby, we arrived. The dark clouds had followed us all the way to Vermont, and as we parked in Gramp's gravel driveway, the heavens opened up. We left the luggage in the car and made a mad dash for the cabin, with Stubby running ahead, barking. Nanny was there with the door open, welcoming us back, and by the delicious smells coming from the kitchen, I knew dinner had already been prepared.

"A certain someone came by for you about an hour ago, Callie," Gramp said, handing me a small bouquet of wildflowers. I smiled and grabbed a mason jar from the cupboard to put the flowers in. I walked back to my room and put the flowers on my nightstand. The pretty little bouquet made me hopeful for the summer ahead.

Eventually, the rain let up enough for us to go back out to the car for the luggage. As the clouds broke, steam rose from the gravel road; it was going to be a muggy evening. I glanced toward the Wilsons' house to see if anyone had ventured outside. Tommy and Sarah were out playing with Freckles in Mr. Silk's yard. They waved in my direction, but there was no sign of Wyatt.

I walked in, unpacked my bags, and changed into running clothes. I ran my usual route—up the gravel road and past the vegetable farm, waving at the woman that owned the place. She looked even older than I remembered. I ran out to the main road and back, slowed to a walk, and passed Mr. Silk's. Next stop: the Black Forest, my tree.

The forest was getting thinner; I could see straight through to the other side where many trees had been cleared and new cabins were being built. I sighed deeply. With my hands over the initials on the tree, I leaned to stretch my right calf, thinking back on the first day I met Wyatt here.

While I stood stretching, I noticed that the undergrowth had remained clear around my tree, which made me smile. As if reading my mind, Wyatt materialized.

"It is easier to get to your tree, don't you think?" he asked, smiling.

"It is, yes, and thank you for the flowers," I submitted shyly.

"What flowers? Must be your other boyfriend," Wyatt joked.

I gently slugged him in the shoulder.

"I'm glad to see you again. Wanna walk a little bit?"

I nodded my head, and we walked up Camp Road toward Lake Road, past the farm.

"So what really happened?"

I knew what he was talking about. I began with the snowstorm knocking the power out, and how we all sat by the fire for the afternoon. "Plus, I never did tell my mom I was meeting you there. I tried to call you after the power was up and running in our part of town, but apparently, it still wasn't working at your house. I kept getting a busy signal." The words came out in a rush.

"I got there at one thirty, an hour later than we planned, because I got stuck in the snow on Camp Road. I thought maybe you had made it to the mall but decided not to wait any longer and left. That's what upset me the most, the thought of you not caring enough to stick around a little longer just in case I would show up," he said while staring down at his feet.

"I would have been there if I could have, but Mom didn't want anyone out on the roads with the snow being so bad."

"Yeah, well, my dad gave me hell for trying to meet up with you, and I had my car privileges taken away for a week."

"Sorry I wasn't there."

"Well, you're here now; that's all that matters," he said, kissing me on the cheek.

ଔ   ଔ   ଔ

Our summer break started, and we moved along as if we were never apart. July 4th came and went with our annual family reunion. We had our big volleyball tournament in the Wilsons' yard against the Silk family. This time we had the Wilsons play with us. Wyatt, Tommy, and Sarah were on the Lamplys' side, while Mr. and Mrs. Wilson and Samantha were on the Silks' side. Great food, and the fantastic fireworks punctuated the evening.

Aunt Marilyn reported seeing Jimmy and Riley walking the gravel road together past Aunt Doris and Uncle Oscar's camp recently. Apparently, Jimmy had a change of heart and decided to put all his eggs in one basket. Tyler had left for Beirut on December 28th, so Jimmy was in the clear for now. I could tell he was a little worried about seeing Tyler, but relieved when we found out that Tyler wouldn't be around for some time.

Around the 29th of June, I saw the happy couple together for the first time. It was pretty harmless to start: they fished and water-skied. Then it started to look like more. They were going to the state park and hanging out on the beach all day. I no longer had my canoeing bodyguard for crossing the lake.

One night, Jimmy walked around the cabin preparing for a movie date with Riley as I peppered him with questions. Leaning against the doorframe of the bathroom in the camp, I asked, "So have you thought about what's going to happen when

Tyler comes back? You and Riley seem to be getting pretty close. Aren't you worried at all about how he'll react to this?"

Jimmy stood in front of the bathroom mirror, inspecting his image. He proclaimed, "As far as I'm concerned, it doesn't matter. Riley told him before he left that she's not going to date him exclusively. She told me he was fine with that."

This sounded pretty suspicious to me. I would have been really surprised if she actually said that to him, but for whatever reason, Jimmy believed her.

"Mrs. Wilson said that Tyler will be back in August. Doesn't that worry you at all?" Jimmy left the bathroom. I followed him to the kitchen, where he grabbed Gramp's keys.

"Nope. I'm a big boy. I think I can handle it," he said, then left the camp.

CHAPTER 26

As the days flew by, I began to feel like part of Wyatt's family. Even Tommy and Sarah had accepted me and had forgotten about last summer's embarrassing wardrobe malfunction. Wyatt told me that Samantha had moved to a nearby apartment after her twenty-fifth birthday. She got a job and was now working as a teller at People's Trust Company in Enosburg. Now that Tyler and Samantha were gone, he'd moved into Samantha's space in the basement.

One afternoon in late July, while Wyatt and I were jogging around Franklin—apparently he'd been working to build up his mileage—he mentioned that his parents were going out for a quick dinner before seeing an eight o'clock movie, and that he had to watch his little brother and sister.

"You think you can come over and hang out for a while?"

"I can try. I'll come up with some excuse." Butterflies bounced around my belly as I wondered how I was going to pull this off.

The day was hot, so we ended our run by jumping right off the end of Gramp's dock in our running clothes. Stubby made a mad dash and jumped off, as well, snorting and paddling toward us. We sat on the embankment, tossing a stick in the water for Stubby to fetch. Wyatt had to get home to watch his siblings, so I walked him up the embankment and noticed that the sandy shore of the lake had eroded more; I was stepping on more rocks than last summer.

Once back at the cabin, I opened the screen door and hollered, "Mom, can you bring me the soap and shampoo? I'm gonna shower in the lake." I heard her open the bathroom cabinet and tear the wrapper from a new bar of Ivory soap. She handed it to me at the door.

଼ଃ   ଼ଃ   ଼ଃ

The smells I encountered as I left my room were delicious. Dad was grilling steaks, and I started calculating how long this dinner was going to take. The clock suggested that it was nearing six, which meant we wouldn't be eating until seven. I wondered what time the Wilsons were leaving. If their movie started at eight, they would have to leave by six to eat at seven thirty. Running the numbers through my head, I heard a car approaching and saw the Wilsons driving Tyler's truck past our back window.

We sat down to eat at seven and enjoyed a steak and potato dinner. I had one eye on my dinner and the other on the clock. The conversation was light, and at one point, Dad said we should all go for ice cream. Jimmy quickly asked if we could go to Stewart's because Riley was working the late shift tonight. Mom and Dad agreed and asked if I'd like to bring Wyatt. I told them no, that he was out with his parents tonight for dinner. *I'm a terrible liar.* The guilt was already getting to me. Jimmy helped clear the dinner dishes from the table and seemed to be rushing us along. I could tell he was anxious to see Riley. Finally, Dad got everyone moving to the car as the clock read eight thirty. I hung back at the door.

"Something I ate isn't agreeing with me," I told them. "I'm just going to hang here."

Mom and Dad looked at each other, and then back at me. "Well, Nanny and Gramp are here if you need anything. You want us to bring anything back for you?"

I shook my head. "Nah, I'm good."

Jimmy was in the car, honking the horn for Mom and Dad to hurry up. I went back inside to plan my next move. It was now eight forty-five, and I was running out of time. I grabbed my flip-flops and told Nanny and Gramp that maybe a walk would settle my stomach.

"Okay, dear. We'll probably be in bed when you return, so I'll say goodnight now."

I walked over and kissed each of them on the cheek. Gramp offered, "Have a good walk." I saw that little twinkle in his eye, which gave me pause. *Does he know something?* I hesitated for a split second, then turned to leave.

I jogged around the Wilsons' house and gently opened the sliding glass door to Wyatt's new lair. I could hear the TV on upstairs as I slid the door closed. I quietly walked up the first set of stairs to the landing at the front door and peeked up the second set of stairs to look for Wyatt—all the while trying not to be seen by Tommy and Sarah. Wyatt sat on the couch with his back to me, but one of the stairs creaked, causing Wyatt to turn toward the sound. When he saw me, he grinned and raised one finger.

"I'm gonna head downstairs for a while, guys. If you need me, just holler."

They mumbled, "Mmhmmm," too captivated by the TV to turn and acknowledge him. He walked down to the landing and grabbed my hand as we descended into the basement.

We sat on his couch and he leaned in to whisper, "What do you think of the place?"

"It looks like a bachelor pad," I said, giggling.

Still holding my hand, he stood and pulled me up off the couch. "Wanna see the rest?" He swept his free hand in front of him like a magician to indicate the space we were standing in. Then he led me back to his bedroom. Feeling anxious, I followed. My palms were starting to sweat, and I let go of his hand, embarrassed. He left the bedroom door open so he could listen for his brother and sister, and we sat on his bed. "So, this is my bedroom."

Ski posters decorated the walls, and a small dresser, with a mirror attached, occupied one corner. On the dresser sat a pile of letters. Curiosity got the best of me. I picked up the top envelope, recognizing the handwriting, and asked, "Did you keep all my letters?"

He began to blush. "I did, yeah." Looking adorably self-conscious, he continued, "I read and reread them, just waiting for you to visit. I felt like reading them somehow brought you back to Vermont. I could hear you as I was reading. I know that sounds so corny, but I really missed you." He got up off the bed, took the letter from my hand and set it on top of the pile. "I really, really missed you." He brought both hands up, placed them on either side of my face, and kissed me.

A tingling sensation began to spread from my head to my toes, and my face reddened in anticipation of his next move. My breath began to quicken as he caressed my back, one hand traveling upward. I wanted him to touch me. My skin was on fire as he placed his hand on my breast. I thought I was going to combust. His other hand traveled up my backbone inside my T-shirt and tried to undo my bra. He fumbled with it, and eventually, I had to take matters into my own hands, undoing it myself. Both of his hands were now under my shirt, feeling all of me.

We heard footsteps upstairs and froze. The footsteps went down the hall, and soon we heard the flush of a toilet and footsteps receding. We continued touching each other as he pulled me to his bed. Side by side on the bed, panting, not able to get our breathing under control, we wildly groped each other.

Fully clothed, he climbed on top of me and started to move his hips. A deliciously warm, tingling sensation began to spread from my hips down to my toes. He was kissing my neck, and still, we pressed our hips into one another's. My breathing escalated; the rush of exhilaration coursed through my body, leaving every millimeter of my body hypersensitive. Before long, with a few more furious bumps and grinds, he was breathing fast and furious. Then he uttered a groan, falling to the side of me. He lay on his back, and I could feel his heart beating through his shirt.

As our breathing relaxed, he stood and walked to the bathroom while the numbers on the clock clicked to ten. *Oh crap, his parents will be home soon.*

"Wyatt," I heard Sarah yell. "Tommy says he won't make popcorn! Mom said we could have some. Wyatt, can you make me some popcorn?" Footsteps fast approaching, I rolled off the bed to hide on the far side as Sarah barged into the bedroom. "Wyatt, are you in there?" she yelled, knocking on the bathroom door.

The rush of the water could be heard through the bathroom door as he flushed. He opened the door, a little bewildered. "Sarah, what is it?" he asked, looking wildly past her.

"Can you make me some popcorn? Tommy won't do it, and Mom said we could have some."

With his hand gently pushing her out the bedroom door, he turned to see me poised on my hands and knees. "You go back up. I'll be right there, and I'll make you some popcorn."

Her footsteps faded up the stairs. "I told you we could have some," she said tauntingly to Tommy as she returned to her spot on the main floor.

Wyatt turned to gather me in a bear hug, smiling. "Thanks for seeing me tonight. I was watching the clock, and it was getting late. I thought you weren't going to make it."

"I didn't want to let you down twice," I said with a kiss. He walked me to the door and slid it open for my getaway.

As I walked back to the cabin, that familiar red truck crept down Camp Road. Inside camp, there were only a few lights on. One in Mom and Dad's room—Mom was probably reading, and the other in the kitchen.

"How was your walk?" Jimmy asked from his seat at the counter, enjoying the remainder of his ice cream. By the tone of his voice, I could tell the jig was up.

"Fine," I said flatly, unwilling to give him the satisfaction, as I walked past him to my room. After donning my pajamas and brushing my teeth, I encountered Jimmy standing at the bathroom door.

"Saw Wyatt walking into the Wilsons' house just as we were leaving for ice cream tonight."

"Hmmm," I said, affecting disinterest.

"Maybe his dinner didn't agree with him either," Jimmy chided.

CHAPTER 27

For the next few days, I tried to avoid my brother's knowing glances. Riley was taking up a lot of his time, which helped my cause. When she wasn't working at Stewart's, she was over at our cabin; when she was working, Jimmy always found an excuse to see her at Stewart's.

One late night in early August, I woke to the sound of people jumping in the lake. There was a lot of giggling, so naturally, I had to investigate, wondering which of the Wilsons were frolicking in the lake tonight. Quietly, I left camp and walked down to the dock, remembering with a flush the last time I did so. From the bottom step, I could hear them whispering. I heard the swish of the rope and the splash of someone entering the water. As they exited the lake, I followed the shadows with my eyes. One figure rejoined the other waiting at the rope. There was something very familiar about this figure, and I gasped. The image of my brother naked, skinny-dipping with Riley, would be forever seared in my brain.

ଔ   ଔ   ଔ

Our summer was quickly coming to an end, and that familiar melancholy feeling had begun to wash over me. *Too fast.* I walked to my tree in hopes of seeing Wyatt, but the drone of the lawn-mower motor told me he was busy. He moved in parallel lines up and down the field as I left the forest. I waved to him as I came into the clearing, and he stopped the engine. "Got room for one more?" I asked. He moved forward and patted the spot behind him.

I hopped on and wrapped my arms around his bare chest. We tried to have a conversation while mowing, but hearing was difficult. He yelled to me that Tyler had called a few nights ago to tell them his leave would start on the 16th. *That's tomorrow.* I inhaled sharply and thought, *crap, I wonder if Jimmy and Riley know this.*

Wyatt parked the mower in the garage next to my grandfather's Cadillac. "What's with your granddad and Cadillacs anyway?" he said, pointing to the beloved car.

"It's just that he's always loved the roominess of that car, and having the status symbol doesn't hurt either."

He grabbed his shirt from the hood of the car and put it on as we closed the garage door. We walked to the embankment between Mr. Silk's and Gramp's camps and sat in the shade. From a distance, we could see Jimmy and Riley canoeing across the lake to the state park, as they had often done the past few weeks. Without anyone around to overhear our conversation, we talked about the complicated lovers' triangle between Tyler, Jimmy, and Riley.

"How do you think Tyler will feel when he comes home?" I asked, watching the canoe.

"I'm not sure. He really likes Riley a lot, and I don't think he knew she was serious about seeing other people. I think he assumed she was just trying to get a rise out of him."

"So she really did tell him? She said, 'I want to see other people'?" I asked, dumbfounded.

"Yeah, sorta. She really didn't come out and say it like that … it was more roundabout, but I could tell what she was trying to say."

"How did Tyler react?" I asked, wide-eyed.

"He said, 'Knock yourself out.' He played it off like she was kidding, but apparently, she wasn't." Wyatt picked up a rock and threw it in the direction of the canoe. "Believe me; I'm not going to be the one to break it to him."

Later that night, after Jimmy had walked Riley home, I told him that Tyler was coming home tomorrow. Rather than react, he ignored me, picking up a crossword puzzle to work on. He was walking around the kitchen in search of a pencil when I asked, "Doesn't this bother you?"

"Nope. As a matter of fact, I welcome it."

I dropped it and left to play solitaire at the dining-room table. *Tomorrow is going to come soon enough. I hope he's ready.*

CHAPTER 28

As we returned to camp from a visit with Aunt Doris, a change came over Jimmy. We'd been fishing and had given our catch to Aunt Doris for a fish fry with Aunt Marilyn and Uncle Oscar. *Thank God! I don't think I could eat another fish this summer.* Jimmy dawdled about, anxious and very short-tempered. I could tell there was a lot weighing on his mind.

It was a beautifully clear evening, so we ate dinner outside at the picnic table. All of us were enjoying the company and ambiance. That is, all of us except Jimmy, who hardly touched his food. Even the strawberry-rhubarb pie didn't entice him. As the rest of us enjoyed the pie, that familiar red pickup truck wound down the road. Dad waved at Mr. Wilson. "Looks like Tyler made it home safe and sound," he said, oblivious to the pain my brother was experiencing at the mention of Tyler.

The next few days were quiet. I didn't see Wyatt, but I assumed he was busy with his family reunion. On the third day of Tyler's leave, during my run, I noticed two people walking down the road carrying a bag of tomatoes from the vegetable stand in front of the farmer's house. *I wonder if they paid using the honor system?* In Vermont, if no one manned the vegetable stand, you just put the money in a shoebox and took what you paid for. Just past the vegetable stand, I heard them. It was Tyler and Riley.

"So you really are dating him?" Tyler said, louder than expected.

"Tyler, I tried to tell you before you left: it's just too hard when you're not around."

He began to talk but stopped and glared at me as I ran by. He looked so angry; I could feel his poker-hot glare boring into my back. He remained silent until I ran past—out of earshot. I turned right onto Camp Road and went to my tree to cool down. Stretching by the tree, I lingered long enough to see the two of them walking down Camp Road with the tomatoes. Tyler had picked up his pace, with Riley jogging to catch up.

"Tyler...Tyler, slow down, please..."

He whipped his head around. "Jesus! Seriously, Rye? What am I to you, some kind of toy? I'm not something you can just play with and drop by the wayside when you get bored!" Instead of following Tyler back to the Wilsons', Riley went home. Tyler maintained his fast pace back to his camp and marched through the front door, slamming it shut. *This cannot be good.* I made a beeline for camp and tried to find Jimmy, but he was nowhere to be found.

"Where'd Jimmy go?" I asked Gramp as he fed Chip and Dale.

"He went to see Riley. I think that boy's in love."

There were a few hours of calm before the storm when Jimmy finally reappeared, whistling. Tyler had been waiting and was ready to pounce. As soon as he saw Jimmy, he threw the front door open and yelled, "HEY!"

Jimmy's whistling stopped immediately.

Tyler ran down to confront Jimmy. "I hear you've been messing around with Riley while I was gone."

"Listen, Tyler, I don't want any trouble," Jimmy said calmly.

Tyler continued to encroach on Jimmy's personal space. "Well, you asked for trouble the minute you tried to fuck her," he accused in an eerily calm voice, punching my brother in the gut without warning.

Jimmy doubled over, grabbing his stomach.

Tyler screamed, veins bulging from his neck, "I don't want to see you anywhere near her! Get the fuck out of here and go back to Connecticut where you belong!" Seething, Tyler turned to go just as Jimmy caught his breath and ran toward Tyler at full speed. He dropped one shoulder, slamming directly into Tyler's back, knocking him to the ground. Jimmy threw wild punches at Tyler's face, one connecting with Tyler's lip, causing the blood to flow freely. Tyler's fist violently made contact with Jimmy's cheek and instantly raised a softball-sized lump.

Hearing the fight, Mr. Wilson rushed out to grab Tyler by the shirt collar, like reining in a disobedient dog by the scruff of his neck, and pulled him off Jimmy. They were both a mess of bloody bumps and bruises. Jimmy tried to throw a final punch at Tyler, but Dad had come around to see what all the commotion was about and grabbed Jimmy by the arm to wrangle him back to camp. It was mayhem, as they each had to be dragged forcibly back to their homes, kicking and screaming obscenities at one another.

Jimmy wouldn't let anyone care for his cuts and bruises. He couldn't sit still and paced inside. Finally, Mom got him to sit at the kitchen counter to put a bag of frozen peas on his cheekbone. There was no discussion; we all knew what the fight was about. It was bound to happen sooner or later. The real problem was that it happened at the end of our vacation.

Later that evening while Mom was getting the camp cleaned and clothes packed, I overheard Mr. Wilson and Dad talking in the back of camp.

"Hey, Rit. Sorry about what happened this afternoon. Tyler has been a wild man since Christmas break. I think he's seen a lot of awful things go down in Beirut, things he won't talk about with us. Being on the other side of the world has changed him. We received letters from him about how excited he was to come home and see Riley. I don't think he planned on it playing out this way. He really thought he still had a chance with her. This whole thing with Jimmy has really messed him up. I hope Jimmy is all right and that this doesn't ruin our friendship. Mary and I always look forward to your visits in the summertime, and Wyatt is just crazy about your daughter."

Dad laughed. "She's just as crazy about your son. No hard feelings, Sam. Things have a way of working themselves out. Take care of that boy of yours; we'll keep him in our prayers as he heads back overseas." The two men embraced and went back to their respective homes.

After Dad returned, preoccupied with retelling the conversation to my mom, I snuck out to my tree in hopes of seeing Wyatt. Much to my chagrin, there was only a note.

Callie,

I couldn't come see you tonight, but know that I wanted to. We knew this confrontation was coming, but it really sucks that it was today. Tensions are super high in the house, and it wouldn't be fair to Tyler if I were to fraternize with the enemy tonight (though I do enjoy fraternizing with you ☺). I'll miss you. Travel safe.

-W

CHAPTER 29

Leaving the camp the next morning proved arduous, as Jimmy was in a lot of pain. The physical damage was nothing permanent, but his pride was another story. I was pretty sure Jimmy didn't get a chance to say goodbye to Riley last night— another reason for his foul mood. We got him situated in the front seat of the car with Dad, and I got in the back with Mom and Stubby. My parents both agreed that Jimmy would have a more comfortable ride up front, and I didn't mind being in the back with Mom, because she spent most of her time reading, giving me the opportunity to daydream out the window. Jimmy held one bag of ice to his cheek and another to his hand; he fell asleep with his head against the window, a bag of ice between his cheek and the glass. This was going to be a long ride home.

Dad drove home faster than ever, knowing that Jimmy was uncomfortable. When we got to our garage and started unloading the car, Jimmy hobbled slowly to his room. I walked in behind him and put his bag on the floor of his bedroom.

"You okay? You hardly said two words during the car ride home," I noted, concerned.

"I'll be fine. Could you close the door on your way out?" he said curtly. I went to my room with my bag and started to unpack. My first instinct was to find a pen and paper to write Wyatt a letter; I missed him already.

Dear Wyatt,

I'm so disappointed that we didn't get a chance to see each other before I left, but I get it. As usual, the summer went by way too fast. There's nothing left for me to do but hurry up and wait for winter break. Hopefully, I'll be lucky enough to get back up there to see you again soon. I know that you have a lot going on, now that you're a big college man. I just hope you don't forget about me with all those college girls around. I'll be heading into my senior year FINALLY. Then I'll have to start the process of submitting all of my college applications.

The letter continued on about all the things I didn't have time to say. I wanted a do-over. I started to daydream about the time we'd spent alone in his room. I would have given anything to have that time again.

I scratched Stubby's soft, beige head as he lay next to me. "What am I going to do with all this time on my hands?" He lifted his head and sneezed.

Soon after we returned, Jimmy began receiving a steady stream of letters. It seemed that Riley had started writing.

ᘓ　　ᘓ　　ᘓ

The days passed, and we continued to watch the news closely as a family. We had settled into a routine of late; eating an early dinner while watching the evening news. We listened as the newscaster described the situation in Lebanon. The Marines had sent troops over in August, 1982 and were plagued with problems from the beginning. The body count was growing, as was the civil unrest. Eight hundred Marines were ordered to Beirut to help withdraw the Palestinians. According to sources, the Marines left Lebanon on September 10th, only to return on the 29th to strengthen numbers. At this point, the first Marine casualties were reported. On April 18th, 1983, a suicide bomber killed sixty-three people, including seventeen Americans President Reagan tried to keep the peace but was met with much resistance.

Dad shut the TV off. That was not good news, and I could tell from the look on Mom and Dad's faces that they were worried about Tyler. He had been back in Beirut since August 23rd, and Wyatt had written to tell me about a letter written by Tyler describing the bloodshed he had witnessed. He mentioned that a couple guys from his unit had already been killed during this tour. My stomach was churning as I went to bed.

On September 6th, while I sat in my biology class, my parents made the forty-five-minute drive to take Jimmy back to school. When I got home, I found that I had the house to myself for a change. It was a strange transition for me when Jimmy left for school, making me feel like an only child.

With curiosity as my culprit, I found myself walking into Jimmy's room. I searched his nightstand, under his bed, on his dresser, and inside his dresser drawers—but couldn't find the letters. I knew for a fact she had sent four letters; I brought them into the house. That didn't count the times he fetched the mail first. I thought there had to be at least eight letters, so I continued my search. I checked his nightstand: nothing. Then I sat on his bed to think. Sitting adjacent his closet, I decided to open the door and look under a pile of clothes he had tossed in the corner. Jackpot! I carried the shoebox to my room and checked the dates the letters were mailed so I could start at the beginning. He would be ticked if he knew I was reading his mail, but I continued anyway.

Dear Jimmy,

I don't know where to start with this letter. "I'm sorry" doesn't feel quite right, but I am. I feel awful about what happened between you and Tyler. I had been dating Tyler for two years before you came into the picture. We were pretty close, and I thought I was in love with him. Then I met you, and my feelings started to change for him; he could tell. I mean, I was sixteen when I first started seeing him, just a kid! Then you came along when I was eighteen. I guess as I got older, I could see that my relationship with Tyler was changing. He was talking about "our" future, and that scared me. When I met you, I thought, THIS is my way out of that relationship, and told Tyler that I was falling for another guy. The beautiful thing was that you were here during the summers, and if it didn't work out, I always thought I could fall back into my routine with Tyler.

He wasn't having any of that. He was pretty clear on how things were going to be; I was his and no one else's. If anyone got in the way of his happiness, he was going to make their life miserable. I knew this from the start, yet I let it go on without telling you, and for that I'm sorry. I've only received one letter from him over the past month and a half. It was short and not too pleasant. He is still holding on to hope that he and I can get back together, and he is willing to wait for me. Isn't that funny? He'll wait? I'm the one here, stateside, doing the waiting. Waiting for him, waiting for you, waiting for something to go right in my life. I don't want to wake up when I'm thirty, alone and still working at Stewart's, without anything to show for my life. Please write back when you can.

Love,

Riley

Wow, Jimmy had his work cut out for him. The next one I read had a lot of responses to questions that Jimmy must have sent her. From what I could gather, he was willing to work on a relationship with her and wanted her to take Tyler out of the equation because Tyler was away. Hard sell, but I think he was wearing her down. By letter four, she had agreed to send Tyler a *Dear John* letter, basically informing him that their relationship was over. She was feeling awful about it, but thought it was for the best.

I picked up the second-to-last letter and perused the words until I saw a line that caught my eye:

I'm coming to visit you at school. I have a few days off coming to me since I pulled a few double shifts at the shop. I was thinking about coming up around the 20th of October for a long weekend. Do you think your roommate would mind? I was thinking about that night we went to the rope swing, and I—

"What are all those?" Mom asked suspiciously, making me jump. *When did she get home?*

"Uh, these? Nothing ... just letters I've gotten over the summer," I lied, quickly putting the letters back in the envelopes and then back into the shoebox.

Mom picked up one letter that had slipped out of my hand and read Riley's return address out loud. "Wyatt, huh?" she said with a raised, disapproving eyebrow.

I looked down at the shoebox. "Yeah, I know, but he never talks about her and what happened over the summer. I was trying to put all the pieces together." I took the letter from Mom and put it in the shoebox with the rest, and then stood up and said, "Okay. I'll put 'em back." I walked back into Jimmy's room and placed the shoebox back under the clothes in his closet. Mom followed close behind.

"Those are personal letters, Callista, and I would appreciate it if you would not go snooping around your brother's room. He would be very upset if he knew what you were up to. Just leave his stuff alone, understood?" Mom said sternly.

"I just thought if I read …"

"Nope, no more reading," Mom said, cutting me off. I walked past her into my room and flopped onto my bed. Mom walked in and sat next to me. She placed a hand on my knee, and after a brief silence she asked, "Have you heard from Wyatt lately? Are the Wilsons getting any letters from Tyler? I'm sure his parents are worried sick about him. This conflict in Lebanon is really upsetting."

"Yeah, I've heard from Wyatt a few times." I said as I sat up next to Mom. "He's keeping busy at the University of Rhode Island. He says he's going to be home for Thanksgiving and then Christmas until January 23rd. Are we going up to Vermont for Christmas this year?" I asked hopefully.

"I'm not sure that's going to work out this year," Mom said as she stood and walked toward my bedroom door. "We'll see what Dad's work schedule looks like," she said as she left my room.

Being a teacher gave Dad a lot of time to travel in the summer, but during the school year, we had to plan things around his mandatory teacher in-service days. Sometimes planning got tricky around the holidays. Even though the kids were out of school, there were many days Dad had to be present.

CHAPTER 30

Evenings had become cooler. It was October already, and I could feel the excitement of the holidays building.

I had occasionally been going out with my friends on the weekends, and watching the way the girls my age acted around boys embarrassed me and reinforced the fact that I was glad that I didn't have to worry about that anymore. Wyatt continued to write to tell me how much he missed me and that none of the girls at school compared to me. The letters I looked forward to most were those in which he got deep, talking about the future. An image of that future came to life in my mind; me getting accepted into college, sharing our college experience together, graduating, marrying, and having a family.

Does Jimmy feel this way about Riley? I looked at the calendar on my bedroom wall and noticed the date. October 22nd, Jimmy and Riley's rendezvous weekend. *I bet Mom and Dad don't know. I wonder if she sent Tyler the letter yet.*

Jimmy made his weekly phone call home. Strangely, he called earlier than usual. *The call was probably early so he could spend the remainder of the weekend with Riley.* He routinely called on Sundays at five, before he went to dinner. This week, however, he called at noon on Saturday. My parents thought that seemed odd, but Jimmy made up some lame excuse, saying that he had a group project due Monday so they all decided to meet Sunday.

It was the only time they all had free to meet. He talked to Mom and Dad briefly, and I got on to say hi.

"How's your weekend?" I asked. I walked around the corner of the kitchen, stretching the cord into the pantry and partially closing the door. "Doing anything fun?"

He didn't budge on providing any information and remained vague about everything related to college.

"Heard from Riley lately?" I asked, pushing the envelope. Again nothing. "Have fun, and don't do anything I wouldn't do."

Jimmy listened quietly for a minute. "Okay ... put Mom back on." So I did, and they said goodbye and hung up.

"Must be that project is really important for him to plan ahead and call, knowing he'd be busy when he usually calls home. He's such a responsible young man."

I replied with a hmph, thinking to myself, *oh, he's good.*

The next morning, I stayed in bed as long as possible, hoping I wouldn't hear the shower running. Like clockwork, though, the shower was turned on—my cue to get ready for church.

On a crisp fall morning, we parked the car and walked into the building, ready for worship. As we entered, I noticed an eerie silence. People were whispering, and I got a queasy feeling in the pit of my stomach.

We all stood to sing the first hymn in unison, after which the minister took to the pulpit and said, "Good morning, please take your seats. It's been reported that there was another bombing in Lebanon early yesterday morning; therefore, I'd like to begin our service with a prayer." Gasps issued from all corners of the congregation; we were stunned by the news. I couldn't even concentrate on the remainder of the service. My mind refused to stop whirling. The service ended, and we rose for the last hymn.

We greeted the minister at the door as we left. "You wouldn't happen to know where in Lebanon the bombing took place, would you?" I asked.

"Sorry, I don't have any details. Just say a prayer that this warfare will end soon," he recommended as he wrapped both his cold, clammy hands around mine.

The car ride home was quiet, and we were all on pins and needles. The radio droned on, and we were grasping for any details we could get. The reporter kept repeating, "Please stay tuned to your local station for details as they unfold." We waited for what seemed like an eternity for Tom Brokaw to speak to us on the *NBC Nightly News.*

"We begin our nightly news program with a report from Beirut, Lebanon. This morning at 6:20 a.m. on October 23rd, 1983, there was a bombing in the town of Khalde, Lebanon. It's been reported to our news agency that a truck carrying several tons of explosives entered the Marines' compound. The explosives leveled a four-story building holding sleeping Marines. Snipers are making it difficult for rescuers to search for survivors. Hundreds of Marines lost their lives. No group is claiming responsibility at this point. We will continue to keep you updated as more details come in. In other news…"

We sat stunned. "He didn't say what post, though, right?" I asked.

My parents didn't answer my question. I saw a worried look exchanged between them. "We'll have to wait and see as details come in," Dad said.

I felt sick to my stomach. I wanted to talk to Wyatt. My next thought went directly to Riley. *Has she heard the news yet?*

No new details surfaced during the night, and I grew angry with the news anchors; they just kept giving us the same information. Every channel we turned to said the same thing, although worded slightly differently. Frustrated, we turned the television off deciding to wait until morning for more news.

CHAPTER 31

The TV murmured as I entered the kitchen.

"We now have new reports on the Beirut bombing. While on a 'peacekeeping mission' in Beirut yesterday, two hundred forty-one Marines and sailors of the 24th Marine Amphibious Unit perished. The Mercedes-Benz truck we reported on yesterday was carrying five tons of explosives. It had stopped at the north checkpoint outside Beirut International Airport at Khalde, Lebanon. The guard at the checkpoint failed to notice that the truck sat lower than a normal Mercedes-Benz truck, and therefore did not notify anyone about anything peculiar at his station. Behind the checkpoint, most of the Marines were asleep in their compound. Those that survived the attack have the task at hand to look for any survivors in the rubble."

The screen went black as the news switched to a commercial break. I realized I'd been holding my breath listening to this horrible news and began to breathe again. I remembered Wyatt saying something about the number 24 and Tyler in the same sentence. *Could it be that was his unit?* When I turned around, I saw Dad trying hard to hold it together. I slowly wrapped my head around the fact that Tyler could be dead.

"They said there were survivors; the news guy just said that. Tyler might be okay." Mom got up off her chair, reached for a tissue on the kitchen counter to blow her nose and then poured a glass of water. Dad followed her to the cabinet to retrieve a glass for himself and they started talking quietly to each other.

"Do you think I should call Jimmy?" Mom asked.

"I'll call him tonight," Dad answered.

Jimmy came home for the weekend on the 28th and said he had heard from Riley earlier in the week. She said that she was aware of the attack, but had not heard from the Wilson family yet.

It's strange how holidays keep coming regardless of what's happening in the world. My mom had a childlike love of the holidays and celebrated every holiday regardless of its significance. Flag Day? Flags adorned our front yard. National Donut Day? No problem, fresh donuts on the table. On Groundhog Day, there would be a plate of sugar cookies in the shape of groundhogs with little mini chocolate chips for eyes. This particular holiday, Halloween, came and went without any fanfare or celebration. I stayed home that night and handed candy out to the neighborhood kids to try to keep my mind off of Tyler. The phone rang as I closed the door on yet another Michael Jackson accompanied by a mini Madonna.

"Hello?" I said, answering the phone.

"Hi, Callie, it's Gramp. Happy Halloween. Can I speak to your dad, please?" sounding unusually pleasant.

"Sure, hang on a sec." I quickly got Dad on the line. My dad took the phone call from his office in the basement. I pretended to hang up, but stretched the receiver cord to its breaking point and walked around to the pantry to listen in.

"Rit, it's Dad. I got news about the Wilson boy. I spoke to Oscar today, and he said he saw a military vehicle come down Camp Road while he stood at the pump. He said he watched two Marines in uniform drive past. The car stopped at the Wilson house. Oscar said he watched Sam catch Mary as she collapsed at the front door. Thankfully, the men in uniform have done this a time or two and helped Sam support Mary as they went inside for a brief visit. That poor boy was only in the military for a short time. Do you know they couldn't find Tyler's body for several days? He was trapped under the rubble of the building. I mean, he was sleeping, for God's sake! The kid didn't have a chance. It's a crying shame that it had to end this way for him."

I didn't want to hear any more details and quietly hung up the receiver. I leaned my back against the wall and slid down until I hit the floor. With my legs outstretched, head resting against the wall, I closed my eyes. Tears I couldn't stop had begun to descend my cheeks. I felt awful for Wyatt. I can't imagine losing a brother or Mr. and Mrs. Wilson losing their son. Poor Riley... after all, he was her first love. *I wonder if he ever got her letter. How do you live through something like this?* Profound sadness had taken me over.

I heard my dad's footsteps coming up the stairs, and quickly wiped my face as I rose up from the floor. Dad came through the basement door and stood next to me. He squeezed my shoulder, slowly shaking his head. "He didn't make it," he said with a sniff and walked past me to relay the message to my mom. A moment later, he picked up the phone to dial my brother's dorm. I listened as Dad cleared his throat before he gave Jimmy the details.

After he hung up, he said, "He didn't take that well. Everything that happened between them is weighing on him heavily. I think we need to go up for the funeral to pay our respects. All of us." He looked at my mom as she walked into the kitchen and into his open arms. Poor Mom, tears were streaming down her face with no sign of stopping.

Several days went by; we moved through our daily routines on autopilot. Gramp called with news that a service celebrating Tyler's life would be held at the Franklin United Church on November 5th at four in the afternoon. Jimmy came home on November 3rd. We packed and made the trip to Gramp and Nanny's winter home in Franklin. When we arrived, Jimmy asked Gramp if he could use the Cadillac to visit Riley and was gone for several hours. We waited patiently for his return, eager to hear how she was faring. After we'd finished a quiet dinner with our extended family, Jimmy returned with several books in hand. He had been at the town library most of the evening since Riley hadn't been up to seeing visitors.

"What are those for?" I asked Jimmy, pointing to the books.

"I want to say something at the service. I need a little help getting started, so I thought some of these books may help me out."

"What do you want to say?" I asked, surprised.

"I don't know. I just know I have to say something."

My eye was drawn to a poetry book tucked under his arm, among others.

"What's that for?"

"I noticed it on the bookshelf. I thought it might help get my thoughts in order. I just feel like something needs to be said. We'll see what I come up with. I don't want to just sit around doing nothing."

I wished him luck and left him to scour the books for the right words.

CHAPTER 32

The following morning, we all got up relatively early. Jimmy finished putting his thoughts on paper, while Mom and Dad dressed for the upcoming service. I decided to put on my running clothes and run to camp. The long run would help clear my mind and help me to decompress for the time being. I slowed to walk past Gramp's camp, Mr. Silk's, and the Wilsons'. There was a lot of activity today, with several cars in the driveway and the house lit up like a jack-o'-lantern. I continued walking toward my tree.

Wyatt was outside in the backyard taking out the trash when he spotted me. He walked to my tree, and when he was close, I opened my arms and enveloped him. He began to sob as I stroked his back. He fell apart in my arms. My throat tightened, and I began to weep silently; I was trying to hold it together for him. I felt as though I needed to be strong for him in his vulnerable state. I was his only outlet to express his loss.

"I'm so sorry, Wyatt," I whispered in his ear.

He didn't speak for a few minutes while we continued to hold each other. He used the back of his hand to wipe his face.

"How are you holding up?" I asked gently.

"Not very well," he said, his voice cracking. "This is the worst thing imaginable," he said. Tears streamed down his contorted face. With a big sniff, he said, "My mom is pretty much catatonic. She's taking sedatives to numb the pain, like they're candy." He began to pace back and forth, running his hands over his face.

Finally, he grew still and clasped his hands behind his head letting them rest there.

"Let me know if there's anything I can do for you or your family," I said. I reached out to him and placed my hand on his chest.

"I'm just glad you're here," he said, reaching for my hand.

"I'm gonna head back now, but I'll see you at the church in a few hours." I gave him one last hug. I had walked past him toward camp when I heard him rushing up behind me.

"What if I can't do this?" he said frantically. "What if I can't say goodbye to him?"

"It's going to be okay. Tyler would want you to be there. You can do this."

"I don't know ..." he said, taking a deep breath.

Looking at him, I wasn't so sure he could do it. He looked like a little boy—eyes wide with insecurity and self-doubt. It tugged at my heart. With a weak smile, I left him standing there; a little boy lost without his big brother. *Too much.*

As I walked briskly back home, I could picture Wyatt and Tyler playing catch in the field by my side. I imagined Tyler teaching Wyatt how to catch a football, how to cast a fishing pole, the two of them talking quietly at night about their hopes and dreams. *Unbearable.*

Running now, I felt a crushing weight on my chest. Unable to breathe properly, sobbing uncontrollably, I needed to walk the length of the driveway to get myself under control before going inside. A long, hot shower helped to calm my nerves, and when the time came, Mom and Dad met Jimmy and me in the driveway.

We parked at the church and walked in, Jimmy clutching several papers in his hand. The whole town showed up. The front of the church was decorated with wreaths of red, white, and blue flowers on stands. There, next to the pulpit: a large stock photo, taken during Tyler's time with the Marines. He looked noble in his uniform. Tyler's casket was draped with an American flag. His family sat in the first row, with Mr. Wilson's arm protectively around Mrs. Wilson. Samantha had her arm around Tommy, and Sarah sat next to Wyatt, holding his hand.

When the congregation was seated, the minister began the service. "Thank you all for coming today to celebrate the life of an extraordinary young man. He lived and died for this country and for what it stands ..." Mrs. Wilson's muffled cries echoed throughout the church. We sang several hymns including "Amazing Grace." I was moved. The minister offered a lovely eulogy, and invited people to come forward to say a few words. To my surprise, Wyatt walked up to the pulpit first and began to speak.

"Today is a really hard day for me. I feel like I have lost my best friend. We can't really understand why he was taken away from us so soon. I wanted to share with you all that even though my brother was bullheaded and stubborn, he was also very bright, kind, giving, and loving. If we take nothing else from his passing, just know this: life is a gift. If we don't live it with purpose, with our full potential, then we've wasted it," he said, not bothering to wipe the tears sliding down his cheeks.

"He took this life very seriously," Wyatt continued, "but I have many memories of the fun and mischievous Tyler. One night when I was little, I heard the water running and went outside to find Tyler watering the lawn. I said, 'Tyler, it's bedtime; why are you watering the lawn?' He told me he was waking the night crawlers. I had no idea what he was talking about, so I sat on the front steps, watching.

"When he finally turned off the water, he smiled at me and said, 'Earp, now we wait.' No sooner than he spoke, I could see these big, fat worms coming to the surface of the lawn. I was amazed!"

Wyatt looked as though he was transported back in time as he spoke. "I thought Tyler had these special powers to summon the worms from the earth," he admitted with a restrained chuckle. "He was, and always will be, my hero. Fishing with Tyler was always an adventure, and I'm going to miss that part the most. I love you, T," he finished, his voice breaking. Sobs escaped him as he walked back to the front pew. His dad stood to hug him and caressed the back of his head—a beautifully intimate gesture.

I'm proud of you, Wyatt. That had to be the hardest thing he had ever needed to do; I was sure Tyler was proud.

The minister stood and asked if anyone else wanted to share a memory before he closed the service. My brother stood and approached the pulpit. The minister nodded and sat back down, indicating to my brother he could continue.

"Tyler and I didn't exactly see eye to eye, but I believe deep down he was an honorable man. I am especially emotional about the last time I saw him and felt compelled to speak today. I was racking my brain last night, trying to come up with something appropriate for this service. Instead of reciting a poem from someone else, I decided to write my own."

Clearing his throat, he began:

A young man of twenty-one, planning for life ahead

The oldest Wilson son, what an interesting life you've led

Don't grieve for me, he would say:

I may be free, but you need to be strong today

I've lived my life for all it's worth,

With friends and love and war.

I've been living my life for this moment since birth

Please don't ask what for.

Don't question what could have been

I need to heed the call.

God has a plan for me to begin.

It's time to leave you all.

I found my peace that fateful day

Among the bunks of brothers

Please watch my family grow, not stray,

And work toward peace for others.

At the end of Jimmy's poem, the minister boomed, "Amen." The congregation followed suit. Jimmy walked back to his seat, folded the poem up and placed it in his breast pocket. Riley, who I hadn't seen when we walked in, was weeping uncontrollably from the back of the church next to her sister and grandmother. When the minister indicated it was time for us to rise for the last hymn, I turned to see Riley in the back of the church, clutching herself, sobbing.

One by one, the family members walked to the casket to touch it one last time before the burial. We all walked to our cars and followed the procession to the burial site. This part of the funeral was just for close family and friends. We were privileged enough to be invited. When we entered the burial ground, we passed seven imposing Marines with guns, ready for the salute. We all stood around the casket as the minister offered his final words: "Ashes to ashes, dust to dust …" He gave a short prayer; then three volleys were fired. The firing line was brought to the position of present arms. Then the casket, holding the Wilsons' oldest son, was lowered into the ground.

As the trumpeter began playing Taps, two Marines folded the American flag and presented it to Mrs. Wilson. I would never hear Taps again without thinking of the anguished look on Mrs. Wilson's face.

Family members were trying to be strong for Mr. and Mrs. Wilson, but I heard them smothering their cries. My heart was heavy as we left the gravesite. The Wilson family left first, and the extended family and friends followed. As we drove off, I could see one person left at the gravesite: Riley.

We went to the Wilsons' for a gathering after the burial. Neighbors brought food and drink. People sat upstairs in the kitchen, in the living room, and out on the deck by herself sat Aunt Marilyn. Watching people was interesting. Some had not attended the funeral or the burial and were stopping by to pay their respects; others seemed like vultures, coming to the Wilsons' home in hopes of watching drama unfold. Little did I know: we were about to have front-row seats.

CHAPTER 33

Everything was going as could be expected. Samantha supported Mrs. Wilson as they walked arm in arm to her mom's room. I saw Samantha shake a Valium from its bottle into her mom's hand and offer a glass of wine. Samantha quietly closed the door and returned to the living room. Tommy and Sarah were sitting outside with their dad, listening to people share stories of Tyler as a boy. Wyatt, Jimmy, and I sat at the kitchen table staring at each other, not knowing what to say. Out on the deck, Aunt Marilyn was having an animated conversation … with no one. It appeared that she was the only person out there. As I stood to investigate, the front door suddenly burst open, and Riley came staggering in. She must have gone home and found the liquor cabinet, because she was a mess; dried streaks of mascara lined her cheeks, her eyes wild and bloodshot.

"Tyler!" she called out when she came through the door. Jimmy jumped up and ran to Riley's side, quietly urging her to keep it down. "Where is he?" she slurred, having a momentary mental breakdown. Jimmy put his arm around her and tried to guide her to the sofa, but she was having none of that. She shook him off, stumbled through the kitchen and down the hall by the time Jimmy reached her again.

"Where you going?" he asked, as gently as possible.

"I'm gonna see if he's in his room." They continued to walk down the hall into the room Tyler used to share with Wyatt. She sat down on his bed, and Jimmy sat next to her.

"Riley," he said, making her look at him. "He's not here. He's gone. He won't be coming back. Don't you remember where we all were earlier today?"

Recognition was coming back to her face.

"Rye?" Jimmy said with concern.

She looked at him, eyes dilating, raised her open hand and slapped him across the face. "*Don't call me that! Don't you ever call me that!*"

The tears began to fall again. She let out an inarticulate cry of pain. Her body shuddered with each sob, and she was consumed with grief. "Make it go away. Make it go away," she said as she rocked herself back and forth on the bed. "I can't handle the pain."

Jimmy inched closer and took her into his arms like a father holding a child. "Shhhhh," he said, in attempt to soothe her. She wrapped her arms around his neck and sobbed until her last tear fell; she was tapped dry. He laid her down on Tyler's bed and pulled a blanket over her shivering body.

"I don't want to feel the pain anymore." She sounded like a frightened child.

"Close your eyes and rest. I'll be in the other room when you want to go back home."

"It still smells like him," she said, holding the blanket up to her face as she drifted out of consciousness.

Jimmy walked uncomfortably back into the kitchen—his hand raking his hair, making him look like a mad scientist, his eyes dilated and wild with tears on the verge of escaping—and sat down.

ର   ର   ର

We left the next day and tried to continue on with our lives, tried to act like nothing happened—but we all knew that things would be different, and that our visits to Vermont would forever be changed.

Christmas was not as magical that year. We didn't drive to Vermont; instead, my grandparents came to us. During the holidays, I came across an editorial in the *Newtown Bee* about the invasion of Grenada, or "Operation Urgent Fury." It described in detail the act of terrorism that took two hundred forty-one Marine's lives. The fact that those soldiers died on a peace mission was beyond my comprehension. The article claimed that "these men were destined to die," as if those higher-ranking Marines knew the grim outcome, but went in anyway.

Stunned, I shook my head at the senselessness of it all. *How could this have been allowed to happen?* I cut the editorial out of the paper, made a copy at school for Wyatt, and mailed the original off to Jimmy.

CHAPTER 34

March, 1984

I had turned my attention to school and was taking my final exams, hoping that all the studying would keep my mind busy and make the time pass quickly. If the months would fly by, I could get back to Vermont and see how the Wilsons were doing. I could see Wyatt. Despite my efforts, though, the months seemed to be going by more slowly than usual.

Jimmy had been home just about every weekend since Tyler's death. I thought he needed the comfort of having family around after seeing how quickly life could be cut short. He opened up to me a lot more about Riley and how their relationship was going. Needless to say, they hit a rough patch after the funeral. He'd written to her several times, but she wasn't responding.

"I decided, after not hearing from her for a while, that I would drive up and surprise her over Valentine's Day weekend."

"Really? How'd that go?"

"She was really surprised and not too crazy about me being there at first. Naturally, I won her over with my wit and charming personality."

"Did you bring her any gifts?"

"Roses, chocolates, and a card."

"Yeah, I'm pretty sure the gifts were what won her over." Hearing Jimmy's laughter again made me smile.

"She cut back her hours at Stewart's after Tyler's death, so we had a lot of time to talk. Megan's picked up the hours until Rye feels up to going back full time. One night, we were sitting out on the back porch stargazing and contemplating life when she went inside for something. She returned with an envelope in her hand, and naturally, I thought she bought me a valentine, but this letter wasn't for me. She told me to look at the front of the envelope. In big, bold red print it read, RETURN TO SENDER, with the name Tyler Wilson on the front. "This letter was to tell Tyler about our relationship, but it never made it to him."

Jimmy seemed reassured. "Riley was visibly relieved that he hadn't received that letter. She told me that secretly, her biggest fear was that Tyler thought he was all alone when he died." Finally, he and Riley could move forward. This solidified their love for one another.

I got a letter from Wyatt. He said that writing about Tyler made him feel like Tyler was still around. He told me the story that Jimmy had shared about Tyler and the high school coach. Apparently, Tyler had truly been in love with that woman and always felt bad about the gossip which had caused her to take a leave of absence and eventually quit. He told me about the boy Tyler had punched hard enough to put in the hospital for four days. I guess Jimmy was lucky to have walked away with a few bumps and bruises. But that wasn't all Wyatt had to say:

...The countdown has finally begun! I'm so looking forward to our summer with each other! Even though I'll be working part-time at Stewart's to help out Riley and her family, I promise I won't let it interfere with our time together.

I thought that was noble of him, but I was sad that our time together would be limited.

...Hey, funny thing happened the other day when I was out running errands for my mom. I was driving past the cemetery, and, well, I'm not sure how to put this, but your Aunt Marilyn was there. Is she all right? She was by herself standing outside the gate in the creepy part of the graveyard. You know, the place where the small tombstones are covered in weeds, falling apart and whatnot? Well, she was standing over one headstone having a big conversation with the grave. I swear it looked like she was having a full-on conversation, all animated with her arms gesturing and all. Just thought it was weird. Do you know anyone buried there?

Huh. It seemed over the years she'd started displaying some strange behaviors. Mental note: have a chat with Aunt Marilyn.

ೞ ೞ ೞ

Mom and Dad had been closely monitoring the progress of a memorial in honor of the Marines lost in the attack that took Tyler's life. News had spread about the planned memorial, attracting donations on a national level. The Marine Corps Base Camp Lejeune offered to commission four-and-a-half acres of highly visible and publicly accessible land for placement of the memorial. Exciting news.

My parents remained abreast of any new developments, and they felt like they could finally contribute to something worthwhile. Jimmy had become very involved in this process, as well, which I found interesting, and was contacting friends in Connecticut for donations. I loved seeing our family work together toward something that was important to the Wilsons and the community of Marines. We were all more connected after Tyler's death, and in a way, it felt like we were on the cusp of something momentous.

CHAPTER 35

May, 1984

I was getting excited to finish up my high school career. With all the senior activities, I had been super busy—on pins and needles waiting for my acceptance into college. I chose to remain in state and most likely would attend the same school as Jimmy. Hopefully, I would know where, for sure, by the end of the school year.

I got an interesting letter from Wyatt in mid-May. He sounded excited for our visit this summer, mentioning something about having some plans for us, but didn't give any details about what he had up his sleeve. I didn't mind the suspense; I was just happy that he had something to be excited about after the year he'd endured.

As the month slowly passed, I started receiving invitations to graduation parties. Most I declined because I would be in Vermont for two months of the summer. One invitation piqued my curiosity because it was from that boy who'd dropped a note on my desk junior year. We hadn't spoken since that day, but I figured he had invited the entire class. Depending on when we left for Vermont, I would probably be able to make it. The date of the party was June 26. I walked into my mom's room carrying the invitation.

"Hey, Mom, did you and Dad decide when we're going to camp this summer? Have you talked it over with Nanny and Gramp yet? I just want to give Wyatt a heads-up," I said nonchalantly, as I sat on top of the dirty clothes hamper.

Sitting on the hamper reminded me of the time Jimmy and I were playing hide-and-seek years ago. I had run into Mom and Dad's room looking for a place to hide when Dad opened the hamper and ushered me in. Jimmy never found me.

"June 25 through August 22."

Guess I'm not going to that graduation party.

Mom continued, "I just got off the phone with your grandparents, and Nanny says that they'll probably stay at their home in Franklin and drive down for a few visits. She says, and I quote, 'I'm no spring chicken anymore.' Besides, it's getting harder and harder for her to climb the dock steps."

"Okay. I'll give him those dates then. Did I tell you he's working at Stewart's this summer part-time? So you won't have to worry about us spending too much time together."

"I don't worry about you guys spending too much time together," she said, with a wave of her hand.

"Really? So I don't have to worry about you sending Jimmy to the movies with us?"

"Well, you're a big girl now. I suppose you can go unchaperoned."

Smiling, I went to my room and wrote Wyatt a letter. I told him I was very curious about his plan for the summer and loved to hear his excitement in the last letter he'd sent. Then I told him about the party I was invited to and how surprised I was to be on the list. Deep down, I was hoping Wyatt would get a little jealous. I told him in the letter about the boy dropping a note on my desk junior year and how rude I was to him. I told him that the boy had moved on to the next girl's locker, so I knew he wasn't real serious about getting to know me.

About a week later, at the beginning of June, I got a response from him.

Dear Callie,

If you're trying to make me jealous, it's working. Who is this guy, and where does he live? Maybe I need to pay him a visit.

I smiled in spite of his empty threat. The letter continued with news about his parents.

I recently came home for a weekend visit because my pop had called and said he was worried about Mom. She was struggling. She was walking around the house like a shell of her former self, not showering or eating, and not sleeping unless she was in Tyler's bed. I tried to get her to go for walks with me while I was home, but she would get as far as the Silks' and turn back, saying she needed to rest. It's so sad to see her this way. He's gone now, and we have to move on with our lives. It's going to be hard most days, but knowing Tyler, he wouldn't want us to wallow. I just have to be strong for my parents now. Lately, she has been trying to get back to herself, because we have an announcement:

Samantha is engaged! I didn't even know she was dating anyone. This should give my mom a reason to get up in the morning. She is consumed with getting the wedding details just right. Samantha is marrying some guy named Brian, who's thirty, never been married, and has a career. Mom is over the moon about that. Samantha doesn't have the best track record when it comes to dating. I think they've set a date for sometime in December. I know what you're thinking: no, she's not pregnant. They just think it's the right time for them. She's twenty-five, and he's thirty, so why wait? My parents seem to like Brian, though the jury is still out until

I meet him. So things are looking up in this neck of the woods. I really, really miss you. Counting down the days.

Love, Wyatt

I read the letter a second time, folded it up, and put it in the shoebox on my closet floor. Seeing as we were going to be there the following week, I didn't bother to write another letter. I wondered what it was like to plan a wedding. It must be exciting: figuring out all the details, finding the right dress, deciding where the reception would be held, and what the bridesmaids would wear. I got butterflies in my stomach just thinking about that possibility for me someday.

"So, what did he have to say?" Mom said, as she placed folded laundry on my dresser.

"Who?"

"There's only one person in this world who can put a look like that on your face."

I played coy. "What look?"

"The dreamy, faraway look," she said, putting my socks in my drawer. I laughed as she walked out the door, batting her eyelashes at me.

The night before we left for camp, I couldn't sleep. *Here's hoping my dad has a lead foot in the morning.*

CHAPTER 36

No such luck. Construction on the highway delayed us, and we didn't get in until three forty-five. I was screaming in my head, *GET ME OUT OF THIS CAR!* From the look on Jimmy's face, he felt the same way. As we arrived, I barely gave Dad time to put the car in park before I flung the door open and ran toward camp.

Just as I was hoping, Wyatt was outside mowing the field. He looked taller, and I thought he'd added ten pounds of muscle. My blood was pumping. He waved from across the field, but I'd have to wait to give him a proper hello, as he still had to finish mowing.

I helped Mom and Dad with the bags, and Stubby ran straight over to Freckles, barking his brains out. As usual, Freckles wouldn't have anything to do with him and just rested his head on the ground. Stubby, in a huff, trotted back to camp. We went in, and Dad planned out our meal by making a list for the grocery store. On his way out, he suggested to Mom that we invite the Wilsons over for dinner, and she agreed. Dad took his pen out and added a few more things to his list.

When Dad left for the store, Jimmy went down to Riley's, and I took the opportunity to go outside and find Wyatt. Perfect timing: he was driving the mower back toward Gramp's garage, looking very happy with himself. He was holding one hand behind his back, and I knew what was coming.

"For the young lady," he said, bowing and handing over a bouquet of wildflowers.

"They're beautiful. Thank you," I said, wrapping my arms around his neck. We leaned in and shared a lingering kiss that I'd dreamt about since we last saw each other. I pulled away and asked, "Are you and your family doing anything for dinner? Dad went to the store for some steaks and added a few more in hopes that you guys could come over."

Placing his hands on my hips, he gently pushed me aside, and smiling, he said, "I thought you'd never ask. I should go home real quick and shower. I want to be presentable. See you in thirty minutes?"

I nodded my head, and he took off for his house. I told Mom that the Wilsons were coming for dinner, and we got all the plates, silverware, drinking glasses, and napkins ready. Then we started working on the side dishes. We made Mom's cabbage salad—do not call it coleslaw. Then we shucked the corn, and as we got to the last bag, Wyatt knocked on the door, looking somber.

"What is it?" I said, setting the corn down.

"Mom's not going to make it tonight. She's not feeling up to it. Ever since Tyler died, she doesn't like to socialize much. She doesn't want the conversation to get uncomfortable." He looked embarrassed.

"That's not a problem, Wyatt. These things take time. Please stay with us for dinner, and if Tommy, Sarah, and your dad would like to join, the more the merrier," Mom said sympathetically.

"Thanks, Mrs. Lamply. I think Tommy and Sarah will be over, but Pop is going to stay and take care of Mom."

Mom smiled. Tommy and Sarah came over, and Wyatt and I decided to play some horseshoes with them. While we were playing, Riley and Jimmy came walking down Camp Road, hand in hand. They released hands when they saw us. Wyatt whispered to me, "I wish they wouldn't do that. My parents just want her to be happy."

I grabbed the next horseshoe and tossed it for a ringer. "I'll be sure to let Jimmy know how you guys feel about it. I'm sure he's just uneasy and doesn't want any of you to be uncomfortable." Wyatt grabbed the next horseshoe and tossed it too far. I smiled. My team won. Sarah and I high-fived each other. We played another game, inviting Jimmy and Riley to join, boys against girls.

"How's that going to work? We're only supposed to play with two on a team," Jimmy asked, confused.

"Doesn't matter. We'll just take turns. Trust me, it'll work. Right now, the score is 1-0 girls, so you boys have some catching up to do," I teased.

Jimmy and Wyatt awkwardly shook hands, and then they decided in which order to play. They decided that Tommy would go first, and then Wyatt, followed by Jimmy. The girls' team would play in the order of Sarah, me, and Riley. We started by having each team choose one player to throw one horseshoe, and whoever threw closest to the post started the game. Tommy and Sarah tossed one horseshoe each, and unfortunately, Tommy's was closer.

The game went back and forth with a lot of playful ribbing. It started to get interesting when Jimmy said, "Let's make a little wager. If we win, you girls have to go jump in the lake, and if we lose, we'll do the same."

Feeling pretty confident with our team, I looked to the girls and then back at Jimmy with a smile and said, "You're on." Unfortunately, the last toss of the game made Jimmy the winner.

Jimmy and Wyatt seemed to have warmed up to each other throughout the game, and after the last horseshoe was thrown, Jimmy and Wyatt charged each other, landing a stronger than expected chest bump and they both landed hard on the ground, laughing. It was infectious, and soon the girls' team had begun laughing with them. From where we were standing, I could see Dad grilling the steaks, and they smelled delicious. "Good game," I said to the boys and shook each of their hands. When I got to Wyatt, he picked me up and threw me over his shoulder.

"Wha...what are you doing?" I said, laughing as Wyatt started running toward the lake.

"We won. You lost."

Jimmy and Tommy joined in by chasing the other two girls. Jimmy managed to pick up Riley, but Sarah was too fast for Tommy. She decided to take matters into her own hands, jumping off the end of Gramp's dock of her own accord. I held on for dear life and managed to make Wyatt fall in with me. All's fair in love and war. Jimmy managed to toss Riley in, but she put up quite a fight, and Jimmy's clothes were drenched.

Mom came out with dry towels for us all, apparently pleased that we were having a good time. When we finished dunking each other and harassing the boys, we went up the embankment for the towels. As we reached the top, we were surprised to see two guests sitting at the picnic table with my folks. Mr. and Mrs. Wilson smiled timidly at us as we took seats in the sun to dry off. They looked like they had aged ten years since I'd last seen them. "Hi, Mr. and Mrs. Wilson. It's so great to see you."

Wyatt walked over to hug each of them. "I'm so glad you changed your mind," he said, as he hugged his mother.

"Yes, well, I needed to get out of the house. It's such a beautiful day, and Tyler wouldn't want me wasting it on self-pity."

The mention of his name felt like a blow to my stomach. Despite the undertone of sadness, we had a great meal with everyone around the picnic table.

"What took us so long to do this? We've been vacationing up here for years. We really need to do this more often," Dad exclaimed, and everyone agreed.

"Next time, we'll have dinner at our place. It would do us some good to have visitors again," said Mr. Wilson. With this new development, we made tentative plans for the following week.

After dinner, Mr. and Mrs. Wilson thanked my parents and bid them goodnight. As they were leaving, Mrs. Wilson walked over to Riley and hugged her. "I'm so glad you are living your life. Tyler would have wanted you to be happy," she whispered. We were all so quiet as we watched this take place that we could hear her every word. Turning around to join Mr. Wilson, she said to Tommy and Sarah, "If it's all right with the Lamplys, you can stay awhile longer."

My parents nodded their heads, so we decided to play another round of horseshoes, because as Sarah reminded the boys, we were tied up now. We continued playing and laughing until it got dark. Riley seemed at peace, and the girls ended up coming out on top and winning the tiebreaker. Together, we decided we would wait for another time to make the boys jump in the lake. Tommy and Sarah said goodbye and walked home, as Wyatt and I walked with Jimmy and Riley down Camp Road, thinking we were just going to walk Riley home. Then Jimmy and Riley asked us if we wanted to build a fire by the rope swing and sit for a while. It seemed odd sitting on the ground around the stone circle of the fire pit with my brother and Riley. Somehow we had gone from being annoying kids to young adults. I guess that death forces you to grow up and look at life a little more deeply.

We sat quietly as Riley took a pack of matches out of the knot in the rope-swing tree and lit the twigs under the logs. I added some dried grass and leaves to the bottom of the twigs, hoping that would help them ignite into flames. Eventually, the fire caught on, and the wood began to burn brightly. We sat staring at the flames for several minutes without speaking, until Wyatt broke the silence.

"Tyler would have loved this night."

I looked at Riley. Oddly, she lifted her eyes to Wyatt and smiled.

"He loved hanging out at the rope swing when it was dark," Wyatt continued. "He didn't think I knew what he was doing when he would make some lame excuse to leave the house at ten at night, but I knew."

We let him continue and just listened.

"I could hear the splash of water as he'd jump from the rope all the way back at our house. He would come here even when no one was around. He was completely at home in the water. I think that's why he wanted to be a Marine so badly," he said, as he threw a loose twig from under one of the surrounding stones into the flames. "Jimmy, I don't mean this to hurt you, but ..." he turned to Riley and continued, "Tyler loved you, Riley. I know at times it was hard for you to understand that. He had a hard time showing his feelings. I think he thought it made him weak." Turning back to Jimmy, he said, "But, Jimmy, I truly think that he would want Riley to be happy, and watching you guys together today, I can tell that she is. My parents feel the same way. He was a stubborn guy, and he would never accept defeat, and that's why you guys butted heads so much. He knew that Riley was beginning to push away and even mentioned it at home. We all knew that he would fight until the bitter end ..."

With this last comment, he trailed off. I couldn't take my eyes off of him. His eyes were filling with tears, but he tried to fight them back. Choking on his words, he said, "It's just not fair that he didn't get a chance to fight back his last day on earth. Those terrorists were just chickenshit. Wait until everyone is sleeping, then blow them up?" Tears emerged from the corner of his eyes now. "I know that if he'd had a fighting chance, he would have made it out and kicked some ass."

I put my arm around him and rubbed his back as he let out a sob. He couldn't deny the tears now. He rested his forehead on his knees, which he had wrapped his arms around. Jimmy got up and added another log to the fire, causing sparks to fly and, swirling, burn out above us. I had an overwhelming feeling that Tyler was there, listening. I glanced around, half expecting him to jump out from behind a tree.

Jimmy sat back down and put an arm around a visibly shaken Riley. Her eyes were brimming with tears as she leaned into Jimmy's chest and closed her eyes. The tears slipped from her eyelids and landed softly on her cheek.

Jimmy spoke first. "I just wish I could have met him under different circumstances. If things had been different, I think we could have been friends," he said, looking down at the top of Riley's head. We sat and listened to the pop and crackle of the fire in front of us.

For the next few hours, we talked about Tyler, and Wyatt told us funny stories of their childhood. Even Riley joined in on the storytelling, and we ended our evening on a high note. "Well, I guess we should call it a night," Jimmy said to us as we stood. Riley kicked dirt onto the embers, and then walked over to put the matches back into the knot of the tree. Jimmy walked Riley back to her grandmother's cabin, as Wyatt and I, holding hands, walked back to camp.

I turned to Wyatt in the moonlight and gave him a big bear hug. We stood there and held each other for a moment. Still embracing, I looked up into his baby blues and said, "Today was a very special day. Thank you." I kissed him briefly.

He stood quiet for a moment, and I could see he wanted to tell me something.

"What is it?"

"I love you," he said with true conviction.

"I love you, too." No truer words had ever been spoken. I felt this so deeply and completely. I hoped my words conveyed the depth of my feelings toward him. That familiar flutter swooped back into the pit of my stomach. *He loves me*, I repeated to myself.

"See you tomorrow?" I asked.

"I have to work until three, but then I'm free. I'd love for you to come by the shop."

"Okay, I'll come by around two thirty. Would you be able to give me a lift home if I run there?"

"It's a date," he said, winking. I walked back to the cabin feeling elated. *He loves me.*

CHAPTER 37

Was that all a dream? I wondered the next morning. I got to the kitchen and made myself a bowl of cereal, reliving last night in my head. I didn't hear Jimmy come in the door and glanced, surprised, toward him, noticing he still had on the same clothes he'd worn last night. I looked at the clock, which read seven. "Did you get lost walking Riley home last night?"

Jimmy just walked by with a sheepish grin on his face and went straight to bed.

I decided I would finish reading the third book in the V.C. Andrews series that day, because I knew there was a fourth installment out. I'd been reading her series for the past several summers, and I *needed* to find out what happens next.

By ten, I decided to change into my running clothes, since that's what I'd be doing later anyway. I went back outside, moved my chair to a shady spot and continued to read until around noon when Jimmy finally got up. He came outside with his shower items and walked down to the lake, whistling.

After lunch, I had just a little bit of my book left to read, and when I glanced at the clock, I could see that I didn't have enough time to finish it. Feeling a shift in temperature, I glanced up to see that clouds were moving into the area.

"Hey, Mom, I'm gonna run down to Stewart's and wait for Wyatt to finish his shift. He said he'd bring me home after that, okay?" I said, walking past her, placing my book on my bed in the back bedroom.

"Okay. Be careful running out on those streets. It looks like it's going to rain."

"I will." I went out the door and started off toward the water pump. As I embarked on my run up Camp Road, it started to rain. *Great.* A car drove by and splashed me with the standing water on the road. *This really stinks.* I laughed at my own thoughts as I ran past the dairy farm. As I was running onto the main road, the heavens opened up, and I was completely drenched. The downpour was so heavy, it was difficult to see. I crossed the road and tried to get as far to the side of the shoulder as possible. I could see Stewart's up ahead, about a half mile. Suddenly, there was a truck barreling down the road toward me. I was bracing myself for the onslaught of standing water as the truck passed, but I wasn't expecting what happened next. As if in slow motion, the truck started hydroplaning, swerved to its right, directly into my path. The rain was falling straight down, and there was no wind, but in an instant, I felt my whole body being pushed. That wasn't even the right word—propelled maybe, or shoved—as if someone had tackled me on the football field. I rolled to the ground on the wet grass and watched as the pickup's passenger-side wheels rolled through the grass off the pavement. The look of horror on the driver's face was evident as he stared at me and overcorrected, managing to get his vehicle back on the road. I could see him looking in his rearview mirror at me as he slowed the truck to a stop on the side of the road. He shoved the driver-side door open and ran to my side.

"Are you okay? Did I hurt you? I didn't even see you there. Are you okay?"

Stunned, I stood up and found that I was fine. I said, "Yeah, I'm okay."

"Can I drive you somewhere?" he asked, concerned.

"No, I'm headed to Stewart's right there. I'm fine." He asked me three more times if I was okay and if I was sure I didn't need any medical attention before he got back into his truck and drove off. I decided to walk the remainder of the five hundred yards to the store. The rain had slowed to a sprinkle as I walked through the door. The bell on the door announced my arrival, and Wyatt looked up from the register with a smile that quickly evaporated.

"How can I help? Callie, wha ... what happened to you?" he said, as he ran around the counter.

"It's raining really hard," I said slowly, in a daze.

"You have grass on your back ... you sure you're okay?" he said, guiding me to the ice cream shop side of Stewart's and into a chair. I caught my reflection in the ice cream case and saw that there was grass on my shirt. My eyes looked wild, like the eyes of a drowning rat.

"I think so ... I'm not really sure what just happened there," I said, staring into space. I went through the whole scenario with him, but saying it out loud made me sound like a lunatic.

"I gotta get her home. I think she's in shock or something. Do you mind if I leave a few minutes early?" he called out to Riley, who was manning the front register. She told him to go. He walked back to where I sat shivering in my chair, took an apron from the wall and wrapped it around me. He carefully walked me to his truck and helped me in. We drove back to camp as I sat staring out the windshield in disbelief. *Could that have been someone moving me off the road?*

"You want to tell me again what happened?" he asked gently.

Again, I went over the details.

"You say someone shoved you out of the way of a moving truck?"

"Yes."

"Did you see who it was that shoved you?" he questioned.

"No. When I looked up, there was no one there." My side ached, and I kept rubbing it. "I think I'm gonna go in and take a real hot shower. Thanks for the ride home. I'm gonna lay low tonight. Do you mind if I take a rain check on our plans?"

He looked worried. "No problem. I'll come by tomorrow to check on you when I'm done with work. I have to open the shop, so I'll be done early," he said, sounding disappointed.

I deliberately got out of the truck and went inside, smoothing my hair to avoid frightening my parents. "Hey," I said, trying to sound normal. They were all in the back dining room playing cards as I entered.

"It was raining pretty hard out there. Did Wyatt give you a ride home?" Mom asked.

"Yep. I'm gonna jump in the shower. Anyone need to use it first?"

My brother popped up and said yes. I met him at the bathroom door as he was exiting. "You okay?" he asked. "You look like you've seen a ghost."

"I'm fine, just freezing from the rain and tired from the run." I pushed past him, carrying my dry clothes and towel. Closing the door behind me, I turned the shower on full bore. The shower billowed with steam as I took off my wet running clothes. Something in the mirror caught my attention. I walked to the mirror to wipe away the steam and saw a large abrasion on my side, red and beginning to bruise. Staring at it more closely,

I realized, in my shocked state, that it looked like a handprint emerging in that abrasion. *What the ...?* I stepped into the shower and let the hot water rush over my body, flinching as it rolled over the scrape. I shampooed and conditioned my hair, filling the bathroom with the scent of wildflowers.

Closing my eyes to rinse my hair, I pictured the truck coming for me one instant and me rolling on the grass the next. *Maybe I just tripped on a rock.* Running my hand down my side again, I could feel the sting of my bruised skin. *That was no trip; someone pushed me.* I wrapped myself in my towel and dried my hair, confused by this revelation. I got dressed and joined the family in several games of cards, not once mentioning what happened to me, but feeling the overwhelming need to speak to Aunt Marilyn.

CHAPTER 38

The storm that had blown through last night gave way to a spectacular day. I loved days like this, when there wasn't a lick of humidity in the air or a cloud in the sky. Dad and I took the tandem bike out for a short ride, while Mom ran some errands. Dad asked if he could take me out to lunch, and I thought all this attention seemed really strange. Dad and I seldom did things together, let alone two things in one day. Nevertheless, I liked the attention, and I let him dote on me. Around two o'clock, we returned home, and to my surprise, decorations covered the yard where we played volleyball and horseshoes. There were streamers and balloons with a sign draped over the volleyball net saying, "Congratulations!" Taking a few moments to process, it occurred to me this surprise was meant for me. I got out of the car and looked at Dad, who had a huge, goofy grin on his face.

"Surprise!" Dad said. As we walked toward our relatives, he said that for our family reunion this year, they'd decided to make it a surprise graduation party for me. It worked; I was completely surprised. We had a great evening with cake and ice cream and gifts, which turned out to be mostly money. Samantha and Brian, her new fiancé, came with Mr. and Mrs. Wilson and their family. Samantha gave me the lowdown on her wedding and told me that her bridesmaids were going to wear red and carry red roses, while the fellas would wear black tuxes. After the wedding, their reception would be at a local banquet hall. I told her I hoped to be invited, which elicited an eye roll.

"My brother is head over heels in love with you; there is no doubt that you and your family will be invited." I grinned from ear to ear after hearing that.

As the party started to thin, I looked for Wyatt. I'd been so busy enjoying the attention that I hadn't seen him in several hours. I could see him sitting on the steps at the front of his house, talking to my cousin, David. *Oh boy, I bet Wyatt is getting an earful.*

"... she comes screaming outside when the thing flew just past her head." It's the bat story.

"I can't help it if I'm not fond of bats," I said, sitting down next to Wyatt.

David, my cousin, chuckled and said, "Good to meet you, Wyatt. Hope to see you around at another one of my family's shindigs." Standing, they exchanged a handshake. "And congratulations, young lady," he said smiling, and proceeded to give me a hug. He gathered up his brothers and sister and led them to the car, where Aunt Shirley and Uncle Fred were waiting. Waving through the open window, Uncle Fred yelled, "Congratulations again, Callie!"

I waved and called out my thanks. Pretty soon, just Wyatt and I were sitting outside watching Mom and Nanny clean up the cake table. Jimmy had already left with Riley, and Dad had gone back to the cabin to check on Stubby.

"That was a good party. You're a big college student now," he said, smiling at me.

"I can't believe that. Four years of high school gone in the blink of an eye," I said, astonished.

"I have something for you, but I want to give it to you when we're alone."

This made my heart leap.

"Let's make a date for later in the week, say Saturday. I want you all to myself. I have to work a double tomorrow so that I can have the weekend off. You can come by to visit, but only if you drive in a car. I can't have you scaring me with another near-death experience."

Saturday. Two sleeps. That feels like an eternity.

Later that evening, I drove into town to get some thank you notes. Seeing as I'd have to keep myself busy for the next few days, I thought writing thank you notes would do the trick, but as I drove past Aunt Marilyn's home in Franklin, I felt a pulling sensation. Something told me it was time to chat.

"Well, Callista, what a nice surprise. Come on in. To what do I owe this lovely visit?"

"First off, thank you so much for the very generous graduation gift and for coming to my party. You shouldn't have done that." I said, oozing gratitude. "I was just running to the store to get some thank you cards when I decided to stop in to say hi. I have something I want to talk to you about, and I'm not quite sure how to start."

"Well, how about at the beginning." she said calmly, walking with me to the plush couch. A picture frame caught my eye. It held a black and white photo of a woman I assumed was Aunt Marilyn holding a beautiful baby who couldn't have been more than a few days old. Picking up the frame as I sat, curiosity bubbled up. "Is this you?"

Gently taking the frame from my hands, she gazed lovingly for a moment, then placed it in her lap. "Yes. My goodness, that was a long, long time ago; feels like another lifetime."

"Is that baby one of Aunt Shirley's kids?"

"No, but you didn't come here to talk about this photo." Clasping her hands on top of the frame in her lap, she continued, "So what is it you want to talk to me about?"

"Let me show you." I lifted my shirt to expose my abrasion. "What does this look like to you?"

Before answering, she flashed a knowing smile, then said with certainty, "Tyler."

"*Seriously?* I thought it might be. I just had this strange feeling."

"*See*, you were open; you listened."

"But what do I do with this information?"

Looking down at her lap, she smiled and nodded. "Just know that he's watching over you. He's quite fond of you and Wyatt." she said with a smirk.

Reaching over, I pointed at the picture frame, shaking off that bone-chilling feeling. "Okay. That's enough about me. Tell me about this photo."

"This is Lilian." She spoke softly.

An unearthly feeling resumed inside me as the recognition registered. "Lilian Julia Metcalf?"

"The very one. She lived for six glorious days."

"Was Travis the father?" All the pieces seemed to be fitting together.

"Yep. To be unwed and pregnant back in the day was highly frowned upon. My parents sent me to Scotland to live with my best friend, Elizabeth, for five months. I had no choice in the matter. They didn't tell anyone. Not even our close relatives know this." I nodded my head, understanding the meaning behind this statement.

"Remember when I told you that Travis was very fragile when I turned down his proposal? Well, when I delivered Lilian, it just wasn't right that her father didn't even know she existed. He was so angry when I told him I was leaving for five months. He wanted to know how I could up and leave my family when they needed me to help out with the store. I couldn't explain the situation and just up and left. He was devastated."

"I bet."

"So here's this extraordinary child we created. It just didn't feel right without including Travis, so I sent a letter describing everything that happened, along with this photo but ... by the time he received it, she was already gone. She got tangled up in her blanket, and died in her sleep. The agony of it all was too much for me to bear, and I needed him to support me, but as it turned out, when I contacted him after her passing, it was too much for him to handle. He made the disastrous decision to end his life. I was heartbroken, losing the two loves of my life in one week. Worst time of my life, ever." She paused then, with a shake of her body that began at her head and ended with a slight spasm of her foot. She looked as though she were shaking off the past like a tangle of cobwebs that she inadvertently walked through. "Well, sugarplumb fairies!" she proclaimed with an embarrassed giggle. "That was uplifting."

℣ ℣ ℣

I woke up to another beautiful day with the sun shining in a cloudless sky. I began my morning by tackling thank you notes, using the list that Mom had composed of all the people that were at my party, but my conversation with Aunt Marilyn still rattled my brain, making it difficult to concentrate.

Two hours in, all I had left to do was address the envelopes. Once this process had been completed, I drove to the post office, and stopped at Stewart's. While eating a yogurt I purchased from Riley at the counter, Wyatt took his break and sat with me with a cup of mint chip ice cream.

"So, what do you plan to do with the rest of your day?" Wyatt asked me, as I fed him a bite of his mint chip ice cream.

Playfully, I said, "Sit around the cabin and pine for you."

His hands reached under the table and grabbed my knees. "I wish I could be there tonight so you don't have to pine," he said, his eyes smoldering. Those words made my insides melt and my knees go weak. I could barely squeak out, "Me, too."

The ring of the bell sounded as someone entered Stewart's; Wyatt's break was over.

"See you tomorrow."

"Not if I see you first," he said, as he walked behind the counter to help the customer. I walked past the front register and said goodbye to Riley. *Hoo-boy…this is going to be a long night.*

When I returned, Mom sat on the dock talking to Dad who, for the moment, seemed to be winning the *bathing battle royale* with Stubby.

"What's going on?" I queried, as Stubby grunted—all the while Dad continued scrubbing his squirming body.

"It seems that Gramp's lead foot has finally caught up with him," Dad said, like a frustrated parent. "He was in an accident last night and was taken to the hospital. So we're going to head over to check on him. It's not life-threatening. He's just bruised and shaken up, but they're keeping him in the hospital to check everything out. You can come along, too, if you want, or stay here with Jimmy."

"I'll stay here. Call us if you hear anything." They left for the hospital, and it was just Jimmy and I for the night. We decided that we would go to the movies to take our minds off of the situation with Gramp. Mom and Dad called to give us an update right before we left for the theater.

"Hi, Callie, just wanted to call and let you know that they are keeping Gramp overnight for observation, but not to worry. He's in good hands."

"Thanks for letting us know. Jimmy and I are going to the movies tonight, and we'll be home around ten if you need us." So off we went to see *Gremlins*, a goofy, entertaining movie I actually enjoyed. We hadn't spent much time together this summer, so this was a nice change of pace. When we got home, Mom and Dad were already there.

"We're going back to the hospital tomorrow. Nanny asked if we would pick her up and bring her to the hospital in the morning, so that's what we're going to do. You guys will have the day to yourselves." That worked out perfectly for me, because in only one more sleep, I'd have my marathon date with Wyatt.

CHAPTER 39

Mom and Dad woke up early to travel back to the hospital. When I got up around eight, the smell of coffee still lingered in the kitchen. Jimmy woke up around ten and asked what my plans were for the day.

"I'm not sure what I'm doing yet, but whatever it is, it'll be with Wyatt. What about you?" I asked.

"Once Riley ends her shift at three, we're going to spend the rest of the evening together, maybe see a movie," he said with a smile. I wondered if that meant the *whole* evening, as in returning home Sunday morning, but didn't have time to ask because my date had arrived; the sound of a boat's motor drifted in from the lake. I quickly jotted down a note for Mom and Dad saying that I was going to be on the lake all day and then out for a while that evening. I said that I hoped Gramp was doing well and I'd see them around eleven. Still in my pajamas, I walked outside as Wyatt docked his fishing boat. He had a lot of supplies for the day, including a cooler, fishing poles, some towels, and what looked like two sleeping bags.

With a raised eyebrow, I asked, "Are we going camping for a week?"

He just winked. "Are you planning on staying in your jammies all day? We've got fish to catch! Hop to it!"

Giggling, I ran back inside and put my swimsuit on under my shorts and tank top. Bolting out the door, I grabbed my flip-flops and yelled to Jimmy, "Have fun with Riley later on!" Excited about our day together and curious to see what he had in store for us, I took the dock steps two at a time.

Smiling broadly, Wyatt extended his hand, said, "Madam," and helped me aboard. With me in the front seat facing Wyatt, he sat in the back of the boat next to the motor to guide us on our adventure. We started out around the lake and then headed for the beach. He took the boat right up on the beach, as there was no dock to tie it to. We climbed out and pulled the boat up farther so it wouldn't accidentally go afloat, and then set up our blankets on the sand.

"I figure we'll hang out, swim, and enjoy the sun for a few hours; then we'll move on from here. How's that sound?"

Butterflies…"Sounds great." I took off my tank top and shorts and laid on the towel, soaking up the sun. Before long, I closed my eyes and daydreamed. Wyatt sat next to me, watching the lake, and when I opened my eyes, he was lying on his side with his head propped up by his hand, elbow in the sand, watching me. I blinked a few times.

"Nice nap?" he asked.

"I wasn't sleeping. I was resting my eyes," I said, blushing.

He laughed. "Come on. Let's go play a little volleyball with some of the kids over there."

I must have had my eyes closed for a while, because the beach was filling up, and a game of beach volleyball had started behind us. We played a few games with some kids I recognized from the rope swing a few years back. We had fun, but I didn't really feel like being in a crowd. Mom used to say she could feel alone in a crowd. That sentiment certainly encapsulated this moment. I really just wanted to spend my time with Wyatt.

"Had enough?" he asked curiously.

I nodded my head.

"Wanna head out?"

Again, I nodded my head.

"Thanks, guys! We're taking off." We walked to the boat, and I climbed in as Wyatt pushed the boat into the water. After he hopped in, he said, "You know if you didn't want to play volleyball, you just had to say so, okay? I can't read your mind." He sounded a little upset.

"I thought you wanted to, so I said yes."

"Listen, if you don't want to do something during the rest of our day together, speak up. I don't want to guess. Just be honest with me."

Eesh, we're getting off to a rough start.

"Anyway," he said, as his tone lightened. "Where were we? Oh, right," he said, pretending to check off an imaginary list. "Lunchtime."

After cruising along the water for a few minutes, we docked at Stewart's. As he helped me out of the boat, he took me into his arms and kissed me spontaneously. Then he took me by the hand and walked me to the store. We sat at a booth inside the ice cream shop and shared a sandwich from the refrigerated section and a bag of chips. Then, of course, we had to end with a scoop of ice cream; mint chip, my favorite. At that point, it was around one thirty in the afternoon, and I was feeling a bit worried about my grandfather. "Hey, Wyatt, would you mind if we went by Gramp's camp so that I can check in and see how my grandfather is doing?"

"I don't mind at all. As a matter of fact, I'm glad you asked." Smiling, we cleaned up the table and walked out to the boat. I climbed in and took my spot before Wyatt quickly returned us to camp. As he tied up to the dock and waited, I ran into the cabin. Jimmy was nowhere to be found, and my note was still sitting on the counter, right where I'd left it. As if on cue, I heard my parents' car pull up and tossed out the note.

"Hi there," Dad said as he walked in.

"Hi. How's Gramp doing?"

"He seems to be doing pretty well, but they haven't released him from the hospital yet. His heart is acting funny. It looks like they may need to keep him another day. They're drawing blood and doing some tests to see what the problem may be. We just came home for a little R and R before we head back over. I think we'll relieve Nanny around dinnertime, take her home, and then head back to the hospital for a few hours. Rather than make the drive back here from the hospital, we're going to spend the night at their home. Do you think you and Jimmy can hold down the fort while we're gone for one night?"

"I think we can manage," I said, as my stomach did a somersault.

"Okay then. I'm gonna take a nap, and we'll be good to go. How's your day going? Did you eat lunch?"

"I just got back from lunch with Wyatt at Stewart's. As a matter of fact, he's waiting at the dock to go swimming. I just ran in to see if there was any news on Gramp. Tell him I hope he feels better soon," I said, as I opened up the screen door to leave. Wyatt had grown impatient, but he smiled as I stepped onto the dock.

"Everything okay?"

"Yep." I filled him in on what my dad had just told me. "My parents are headed back there in a few hours to help Nanny out."

Looking concerned, he said, "I'm sure he'll be fine." But before moving out into the lake, he said, "Do you think you need to stay with your folks? I understand if you think you do."

Immediately, I said, "No, they have it under control. I want to spend the day with you."

Wyatt looked relieved. We decided to swim from camp down to the rope swing. As we swam to shore, I could see some people just leaving the rope. "Perfect timing," I said, as I climbed out of the lake. He ran up the shore past me to get to the rope first. He swung out far, and did his best impression of Tarzan as he let go of the rope and landed with a splash. Laughing, I grabbed the rope, swung out, and let go a tad too early. I almost landed on my back. On my second attempt, I nailed a cannonball. We were having a lot of fun trying to outdo each other's tricks when Jimmy and Riley showed up.

"Hi, guys. It sounded like we were missing out on some fun out here; mind if we share the rope?" Jimmy asked, grabbing the cord.

"Come on in," Wyatt said. Jimmy managed a corkscrew dive.

"Well done!" I shouted from the water. We spent several hours out there playing on the rope swing and in the water. My stomach announced its hunger. I hadn't checked the time in a while and was surprised to see that it was nearly five thirty; no wonder my stomach was growling. Feeling wiped out from all the rope climbing, I said to Wyatt, "I'm beat and starving. Should I find something for us to eat at camp?"

"Nah, I have stuff in a cooler I was going to make for us. You ready to go?"

I nodded. We said goodbye to Jimmy and Riley, knowing that they were headed out to dinner and a movie tonight. As they walked past, Jimmy whispered to me, "I'm not coming back to the cabin tonight, so if you and lover boy want some alone time, you'll have the place to yourselves."

Too tired to swim back to the boat, I walked from the rope swing to Gramp's camp to use the restroom and get a change of clothes. Once I was changed, I closed the camp door and went down to the fishing boat. Wyatt untied it and made one circle around Rock Island. I felt butterflies again as he tied the fishing boat to a tree. We climbed out and over several rocks before we hit a dirt path to a makeshift shelter. *I've been here before.* While carrying the cooler, he handed me a blanket to sit on.

"I was thinking we could have dinner here," he said, as he set the cooler down. He took the blanket from me and placed it on the floor of the open shelter. He opened the cooler and pulled out containers of strawberries, potato salad, fried chicken, and Cool Whip. To my surprise, he'd brought along my favorite soda, peach Fresca.

"How'd you know this was my favorite soda?" I asked in surprise.

"I notice a lot of things about you; I've been paying attention," he said with a wink. "I know your favorite ice cream is mint chip. I know that you love animals. I know that if you don't run almost every day, you get crabby," he said, grabbing my knee. "I know that you have a *fantastic* boyfriend, and I know that you're starving right now. I can hear your stomach growling." With a laugh, he handed me a plate, and in between swatting mosquitoes, I ate my food. Itchy and full, we packed up the cooler with the leftovers, rolled up the blanket and went back to the fishing boat.

"Well, that was a bust," Wyatt said, looking disappointed.

I turned to him and said, "It wasn't all that bad. The food was great."

"Yeah, but I wanted this to be a memorable dinner. I didn't take into account the mosquitos," he said softly.

Scratching my arms, I said, "I'll be reminded of this dinner until the itching stops. Let's go back to my grandparents' cabin. No mosquitoes there. We can hang out, play cards or horseshoes, if you feel like losing again."

"I don't think that will happen," he said with a mischievous grin on his face. We untied the boat and went back to Gramp's, watching the setting sun—my favorite time of day.

"Can we just make one long trip around the lake? I love this time of day."

Happily, he said, "Absolutely."

We spent another hour riding up and down the lake watching the ducks frolic in the water and the herons take flight. I loved being out on the water. As we rode, I watched his face change, like he was deep in thought.

"Penny for your thoughts?" I asked him, as his cheeks began to glow.

"I was just remembering the first time I saw you. Man, did you take my breath away, watching you run with those long, beautiful legs of yours."

I have beautiful legs?

"With one look, my sister, Sam, knew I was a goner." I smiled at this proclamation.

We rode back and tied up the boat on the dock. From the top of the stairs, it appeared that the Impala was gone and the camp was empty. My stomach started to knot. "Do you want to bring this stuff up to the camp with us?" I asked.

"Nah, I'm gonna take the boat back, clean up, and head over in about a half hour."

"See you in a bit. Don't take too long," I said, giving him a quick kiss as I exited the boat. I sat down on the Adirondack chair and watched the boat disappear behind some pine trees, hoping for Wyatt to quickly return—but the minutes passed and I thought, *I had better get cleaned up now or I'm gonna run out of time.* Upon entering the cabin, I wrapped myself in a towel to take to a shower. Under the steaming hot water, I washed my hair and body. I froze when I thought I heard a door creak open. *Crap, where's my towel?* Quickly, I rinsed myself off and stepped out of the shower. *Great, my clothes are in my bedroom.*

"Callie, it's me. I didn't want to scare you," Wyatt said, as I towel dried my hair. The only way to get to my bedroom was to walk wrapped in a towel … right past Wyatt.

"Uh, okay. I'll be right out." I took the towel from my head and wrapped it around my body. As I opened the door, I saw Wyatt sitting at the counter in the kitchen. "Hey there. I just felt sticky from being in the lake. I thought I'd have enough time to shower before you got back. I won't be long."

He got out of his chair and walked toward me. Those crystal blue eyes were staring at me … butterflies … still staring into my eyes, he brought his hand up to the top of my towel where it was tucked in and began to pull it apart.

"Wyatt, I…" *I what? I'm naked? What am I going to say to him right now, stop? No, that's not what I want either.*

He unwrapped me like a present, and the towel fell to the floor. Feeling very exposed, I covered my chest with my arms. He placed my arms at my side and whispered, "You're beautiful." I was blushing from head to toe. I could feel the heat rising. He inched closer and kissed me gently. In a soft voice, he said, "I really want you right now." My pulse was racing. Believe me: this situation had definitely crossed my mind.

"I ... I ..." I swallowed hard. "I've never done this before."

"I've been waiting for you for a long time." He took my hand and started walking toward my bedroom. Feeling exposed, I reached down and grabbed the towel, but he placed his hand on the towel and shook his head. Holding the towel now, he placed it on the bed, and laid me down on it. He was touching my hair, my skin, my everything—I couldn't breathe. My head was spinning. All I knew at that point in time was that I had never wanted something so badly in my life. I sat up, took his shirt off and started to take his shorts off, pulling his boxers with them. I'd never seen a guy completely naked before, let alone the love of my life. I touched him, and he let out a groan. I touched him again, and he said with a smile, "If you do that again, I won't be able to control myself and we'll be done before we even get started."

He got down on his knees and began to kiss my neck. I couldn't get enough of him, and without thinking, I grabbed handfuls of his hair and pulled his face to mine. I could feel his lips part and the sweep of his tongue. Without breaking our kiss, he climbed onto the bed. Then breathlessly, he asked, "Are you okay?" I answered without words and pulled his hips into mine. I was gasping for air, completely submerged in ecstasy. I began feeling that familiar rise of heat and then an exploding wave of pleasure. I was flooded with a warm sensation. We were both panting as he collapsed on top of me. His heart was racing. As I ran my fingers down his back, I thought he'd fallen asleep, but he rolled onto his side. Smiling that devilish smile I loved, he said, "I love you," and kissed my lips.

As he was running his fingers down my arm, I asked, "Did you plan for this tonight? Is that what the sleeping bags were for?"

"Well, I had my hopes, but this turned out even better than I imagined," he said, kissing the side of my breast. "My plan was to take you to Rock Island and seduce you there, but the mosquitoes got to be so bad that I thought my plan was foiled. Then, as luck would have it, your parents and brother were out for the night. 'Lover boy' got to spend some alone time with you after all," he said, smirking.

"You heard that, huh?"

"Uh, yeah. I think he whispered it loud enough to make sure I heard. It's kind of a guy thing."

Gotta give credit to my brother for that one.

He draped his arm across my chest and closed his eyes. "I'm gonna just 'rest my eyes' for a minute," he said with air quotes. I laughed. I could hardly keep myself from falling asleep.

SLAM! My parents' car door slammed shut outside. I bolted upright. *Shit!*

"Wyatt, you gotta get up! My parents are home!" He jumped up and grabbed his shorts, boxers, and T-shirt. He leaned down, and hastily kissed me as he left through the front door, naked as a jaybird. I heard the front door close just as the side door opened. I covered up my body and closed my eyes as my parents whispered their way to my room. I could hear Mom move the curtain aside, and she looked in and then retreated back to the kitchen, whispering to my dad, "She's sleeping, but Jimmy's not home. Must be he's still with Riley." They tiptoed to their room.

I giggled quietly as I pictured Wyatt making a mad dash out the front door without anything on. I hoped he was at least able to pull on his shorts before he got home.

CHAPTER 40

I woke up the next morning feeling sore and achy like I'd been run over by a truck. Remembering last night's escapades, my body began to tingle. I put on my pajamas and went into the kitchen.

"Mornin', sleepyhead," Mom said, as I walked in and glanced at the clock. *Ten thirty, a new summer record for me.* I grabbed a glass of orange juice and sat at the counter next to Dad, who sat reading the paper, drinking his coffee. He'd already made it to Franklin and back.

"Did you have a nice time yesterday? Wha'd you do?"

"I hung out with Wyatt. We went fishing, and nothing was biting, so he bought some things at Stewart's, and we drove to Rock Island to have a picnic."

Mom said to me, "That's romantic."

You have no idea… "Yeah, it was sweet."

Jimmy walked out to the kitchen fifteen minutes after I did. Surprised, I said to him, "What time did you get home from the movies?" I knew full well he did more than just go to the movies.

Not one to be tricked, he said, "We went to a ten o'clock movie and got back around midnight. We hung out at her place for a little bit; then I got home around one thirty."

"What movie did you see?"

"*Rocky III.* Since you guys raved about it so much, we decided we would see it, too." Jimmy smiled, grabbed a muffin from the counter, and walked outside. I just chuckled to myself. *Well played, Brother.*

After lunch, the familiar sound of the lawn mower running caused my insides to jump and went outside to investigate. I walked up to the field and watched Wyatt for a few minutes before he noticed me.

"Hop on," he said. I gladly wrapped my arms around him and rested my head on his shoulder, breathing him in. I kissed his neck.

"Sleep well?" he asked with a smile.

"Yes, I did. You?"

"Mmhmmm," he said dreamily. "After our fantastically stupendous evening, I got distracted and forgot to give you your gift. Can I meet you at our tree in, say, an hour?"

"Sure," I said, hopping off the mower as he slowed. "See you then."

I got back to the house with a big, ol' grin on my face. *Man, do I love that boy.*

"What are you grinning about?" Mom asked, as she walked to the car.

Changing the subject, I asked, "Where are you going?"

"Gramp gets discharged today. His blood work came back clean. They said for him to take it easy and rest at home. So, Dad and I are going back to the hospital now to bring Gramp home. Dad and I were thinking maybe next week Nanny and Gramp could drive up here for the day. Nanny stayed at their house last night and said it was silly for us to stay over, so we decided to come home late last night. We should be home after dinner tonight."

"Okay. See you in a few hours," I said to Mom and Dad as they walked to the car. I sat at the picnic table for a while, watching the activity on the lake. The sound of the mower stopped at the garage, and I heard Wyatt close the garage door. He exited through the back of the garage and walked home.

About twenty minutes later, I walked anxiously to the Black Forest with my heart pounding. Jimmy let Stubby outside as I left and the usual barking ensued. A piece of white paper fluttered in the breeze as I approached my tree. *That's strange. He said to meet him here, didn't he?* I unfolded the note and began to read:

Dear Callie,

I have something I want to give to you to signify my love and commitment to our relationship.

Looking up, I saw Wyatt on his way to meet me with a box in his hand.

"Did you read the note?"

Smiling, I said, "I was just starting to when you walked up. Should I finish reading it now?"

"Please."

I looked back at the note:

You mean the world to me, and I think of you every second of every day. All winter long, I wait for summer so that I can see you again. I know that we are both going to be in college, but please don't think that means I want anyone else but you. I want you to wear this ring to symbolize our faithfulness and commitment to each other. I will wait for you for as long as it takes. Know that I will be there for you always. I promise.

All my love,

Wyatt

I folded the note, and he handed me a box. Inside sparkled an exquisite gold ring with a heart shaped, deep-red ruby in the center.

I looked at the ring and then at Wyatt. "It's stunning," I said, with a note of astonishment in my voice.

He took the ring and put it on my right-hand ring finger. "I love you, Callista Lamply. Let this be a reminder of my promise."

"I love you, too," I said, feeling the weight of the ring on my finger.

ভ   ভ   ভ

The following week, as promised, we had dinner at the Wilsons' house. The Wilsons even included my grandparents, which I found especially sweet. We all got dressed, and Dad brought over a bottle of wine for the hostess. Samantha showed us pictures of the flowers she'd chosen and told us how excited she was for the wedding this winter. As I reached for a picture that was being passed around, Samantha grabbed my right hand.

"Is that a ruby?"

"It is," I said, a little embarrassed.

"It's beautiful. Who's it from?"

"Wyatt gave it to me for graduation."

"Well done, little brother," she said, smiling at Wyatt.

I didn't go into detail about my promise ring, because that was just between Wyatt and me.

Mrs. Wilson seemed happy listening to and discussing the wedding plans. Samantha told us they were having five groomsmen, two being Wyatt and Tommy, and five bridesmaids, one being Sarah. As the evening came to a close, we thanked the Wilsons for the delicious dinner. My parents left first with Nanny and Gramp. They took them back to our camp to spend the night so they could spend the next day with us on the lake. I left last, saying goodnight to everyone.

Wyatt walked me out the door, and at the bottom step, he gave me a big hug. "Our summer is ending too quickly. I hate when August rolls around. This summer has been the best by far, and last night was"—he looked around—"amazing." He cupped my face in his hands and kissed me slowly. "I look forward to another night like that before you leave."

"Me, too," I said breathlessly. "I just don't know how we're going to get the time away from our families to make that happen," I said, stepping back from him. "But where there's a will, there's a way. That's what my dad always says."

He winked at me and said, "See you tomorrow afternoon?" I smiled at him and left his house feeling completely fulfilled.

CHAPTER 41

Wyatt and I spent the rest of my summer vacation together, pretty much inseparable. When Wyatt was working, I would go visit him, and when he was at home, we spent our time swimming, playing cards, boating, or fishing together. Every few days, he had to do some work for my grandfather in the field or around his house for his parents. Since the first time we were together in my bedroom, we'd managed to make it happen three more times—twice in his basement when his parents were out and we were "watching" his brother and sister. The last and most memorable time was the night before I left to go back to Connecticut. That night, my parents took Mr. and Mrs. Wilson to The Abbey to celebrate their anniversary. Wyatt and I knew it would be several hours before they returned, so we planned our final rendezvous. It was an enchanting evening, with the moon out and a slight breeze that kept the insects at bay.

"I want this to be perfect, just like I pictured it in my head," he said, as we took the boat out to Rock Island. "Before we walk to the shelter, I want you to put on this blindfold. I'll help you find your way."

Feeling a little nervous, I let him tie the blindfold over my eyes. He held my hand and escorted me to the shelter. "We're here. Take a seat while I finish the final touches." I heard him strike a match and smelled the sulfur as it burned. "Okay, you can look now." I took the blindfold off and looked around. He had placed two sleeping bags down on the platform and put candles all around the makeshift bed, creating a magical space. I was in awe, mesmerized by how he'd transformed this place, and as he drew me near, he said, "I want this to be a place that you remember in your dreams when you head back home tomorrow."

How could I forget this beautiful place? We lay down together, reliving our first time. Looking deep into his eyes, I could see doubt rising there. "I'll come back to you, Wyatt," I said, as he tightened his arms around me, unable to speak.

"Promise me," he said. "Promise me you'll wait for me." He reached for my hand and turned my ring around my finger.

"I promise." We lay still on our makeshift bed on our backs, looking up into the star-speckled night sky. I made a silent wish that we would be this happy forever as a shooting star streaked across the sky. At that same moment, a fleeting thought that things were about to change crept into my subconscious.

"You remember the night we were in the field watching the lights in the sky?" I asked.

He responded with an "mmhmmm," gently stroking my arm.

"I wanted you that night."

He turned to look at me in surprise. "Really? I didn't think you were ready. It wasn't the right time."

Fiddling with my ring, I thought about this comment. "You're probably right, but the thought did cross my mind."

He smiled. "The thought crossed my mind many, many times," he said, as his eyes began to smolder. He rolled toward me, scooping me up into his arms. This time, I let him set the pace.

We stayed until nearly midnight. I knew my parents would be home by now. We pulled on our clothes, put out all the candles, and rolled up the sleeping bags. He dropped me off at my dock, and before I left the boat, he said, "Remember, it's not goodbye." "Right, bye for now then," I said, as he kissed me tenderly and guided the boat back to his dock.

The next morning, my family left bright and early to get a jump on the traffic. I had a lot of preparing to do before I left for college in two weeks. Strangely, I wasn't devastated about leaving Wyatt this summer. Don't get me wrong, I would miss him sorely, but I knew that as a freshman, I would have a lot of things to keep me busy my first year. Besides, in four months, we would see each other again. *I can wait four months.* The next time I would see him we would be at a romantic location: Samantha and Brian's wedding.

The closer we got to Connecticut, the farther away Vermont seemed. So much had happened this summer: Wyatt and Jimmy became friends; Jimmy and Riley grew closer; Wyatt and I got as close as two souls could. I would say that it was a summer for the record books.

ᘒ   ᘒ   ᘒ

September, 1984

When I'd arrived on campus for freshman orientation, my new neighbor hadn't moved in yet, and I was anxious to meet her. When she did finally make it in time for the first day of classes, she appeared to be a sweet and innocent girl my age. That couldn't have been further from the truth. I went to her room while her parents were helping her move in. I managed to say hi and introduced myself as she unloaded boxes. Her name was Maddie, and she lived in New Haven, which wasn't that far from Newtown. She and her roommate, Liz, were the cutest, most petite Italian girls.

"You have a boyfriend at home, Callie?" Maddie asked me as she plastered posters to her wall.

"Well, not back at home, but at the University of Rhode Island."

"That sucks."

Maddie's mom gave her a disapproving look and uttered a "tsk" under her breath.

"Ah, Ma, why you gotta do that in front of my new friend here," she said, rolling her eyes. I chuckled. Directing her comments toward me now, she said, "Not for nothing, but that's far. How often do you get to see him?"

"Unfortunately, I won't see him until December. My family is headed up to Vermont for his sister's wedding."

"Nice. You should get some action in December then."

My face began to flush, and I thought to myself, *I hope so.* Maddie's mom was disgusted with our conversation and dropped the box in her arms loudly to the floor.

As her mother exited the room, Maddie whispered to me, "Don't mind her. She's probably not getting any at home."

This made me laugh out loud. I'd never had a friend talk like this before. It was so refreshing. Maddie and I were hitting it off, and I was thrilled to have found this diamond in the rough. I left the room and sat in mine with the door open, watching her upset mother walk back and forth. When the last of the bags, supplies, and boxes were moved in, her parents closed the door and talked with her. I sat, stunned, overhearing a conversation I couldn't believe. Apparently, this cute little Italian girl had finished rehab only a week ago for drug addiction; that was the reason she couldn't make it to school in time for freshman orientation.

Maddie was the first person that I'd ever met that actually used drugs. *I must really live a sheltered life.* The idea that someone could look the way she did and be a drug user amazed me. The addicts I pictured had missing teeth and hair, with sunken cheeks. Maddie, though, had a beautiful, round face with freckles across the bridge of her nose and gorgeous, long chestnut hair. She was maybe five feet tall and a hundred pounds soaking wet. I liked her instantly, regardless of her sordid past. Besides, she had just gotten out of rehab, so she was clean now. Her mom opened up the door, and I watched as her parents hugged her and told her that they would be back on Friday to pick her up for the weekend. *That seems odd.*

I stood and walked back into Maddie's room. "Hey. Is it safe to come back in?"

She smiled but seemed a little preoccupied. "Coast is clear." We continued talking and decided to go have lunch together in the student union. I was excited to have my first real friend out of high school. I told her all about Wyatt and how we'd been seeing each other during the summers for the last two years. She told me about her older boyfriend who'd gotten a job in the student union so that he could be close to her.

As we walked through the cafeteria and got our food, we saw her boyfriend, Frankie. He was much older than I was expecting. He had long, thin hair, a scraggly beard and mustache, and his only saving grace was his eyes; they were startlingly blue. I was taken aback when I was introduced to him. I'd been thinking maybe he was just five years older than us, from our earlier conversation, but this guy in front of me looked to be about fifteen years older. We took our trays and sat down for lunch.

"How old *is* he?" I asked, curious.

"He's thirty-two."

"Dang …" I said. He looked like he had lived a rough life in his thirty-two years. Maddie said that she and Frankie did a lot of drugs together. She said that if her parents found out he had landed a job at our college, they would make her transfer to another school. She continued to tell me the story of how she was in rehab for a cocaine addiction and how she was so down, depressed, and just plain sad that she'd tried to kill herself. I was sitting there in shock. She could see it on my face.

"I know that's a lot to take in, right?"

I nodded my head. "I feel like such a prude sitting here with you. I haven't had half the life experiences you've had in eighteen years."

She laughed. "Be happy you haven't. It sucks."

Before going to our first class, we said goodbye and made plans to meet up later in the dorm. My head was spinning with the information Maddie had given me. I had to admit, I was way out of my comfort zone, and trying to digest her life story was difficult. Thankfully, my classes went pretty well for the first day. Maybe this year wouldn't be too tough, but I still had my work cut out for me.

I was getting into the groove of college life. My roommate was interesting. She had a boyfriend named Mark, and unfortunately, she liked to have him around *a lot.* This didn't bode well for studying. The study room in the basement of our dorm was my domain most days. Since my roommate was always with her boyfriend, I felt grateful that I had Maddie and Liz to keep me company.

The week continued with classes and my meals at the student union. Most of the time, I met up with Maddie and Liz. By the end of the week, I saw Maddie packing up a small bag of clothes to bring home to wash.

"Now, why exactly do you have to go home this weekend?"

"Mom and Dad don't trust me yet and want to keep an eye on me to make sure I don't slip back into my evil ways," she said, waving her hands above her head.

"That stinks. I guess I'll see you on Sunday night then?"

She smiled at me and said, "Yep, and if you see Frankie, tell him I'll be back around six."

"Got it. Have a good weekend."

"You, too." She left the building. From the side window in my room, I saw that her parents had pulled into the lot in back to wait for her. Maddie put her bag in the car and got in.

"Mark, stop it …" I heard giggling from behind me. *Ugh, not again.* I grabbed my books and left the room, thinking, *this is going to be a long weekend.*

Happy to see Maddie back at the dorm Sunday night at six, I was sitting on the floor of my room with the door open when she arrived.

"Hi, Cal, did Frankie come by yet?" she asked, unlocking her door.

"Nope, not yet."

Moments later, she emerged with a smile on her face, looking excited. "When Frankie gets here, I'm gonna be busy for a few hours," she said, wiggling her eyebrows up and down.

"Ahhh, got it." Okay, so that life experience I had had; maybe we weren't so different after all.

About thirty minutes later, Frankie showed up, saw Maddie in my room, and with a sweep of his arm, picked her up off the floor and carried her into her room.

Laughing, she called out, "When the dorm room's a rockin', don't come a knockin'. See you in a few hours," and then closed her door.

Liz came back from the library and had her key in the door when I said, "she's occupied at the moment."

"By being 'occupied', you mean Frankie and Maddie are bumping uglies?" This made me laugh. She walked into my room, and we spent the rest of the evening talking, trying to ignore the sounds coming from the other room. By the time Frankie left, it was well past ten, and when the door finally opened, the smell of sex came wafting from the room. *That's some impressive stamina.*

Maddie and Frankie kissed as he left, and Maddie floated into my room with her robe on. "That. Was. Amazing."

Smiling, she lay flat on my floor. We stayed up until midnight discussing our conquests.

CHAPTER 42

Later in the month, I got a letter from Wyatt saying he could hardly wait the two more months until we would see each other again. He went into detail about what he wanted to do to me when I got to Vermont for the wedding weekend. I found it hard not to picture all the things he wrote about in my head. He had quite an effect on me, and I was feeling flushed just reading his words. After rereading the letter, I put it inside my desk drawer to read again later.

"Man, what's gotten into you? Your face is all red," Maddie noticed, as she was walking to the bathroom in our quad.

"I just got a real juicy letter from my boyfriend. He sure has a way with words," I said, fanning myself with my hand. I'd received a note saying there was a package waiting for me in the mailroom of our dorm along with that letter. Thinking it was from Wyatt, I got very excited and told Maddie I was headed back to the mailroom if she wanted to come with me and get her mail, as well. When we got there, someone had posted a sign on the mailboxes that read, "Due to illness, the mailroom is closed today." Disappointed, Maddie and I just looked at each other.

"That's unacceptable!" she said, raising her index finger in the air. She grabbed a flier for homecoming weekend in October and used the backside to write a note back to the mailroom people. She used a red crayon that she found on the floor and scribbled away. When she'd finished, she took the gum she was chewing and stuck it on the back of the note, now attached to the mailroom door. "There," she said, feeling good about her decision. It read, "Illness schmillness, the mail must get through!!" This made us double over in laughter.

"That should do it, Schmaddie," I said, still laughing.

"I do believe you're right, Schmallie." Really, nothing in college was more important than getting mail from friends and family; not getting mail was downright depressing, unless, of course, you had your good friend there to make light of the situation. Maddie had a way of doing that for me throughout our first year of college.

The best part of October was the Halloween party that Maddie, Liz, and I went to. We loaded onto buses and drove to a banquet hall. I dressed as a pimp in a pink tuxedo; Maddie dressed as Elvira; and Liz was a jailbird in black and white stripes with a plastic ball and chain. The party was fun, and we met many new people from our school there. One boy in particular was hanging out with our group. Some of the girls knew him already and got really excited when they saw him at the party. His name was Charlie, and I quickly decided I wanted to be friends with him. We danced and laughed the night away, and after the party, I learned that Charlie lived in the dorm next to ours.

"Hey, Charlie, so you're in Sam May Dorm, right next door to us?" I called to him as he walked toward his dorm.

"Yeah, you all live in Sheridan Hall? Are you on the second floor, also?"

"Yep, room 206," I said, smiling at him.

"I'm up on the third floor," he said, gesturing with a nod of his head toward the dorm behind him. I'll bet I can see your room from mine," he said, pointing to his window. My room was on the second floor in the back corner with a window facing

Sam May Hall. "Thanks for a great night tonight, girls," he said to us as a group.

In unison, we said, "Bye, Charlie."

When I went back to my room, I went straight to the window to see if, indeed, I could see his room from up there. Looking out my window, I saw a figure walk to a window on the third floor, and sure enough, there stood Charlie looking back at me. His room was across the walkway and over four windows. We waved to one another, and I began to think *I could get used to having a guy as a friend.*

Charlie was very spontaneous, and several times in early November, he came to my room at crazy hours to see if I wanted to have some fun. His smile was infectious, and most times I agreed to join him on his adventures. Once, before Thanksgiving break, he came to my room at three in the morning and told me it was snowing. I didn't believe him at first, because it never snowed in Connecticut that time of year, but I looked out the window to see for myself, and sure enough, snow was falling. Giddy at the winter wonderland outside, I grabbed my coat and boots.

"What're you doing?" my roommate asked.

"Go back to sleep," I said, heading toward the door. Charlie handed me a couple trash bags as we ran out, giggling like five year olds.

"What are these for?" I asked.

"For this," he said, tearing two holes in the bag and slipping it over his legs. Waddling away with his shiny, black diaper, he ran, jumped onto the snow, and slid down the hill through the middle of campus. We were at the top of the hill, between the natatorium and the science building, and we tore down the center of the street, whooping and hollering. Kids started coming out of the woodwork, whizzing past us on their own makeshift sleds. *SPLAT!* "Hey, what the heck?" I yelled, looking around. I saw some kids had put down their sleds and were throwing snowballs. The snowball fight became so enormous that the police were called to break it up. At that point, we all made a run for it.

On another occasion a few nights later, Charlie came to my room saying he was hungry and asked, "Do you want to Toddle?" I didn't have a clue what he was talking about until we drove up to the 24/7 Toddle House Restaurant. We Toddled that night, enjoying mounds of the best hash browns I'd ever had at two in the morning. He and I had so much fun that semester.

December was quickly approaching, and I was counting the days until the wedding: eleven to go. The wedding date on the invitation said Saturday, the 8th of December, so my parents would be picking me up on the 6th. I planned to skip school on the 7th so that we could join in all the pre-wedding preparations. I warned Charlie that I was going to be gone and he should not come by my room at three in the morning during that week. "I'm pretty sure my roommate doesn't want to be awakened that early unless your name is Mark."

"Eesh … yeah, not interested in your roommate. Your boyfriend sure is lucky, though. Have fun. Maybe I'll get Maddie to join me on some wild excursions while you're gone."

I felt a twinge of jealousy at his words, but I quickly dismissed it. He was entitled to have fun in my absence. "Yeah, you should do that. Just be careful, because I think she has a very jealous boyfriend that might beat you up if he gets wind of you stopping by unexpectedly."

He said that he wouldn't bother my roommate or my friends while I was gone if I would take one more early morning adventure with him. *Of course I would*. He didn't tell me when it would be, but I knew it had to take place within the next eleven days, or he was out of luck.

The day for my adventure with Charlie was Friday, November 30th. He came to my room at two thirty in the *afternoon*, which seemed totally out of character for him, and he told me to get some warm clothes on and bring my wallet, because we were going to be gone until late Saturday or early Sunday morning. He drove us to the Amtrak station and bought us two tickets to New York City. I loved the city, especially during the holidays, and riding the train into Grand Central Station was exciting. Seeing the city through Charlie's eyes made me feel like a wide-eyed tourist getting off that train. We stopped for a quick bite to eat before my surprise destination, and the suspense was killing me. After we finished our meal, we did some sightseeing; we went to the Statue of Liberty, the Empire State Building, and Times Square, which gave me a lot of time to learn more about Charlie.

"So tell me about your family, Charlie. Do you have brothers and sisters? Do you have any pets? What are your parents like? Do you have family close by?" I peppered him with questions.

"Whoa, whoa, whoa, slow down, sister," he said with a smile. "Let's see, you want to know about my family, huh? I'm not sure I can divulge that information. If I tell you, I'll have to kill you."

"Very funny. Come on, I'm serious. I want to know more about you. So far all I know is that you live in Connecticut somewhere and you like to take early morning trips to Toddle House with a really awesome friend."

"Ha, that is true. I do like to go to Toddle House," he said, gently bumping my shoulder. "Okay, let's start with my family.

I have one sister named Laura who teaches fifth grade at an elementary school in Glastonbury. My parents' names are Tim and Charlene Canfield, and they live in Bethel with our cat, Whiskers," he said, rolling his eyes. "I did not name the cat, my sister did when she was ten. He's probably on his ninth life by now. Good thing my dad's a vet. My mom, on the other hand, is a teacher in Newtown."

"No way, really? What school?"

"It's a little school in the middle of town called Sandy Hook Elementary."

"I know where that is. I used to go past it to get to my friend's house."

"Small world. Yeah, she's worked there for about eleven years now."

It was getting dark, and I had assumed all the siteseeing was my surprise and that surely my surprise was over—but according to Charlie, we hadn't even gotten to it yet.

"The siteseeing was just a bonus. You have to be patient. Your surprise will happen around midnight," he said, chastising me. At about eleven thirty that night, we took a taxi to Rockefeller Center, and I saw a line was forming. "Let's get in line to get your surprise."

"Wait a minute … My surprise is getting tickets to *SNL*?" I squealed in disbelief and delight.

"Hopefully, yes, but in order to get those tickets, we'll have to stand in line until seven in the morning when the standby tickets will be handed out. Are you up for that?"

"Am I up for that? Are you kidding me? It'll totally be worth the wait. I have *always* wanted to do this!" I could hardly contain my excitement.

We met some interesting people in line. Some had obviously done this before and had brought sleeping bags, chairs, and coolers. I was so excited that I was running on pure adrenaline for several hours while chatting with Charlie. By about the fourth hour, I was hitting a wall and leaned my head against Charlie's chest and fell fast asleep. Seven o'clock finally rolled around, and we got our tickets. We had to decide if we were going to go to the dress rehearsal and get back in line at seven fifteen that night or if we were going to go to the live performance and get back in line at ten forty-five. We opted for the seven-fifteen timeslot. We now had twelve hours to kill. We went to get some breakfast and a lot of coffee and began to plan our day.

"Where do you want to go first?" Charlie asked. "The zoo? Central Park? Art museum?"

"Um, let's start with Central Park." We started heading in the direction of the park and walked through, while talking about everything under the sun. "Smile," Charlie said enthusiastically, pulling me in with one hand and snapping a picture with the other.

I told him about Wyatt, and he told me about past girlfriends; it all seemed so comfortable. We grabbed a cab to the Brooklyn Bridge and walked across it to get a view of the Hudson River. As we walked, he casually placed his arm around my shoulder. It felt so natural to be walking this way.

When we took a cab to the Metropolitan Museum of Art, I was growing tired. The museum was spectacular, but I needed a place to rest. We found a quiet spot to sit for a spell, and I think I dozed off on his shoulder again. When it got close to six, we left and bought a few things from a street vendor to tide us over as we hoofed it back to Rockefeller Center for *SNL*. We stood in line inside with a perky, little blond page named Jen.

She was in control of who got to sit where, and we stood as she pulled people from the line to form yet another line. Curiously, we watched her pull several people out, and as she approached us, she said, "You two come with me." We were grouped with the others pulled from line, and within minutes, our group of twenty was escorted to the floor seats in front of the stage. I couldn't believe our luck! The show was hysterical; I hadn't laughed that hard in my life. Between Jim Belushi, Billy Crystal, Julia Louis-Dreyfus, and Martin Short, I nearly wet my pants because of the antics going on. During the entire rehearsal, it felt like the cast members were one-upping each other to see who could make the other laugh first. It was absolutely hilarious, and I was having the best time. Two hours later, after a standing ovation for the players, it was time to go. We hailed a taxi to Grand Central Station and bought tickets back to Connecticut, where Charlie had left his car. By the time we got back to school, I was sound asleep, and he gently tapped my shoulder to rouse me.

"Wake up, sleepyhead. We're back," he said, as I rubbed my eyes. I grabbed my jacket, got out of the car, and walked back to my dorm, where I turned and gave Charlie a giant hug.

"That was the single best twenty-four hours I've ever had. I can't thank you enough." I was absolutely beaming … that is, until he kissed me.

"Callie, I'm so sorry. I just got caught up in the moment. I'm so sorry!"

"Thanks again, Charlie. I'll never forget these past few days." I turned and quickly entered the building. I looked back and saw him standing there with a disappointed look on his face. We waved to each other and went our separate ways.

Walking into my room, I could hear the deep breathing of not only my roommate, but Mark, as well. Ugh. Too tired to care,

I changed into pajamas and hopped into bed. For all I knew, there was some funny business going on during the night, but I was oblivious to it. I slept like a rock and only woke up briefly when Mark tried to leave the room without me noticing. "Bye, Mark," I said, as I rolled over and fell back asleep.

When I did finally get up, my roommate was doing homework at her desk. She turned around when she heard me stirring. "Hey, why didn't you find another place to crash last night? Didn't you know Mark was here?"

"Yeah, I knew he was here, but guess what? My parents paid for my room and board, and last I checked, Mark wasn't even a student here. Why didn't you guys just crash at his apartment?" I asked her, thoroughly annoyed.

"Because when I came here to get my things, you were nowhere to be found. When it started getting late and you didn't come back, we just assumed you weren't going to be back until the morning."

"Well, you know what they say about assuming …" I stormed out to use the restroom. As I brushed my teeth, I decided I needed to take this matter up with our Resident Assistant, Deidra, so I walked down the hall to her room and hashed it out with her. When I returned to my room, my roommate had left for the cafeteria, and I went back to bed. I was past the point of exhaustion, but as soon as I closed my eyes, Charlie's kiss ran through my head. *Should I feel guilty? Should I tell Wyatt about this*? I decided it was a one-time thing and it would never happen again.

I went to Maddie's room after the weekend ended and sat on her bed, replaying what happened. I felt better the minute I sat down.

"So when I got back from my awesome weekend, he kissed me. What should I do about that?"

"First of all, that is a wicked awesome weekend! I just sat at home being watched over twenty-four hours a day. My parents were walking on eggshells. I tried to tell them that I was fine and I really do want to live, so chill out a bit. Second, don't think too much about Charlie. He's your friend, and he just got caught up in the excitement you two just shared. He said so himself."

"What if it's not just a passing thing? What if, in two weeks, he wants to kiss me again?"

"Then you kick him in the balls and tell him to knock it off. That should get it through his thick skull." I loved Maddie.

For the next four days, I didn't see Charlie. On one hand, I was relieved, but on the other hand, I missed my friend; I missed his goofy sense of humor and his spontaneity. I made a mental note to see him after I got back from the wedding.

CHAPTER 43

On Thursday, after my last class let out, my mom drove up to school to get Jimmy and me to take us home. The plan was to leave at six the next morning, and when my alarm went off at five thirty, I was tempted to hit the snooze button. *I hate mornings.* Small talk that early in the morning felt like torture. My mom, on the other hand, was a Chatty Cathy. For my brother and I, this was super annoying, but since we were getting ready to go see Riley and Wyatt all weekend, we endured her chattiness with smiles plastered on our faces.

We left at six, and of course, had to make one quick stop at the local coffee shop so Mom and Dad could get their caffeine fix. *I could have slept another twenty minutes in the comfort of my bed.* When we were finally on our way, Jimmy and I decided to sleep in the back of the car, with the smell of coffee wafting past our noses. Believe me, coffee was so much better than having my dad's cigarette smoke polluting the car as it did in my early years. Thankfully, he had stopped smoking years ago, after I tried many times to get him to quit. I wasn't very subtle about it either. I used to clip articles about lung cancer and tape them to the fridge, and once I took a brand-new pack of his cigarettes and broke every last one in half. Even with all my efforts, he didn't stop until he wanted to do it for himself, cold turkey. That was just something they did in his generation. Many of my relatives smoked for years. Thank goodness that disgusting habit was gone.

Jimmy and I slept off and on for two hours. He had brought a book along to read in the car. Watching him read like that made me want to vomit. I didn't know how people could read in a moving vehicle. I couldn't even read a map without wanting to hurl.

We stopped for an early lunch and then continued on the last leg of our journey, entertaining ourselves with the Celebrity Game. I started. "Molly Ringwald."

"Rick Moranis," Jimmy said quickly.

"Mary Tyler Moore!" Mom exclaimed while clapping her hands.

Jimmy groaned because he knew that meant it was his turn again. "Ah, man…Really? Hmmm. Mmmmorgan Fairchild. Yeah, that's the ticket," he said in his best Jon Lovitz impersonation. Eventually, we tired of this game and started working on the alphabet using only road signs.

Finally, we were at my grandparents' house in Franklin. We were each greeted with a hug. Gramp seemed to be doing really well since his bout in the hospital. Everything seemed to be status quo.

I took a shower and got my dress on for the rehearsal dinner that we were all invited to attend. My heart pounded with excitement to see Wyatt. My brother's expression indicated that he felt the same way about seeing Riley. When we arrived at the restaurant, I immediately spotted that familiar truck in the parking lot, and my heart leapt. Wyatt had told me that his dad gave him Tyler's truck over Thanksgiving break, and he was using it at school. His dad thought Tyler would have wanted Wyatt to have it, and I thought that was a sweet gesture.

As I opened the car door, I had to control my feet, because all I wanted to do was run and jump into Wyatt's arms. We all walked in together, asking the hostess if our party had already arrived. We followed her to our table where I saw Wyatt immediately, sitting next to Brian. Our eyes met, and he smiled so broadly it made *my* cheeks hurt. He pushed his chair back and quickly had me in his arms. We hugged briefly, and he kissed my cheek. "It's so good to see you."

I never tired of hearing him say that. He pulled out the chair next to him and said, "I saved this seat for you." Jimmy would have to wait until tomorrow to see Riley, as she wasn't invited to the rehearsal dinner, and I could see the disappointment register on his face.

"How did the rehearsal go?" I asked Wyatt.

He redirected my question to Brian and said loudly, "Yeah, how did the rehearsal go, Brian?"

Brian blushed and said, "Well, I was about an hour late. I had the wrong time written in my day planner at work. I totally screwed up. I can't make any excuses for it, but just know that it will not happen tomorrow. I can't be late to my own wedding… or there won't be one," he said, and winked at me.

I smiled back at him. "I'm looking forward to the big day. You guys have put so much time and energy into the planning," I said to Brian.

"Yeah, well, I had nothing to do with it. Samantha and Mrs. Wilson did it all. I was just told what time to show up. Eight, right?" he said jokingly, turning to Samantha who, in turn, smacked his arm and rolled her eyes. "I know, I know. It's at six. I was only kidding. Sheesh." With this, he gave her a peck on the cheek producing a smile on her lips.

We went home laughing about Brian's little mishap and looked forward to another celebratory day.

ℭ ℭ ℭ

Feeling refreshed after a good night's sleep, I was ready for the day. As I looked out through the Vermont window, watching the clouds pass by, I began to take notice of the window structure and its unique qualities. A Vermont window, also known as a witch window, casket window, or sideways window, is found almost exclusively in or near the state of Vermont and usually found in older homes. The window was diagonal along the roofline. To me, they looked crooked, placed as an afterthought during construction. For whatever reason, this window made me think of Aunt Marilyn. I never did get around to asking her what she was doing in the graveyard when Wyatt saw her.

I decided that if I was going to run, I needed to do it now, just in case the snow began to fall. I dressed in my winter running tights, adding a few extra layers. Grabbing a hat, known as a toque in these parts, I walked through the front door. With the first breath of frigid air, my lungs ached from the cold. This was going to be a rough run. I decided not to run down to the Wilsons' house, instead, I ran through town, past the local beauty shop, where Mrs. Wilson, Samantha, and the wedding party were getting their hair and nails done; a lengthy process with so many bridesmaids. There was a woman in the group of ladies I didn't recognize, but assumed it was Brian's mom, because she was getting all the bells and whistles done, too.

I stopped at the storefront and tapped the glass. Samantha was getting her hair styled, and she turned her head, smiled, and waved. Sarah, farther back, was getting a pedicure. Smiling, I gave the ladies two thumbs-up and continued on my run. The snow was starting to flurry as I turned back to my grandparents' house.

Grabbing the newspaper, I walked through the front door. Gramp was opening the door as I turned the knob.

"Oh!" I said laughing. "You scared me."

Gramp said, "Your dad and I are headed out for some coffee. We'll be back in a little bit."

As Dad walked by, he grabbed the paper from my hand and said, "I'll take that. Thank you."

"Callie, why don't you shower? I have plans for us," Mom said.

Okay, that's strange. I smiled and went upstairs. My hands were burning under the water from being exposed to the cold. All ready to go, I went back downstairs and grabbed my jacket. "Where's Jimmy?" I asked, looking around.

"Still sleeping, and then I think he has plans with Riley. He's taking her to lunch and then to the wedding later on. We'll meet them at the church. He couldn't wait until tonight to see her," she added, smiling.

"Maybe theirs will be the next wedding we go to. So what's your plan?" I asked Mom, as Nanny walked into the room and grabbed her coat.

"We're going to have a girls' day today. First we're going to get a manicure and pedicure; then we're going to lunch."

Nanny said, "I haven't had a manicure in years, and I don't think I have ever had a pedicure in my life!" She seemed genuinely excited, which made us smile. We got in the car and went to the same beauty shop that I'd seen the wedding party in earlier. When we walked in, Mrs. Wilson walked over to Mom, with her pedicure flip-flops on, and hugged her. The shop had a full staff expecting all of us, ready for the challenge. It was like an assembly line: a few girls at a time got their nails done, then they moved to the pedicure station for toes, then they got their hair done. When one group finished, they rotated. We slipped right into the rotation, minus the hair station.

POP! I turned around just as Mrs. Wilson had opened some champagne and poured glasses for all the girls. With the clink of crystal, we made a toast to Samantha and Brian, and hesitantly, I swallowed the champagne, nearly spitting it out. It burned my throat and warmed my belly. *How do people drink this stuff?* A great start to the wedding day; we shared stories, shed a few tears and had lots of girl talk. Embarrassing girl talk. It all started with Mrs. Wilson.

"Samantha, I think this is a good time to have *the* talk."

"Mom, *pu-lee-ze*, I didn't need it when I was in my teens, and I certainly don't need it now," she teased her mother.

"Well, I just want you to know that most nights of the week, men want sex. It's your duty as a wife to please your man."

"Oh, please, really? You believe that?" Samantha asked, surprised.

"I do. Why do you think your father and I have been happily married for so many years?"

I looked over at Sarah to see if she was listening, but thankfully, the blow dryer covered her head. Mortified, I tried to pretend I wasn't listening, but I felt as though this little speech was meant for all of us.

Mrs. Wilson continued. "There will be times in your life when you and your husband will have your ups and downs. When you're up and he's down and you're out of sync, just ride the wave until he comes up to meet you. It's no fun when you are both in a down cycle, but boy oh boy, are the upswings fantastic; it's worth the ride. Plus, I want lots of grandbabies, so don't waste any time." Satisfied with her little speech, she winked at Samantha to punctuate her remark.

I liked the sentiment, and looking at my mom and grandmother sitting in the pedicure station, their approval was evident.

CHAPTER 44

The time had come for us to pile into the car and get to the wedding. The ceremony was at six in the chapel, which was located at the front of the church. This chapel happened to be the first one built in this area, and as the congregation grew, the church needed to expand. The parishioners didn't want to tear down the chapel, so they built one behind it. The chapel was alluring. Having spent many Christmas Eves here, recalling fond memories, I never tired of its beauty.

As we drove up, the flurries turned into full-on snowflakes and started to accumulate. For people in Vermont, this was nothing to worry about, but those of us from Connecticut got worried. "Oh my, I hope this stops before the reception begins," Mom fretted. We carefully walked to the front of the chapel and opened the door. In the vestibule, the groomsmen were waiting to bring the guests to their seats. I spotted Wyatt as he came forward after seating another guest.

"Are you a friend of the bride or the groom?" he said cheekily.

"The bride," I said with a snicker. He took my mom and me by the arm and guided us to the left side of the church.

As we walked to our seats, Wyatt asked, "Do you know why you sit on the left for the bride?" Mom and I looked at each other and shook our heads. "Apparently the bride's family and friends traditionally sat on the left side of the church because the bride always stands with her groom on the right. Back in the day, the groom wore a sword to ward off anyone trying to steal the bride's dowry, and he would have to have his sword arm at the ready. He would wear the sword on his right hip; therefore, he would have his bride on his left. I've always found folklore interesting." Wyatt looked very proud of his history lesson as he seated us next to Jimmy and Riley, who had already arrived. Leaning in to whisper in my ear, Wyatt said, "If you were my bride, I would fight any man to his death."

Thankfully I was seated, because my knees went weak. He looked so handsome standing there in his black tux and wearing a red-rose boutonniere.

The groom and the groomsmen were dressed alike, but Brian had on a white boutonniere to differentiate him from the others. After all the guests were seated, the music began, and in walked the mothers of the bride and the groom—all elegantly dressed. Mrs. Wilson wore a floor-length gown in a soft golden color, like candlelight, with cap sleeves. She looked stunning. Brian's mother wore a floor-length, muted red dress off one shoulder with a sequined belt. Samantha and Brian had a great gene pool for their future kids to swim in.

As the processional began, the groomsmen entered through a side door and stood next to Brian at the altar. Then bridesmaids walked in gracefully, one at a time. They wore knee-length red dresses, matching the red roses they carried, which had white baby's breath interspersed throughout each nosegay. The processional continued as the bridesmaids sashayed to the front of the chapel.

When the trumpeter began, announcing the bride with a melodic blast, he indicated it was time for the guests to turn and rise. "Here Comes the Bride" began as the doors were opened wide. Many people audibly gasped at Samantha's beauty. She had her hair up on the sides and clipped with baby's breath. Attached was a thin veil that covered her hair to her shoulders. The rest of her hair fell down her back in tendrils. Her gown was a sheath-style dress that hugged every inch of her ravishing body in silk. The dress had a plunging V-neck, with crystals decorating the thin straps. The bodice of the dress had ruching to the side in waves, with the remaining fabric cascading down the side of her dress. She wore a chunky crystal bracelet on one wrist, small crystal stud earrings, and her engagement ring for jewelry. Perfect.

I quickly looked at Brian to see his reaction, and I could see the love in his eyes, which were brimming with tears. As Mr. Wilson, wearing a tux, walked slowly down the aisle with Samantha, grinning from ear to ear, I got a good look at the beautiful bouquet of flowers she was carrying. Red and white roses were bound together with a white ribbon of satin, a perfect touch.

"Who gives this woman in marriage?" the preacher asked.

Mr. Wilson responded, "Her mother and I do." He turned and kissed his daughter, shook Brian's hand, and placed Samantha's hand in his. Mr. Wilson took his seat next to Mrs. Wilson in the front pew of the chapel. The snow was falling fast, and accumulating on the windowsill outside. As the ceremony began, I looked around the chapel to see that we were bathed in candlelight as the overhead lights dimmed. It was breathtaking.

"Before we begin our celebration today, Samantha and Brian would like us all to take a moment to remember those family members who could only be with us in spirit, especially Tyler, whom we lost all too soon. Let us have a moment of silence … Amen," the minister said, followed by a chorus of amens from the congregation. We listened as the minister continued the service with readings from First Corinthians 13:4. "Love is patient; love is kind." After that, and to my surprise, Sarah came forward to sing "Grow Old with Me" by John Lennon, while Samantha and Brian lit their unity candle. I had no idea Sarah could sing, let alone with such a lovely voice. There wasn't a dry eye in the chapel, and after the lighting of the unity candle, the minister spoke directly to Samantha and Brian about their union today and asked them to recite their vows to one another by turning to face each other.

Samantha began with her vows, "Brian, I take you to be my partner for life. I promise above all else to live in truth with you and to communicate fully and fearlessly. I give you my hand and my heart. I'll be your shelter during any storm. I pledge my love, devotion, faith, and honor as I join my life to yours." Brian repeated the same vows to Samantha, and then the minister performed the ring ceremony.

As the minister was speaking, my fingers had begun to unconsciously twirl my promise ring. However, the first image that popped into my head was not of Wyatt, but of Charlie. *He'd look so handsome in a tuxedo.* "By the power vested in me in the state of Vermont, I pronounce you man and wife. Brian, you may kiss your bride." Brian gently hugged Samantha, and they kissed tenderly. It was the sweetest kiss I'd ever seen, and as my vision began to blur, I saw Wyatt give me a quick wink from the front of the chapel. *Geez, what am I doing? What would Wyatt say if I told him about Charlie's kiss? What would he say if he knew I was thinking of Charlie rather than him? Get your shit together, Callie.* The congregation began to clap, cueing the recessional music. Two by two, the bridesmaids and groomsmen walked together down the aisle to exit the chapel, and then the parents, followed by the grandparents and guests. The wedding party formed a receiving line in the narthex, and as we exited into the winter wonderland, we were handed sparklers. As the bride and groom exited the chapel, they walked down the illuminated walkway to the groom's car.

My parents drove me to the wedding reception, and as we walked into the party, it was immediately obvious that Mr. Wilson would be the master of ceremonies for the evening. He called each member of the wedding party by name as they walked across the floor to the head table.

"And for their first outing as man and wife, I'm proud to announce ..." *Mr. and Mrs. Charles Canfield.* "Mr. and Mrs. Brian Doyle!" At this announcement, the groom came in carrying the bride in his arms, both of them waving at the guests. He set her down, and they walked to the head table to take their seats. Dinner was served, but time was moving slowly, and I grew tired of waiting for Wyatt. More toasts were made, and as I watched the best man give his speech, I noticed Wyatt was especially enjoying himself. *What has gotten into him?* After the cutting of the cake and the first dance, I finally got a chance to see Wyatt up close and personal.

"You look beautiful!" he said, overly excited.

"Wyatt, did you have more than just a champagne toast tonight?"

"Maybe a little more than just something for the toast." He was acting so immature.

"Let's have some cake and sit down for a little bit." I had to hold his arm to steady him as he sat down.

"I wanna dance; you wanna dance?" he slurred.

Wyatt looked more like he was doing an interpretive dance of the wedding out there on the dance floor. At one point, he slid on his knees from one side of the dance floor to the other, colliding with a party guest and causing the guest to fall backward onto a table that hadn't been cleared. Dishes were falling to the floor, but Wyatt chose to keep on dancing. He danced up to the microphone, and while the DJ had his back turned, no doubt looking in the direction of the mess on the floor, Wyatt began speaking.

"Let it be known that I love Callista Lamply with all my heart. I don't care who knows it! She's so pretty, and her legs are freakin' hot." People stopped dancing and looked up at Wyatt, then at me. I was mortified. The DJ finally managed to yank the microphone away from him. Grabbing him by the arm, I pulled him from the dance floor.

"Yeah, good idea. Let's blow this popsicle stand." He grabbed my hand and, wobbling, brought me to a coat closet just outside of the reception area. He forcefully opened the closet door and pulled me in. He was trying to kiss me, but it felt more like he was molesting my mouth.

"Wyatt, I have to get out of here. I'm sure my folks will be ready to go soon."

"Not yet. I haven't seen you all night, and I want to *see* some," he said, groping me—not at all the gentle Wyatt I'd grown to love.

"Wyatt, please stop. You're drunk." He began to pull on my dress, trying to take it off of me, when the zipper broke. "Wyatt, what are you doing? Knock it off. I mean it!" He turned me around with a steely grip on my shoulder and forced me against the wall, yanking on the broken zipper. Frustrated, he gripped my shoulder with the bottom of my dress in his hand. I turned my head to yell at him, but he grabbed me by the hair and slammed me against the wall. As he moved his mouth over mine, I felt dizzy, and my ears began to ring. When the ringing subsided, I realized that he had unzipped his pants and was now reaching for my underwear. I felt his hand yank the material, and it was beginning to give way when I screamed, "WYATT, STOP!" and proceeded to kick him with all my might in the shin.

"Yow!" he cried. I quickly opened the closet door to let myself out and slammed it shut. "Callie, wait, will I see you tomorrow before you leave?" he asked, sounding like a little boy from behind the door.

My hands were shaking with fear and anger. I left without saying another word to him. Walking down the hall, I could see my parents looking for me. As we left, my mom smoothed my hair down with her hand and said cheekily, "I trust you had a chance to say good-bye to Wyatt?" Pulling up my sleeve, I nodded, not sure why that made my mom laugh. In the car on the ride home, my parents broke down the evening, laughing at Wyatt professing his love for their daughter. I felt sick.

"How about Sarah? Did anyone expect that to happen? What a voice!" Dad gushed.

"She's been practicing for several months to make it perfect. She was very pleased to be able to give the gift of song to her sister," Mom said. "It was beautiful, and there wasn't a dry eye in the house."

They just droned on and on, while I sat in shock in the back seat, watching the snowflakes melt as quickly as they landed on the windshield. One thought drifted through my consciousness: *Charlie wouldn't have acted that way.*

CHAPTER 45

When we got up the next morning, we leisurely packed our things and ate a small breakfast in the kitchen. I was anxious to leave, when I heard a car pull up. Riley had come to say goodbye. She and Jimmy spent some time in the kitchen, talking softly to one another, and then she left. Jimmy walked her to her car, and I watched as he kissed her goodbye. Just as she was backing out, I saw that familiar red truck pull into the driveway. Wyatt jumped out of the truck without closing the door and came inside without knocking. Surprised, Mom said, "Morning, Wyatt. How are you feeling this morning?"

"Hey, Mrs. Lamply, sorry to let myself right in, but I wanted to talk to Callie before you left. I thought maybe she wouldn't answer the door if I knocked first."

Giving a worried glance to my dad, she said, "That's okay, Wyatt. She's in the kitchen. We're leaving in about twenty minutes."

He walked into the kitchen, looking unkempt. *Good, maybe he didn't sleep well last night after making a total ass of himself.* I didn't make any attempt to get up or acknowledge him. Sitting across from me at the kitchen table, he placed both his hands in his lap.

"I didn't want to miss a chance to say goodbye. Cal, I'm so sorry about last night. You have to know that I wouldn't try to hurt you. I can't bear you leaving thinking I'm some sort of animal," he said, just above a whisper.

I just sat there, listening. I didn't know what to say to him.

"Callie, you know I love you…right? Cal? Say something."

I could hear my parents going in and out of the front door as they packed up the car. Finally, I heard them saying goodbye to Nanny and Gramp—my cue to say goodbye to Wyatt.

"It's probably a good thing I'm going back to Connecticut. I think you need some time to sort things out. In six months, we'll have a clearer view of everything." He stood up as I pushed in my chair and followed me as I walked to his truck. "Bye, Wyatt. Take care of yourself." He just stood there staring at me, and I was beginning to wonder if he was going to leave. I stood my ground until he finally climbed into the truck and I closed the door.

"Callie, don't leave me this way." I could see the pain in his eyes.

"Drive safe." I turned around before I could say anything more and walked into the house.

C&R   C&R   C&R

The snow-packed roads slowed our progress home, causing us to stop several times along the way. Once home, we all unpacked our stuff, and Mom immediately started in on the laundry. In order to make it to our first class the next morning, my brother and I would have to leave the house at eight thirty. Mom carried clean clothes into my room and placed them on my bed, saying, "Everything all right, sweetheart? You were awfully quiet on the ride home."

"I'm fine. Just thinking about school."

"Are you and Wyatt okay?"

"I'm not sure." I got up off my bed and started walking out of my room, but Mom stopped me with a hug.

"Just remember, you're never too old to hug your mom."

"Thanks, Mom. I think I'm gonna call Maddie and see how her weekend was."

As I walked to the phone, I thought, *I wonder what Charlie did while I was gone.* It was around seven thirty when I called.

"Hello?"

"Maddie, it's Callie. How was your weekend?"

"Hey! I thought you weren't going to be back until Monday night?"

"We just got home a little while ago, and I'm bored already."

"How was the wedding? Did you see Wyatt? Did you bang him?" I could hear her cover the phone with her hand and yell to her mom, "Yeah, I know, Ma, it's disgusting. If I had a phone in my own room, you wouldn't have to hear me speak of such filth." She uncovered the phone. "So, did you?"

I laughed, glad to hear Maddie in a playful mood. "I did see him, but, no, I didn't bang him."

"No? Not for nothin', but that's a shame."

I continued to tell her all about the weekend and how beautiful it was. I described in detail the dress, the flowers, and the chapel.

"That sounds gorgeous, but why do I get the feeling you're not telling me everything?"

Taking a deep breath, I said, "Because I'm not. I'll have to tell you about it when I see you." We went on talking about what she did all weekend, which was a whole lot of nothing. She said she felt like a prisoner in her own home.

"When you coming back to school? Tomorrow?" she asked hopefully.

"Yeah, I'll be driving in on two wheels to get to my first class at ten. Wanna meet in the cafeteria for lunch?" I asked.

"Sounds good. See you then. Bye, Schmallie."

This made my heart happy. "Bye, Schmaddie."

ଔ   ଔ   ଔ

The next morning, Mom drove Jimmy and me back to school, dropping us off at our dorms. Walking down the middle of campus to get to class, I heard a familiar voice call my name. I stopped and turned around to see Charlie running down the hill. He was breathless when he reached me.

"Hey ... what's up? You have a good weekend? How was the wedding?" Charlie bombarded me with a zillion questions. I didn't have a chance to answer one before he asked another.

"Hey, Charlie, I'd love to stay and chat, but I'm gonna be late for class. Can I see you later on?"

"Sure," he said, but didn't tell me when, which meant it would probably be at three in the morning. I smiled as I walked to class. Biology class dragged on; when it finally ended, I was starving and couldn't wait to catch up with Maddie in the cafeteria.

Later that day, I decided to walk over to my brother's dorm, which was in the same upper quad as mine.

"What is a molecule?" someone yelled as I walked through my brother's open door.

"What is glucose?" Jimmy and his neighbor were playing *Jeopardy* while watching the show in separate rooms simultaneously. Both of their doors were open, and they were both lying on their beds, watching TV. An amusing scene.

"Hey, can I come in for a sec?"

He nodded and yelled, "What is amber? Aw, crap. Whatchu want?"

"Before we left, I meant to ask you about the memorial fund that you, Mom, and Dad have been working on for the Marines. Any word on how that is going?"

"We're still working on it. I'll probably have some idea on how it's going by the end of the school year. What is Zantedeschia? Boom!"

"What? You're cheating over there," a voice called out from the adjacent room.

"Okay, just checking. Thanks. I can tell you're really busy here," I said sarcastically and turned to leave. As I walked down the hall, I heard the neighbor yell, "Was that your sister?"

Jimmy said, "Yeah, why?"

"I thought you said she was fat and ugly?"

Jimmy laughed. "That was just to keep you away from her." I just shook my head as I continued down the hall.

ભ ભ ભ

Just as I suspected, I had a visitor at three that morning. "Wanna Toddle tonight?" Charlie asked.

"I suppose so. Give me a sec."

We drove down to Toddle House, still wearing my pajamas, and went inside. The place was really quiet.

"Hey, um…I just wanted to tell you again that I'm sorry about the other night. It's been bugging me since it happened. I don't want to mess up what we have. I just got carried away. Sorry."

Honestly, that was the furthest thing from my mind, and for a second, I thought he was talking about Wyatt. "Wait, what?" I asked, confused.

"Cal, do I really have to spell it out for you? The day we got back from SNL, remember?"

"Oh, that. Charlie, it's fine. I mean, who can resist this?" I joked disparagingly as I waved my hands down the front of my body. "That day was spectacular! Thank you again for all you did." Relief washed over his face. We went on to talk about what happened over the weekend. I told him all about the wedding.

"Can I ask you something," I ventured, "as a friend who happens to be a guy?"

"Shoot."

Trying to figure out how to explain what happened with Wyatt was more difficult than I imagined, but I began anyway.

"Have you ever had too much to drink out on a date?"

Looking concerned, he said, "Yeah, once. It wasn't one of my finer moments. Why do you ask?"

"Wyatt was really drunk this weekend, and he was acting really weird."

"Like what?"

Feeling uncomfortable, I wondered if I was crossing a line.

"Callie, you can talk to me about anything. Don't be embarrassed. I won't judge."

You might. "Wyatt was, well, really physical at the reception. I'm not sure how to put this. He was being really rough and was trying to get my dress off in the coat closet of the reception, even though I was telling him not to."

Alarmed, Charlie asked, "Did he hurt you?"

"Well, no, not really. He just never acted that way before, and it scared me."

"Cal, tell me the truth. Did he make you do anything you didn't want to do?"

"Charlie, I'm fine. I think I hurt him more when I kicked him in the shin."

Smiling, he observed, "That's my Callie! If he scared you, then he deserved whatever pain you doled out." *My Callie, I like the sound of that.*

Reaching across the table, he grabbed my hand to stop me from ripping the napkin I had been shredding unknowingly. "Cal, if you want to know if I'd behave like that on a date, the answer is no. I have more respect than that. And if I were on a date with you, just know I would never do anything to hurt you."

Butterflies. "Let's stop talking about me. What did you do with your time while I was gone?"

"Promise you won't get mad?"

Uh-oh. "Charlie, what did you do?"

"Okay, just to set the record straight, you were gone for almost a week."

"Just tell me."

"Maddie and I went out one night. She was dreading the upcoming stay with the warden and wanted to have some fun before the weekend, so we went bowling."

"I'm not mad. Why would I be mad?" *What? Hell yes, I'm mad*!! I felt betrayed. Letting go of my hand, he told me about the rest of his weekend.

It was getting late, and I was too tired for an argument. "I gotta get some sleep. I have to present tomorrow in a small group."

"Eesh, good luck with that," he offered as he paid the bill.

After walking me back to my dorm, he pulled me in for a friendly hug. "I'm worried about you. When Wyatt is in the picture, go with your gut. If it doesn't feel right, it's not." With one last squeeze, he let me go.

CHAPTER 46

The month rolled on slowly. When I went home for Christmas break, I promised to call Charlie and Maddie. The thought of Maddie and Charlie spending time together without me was like a festering wound, and on Christmas, I couldn't take it anymore and decided to call Maddie.

"Hey, Maddie, Merry Christmas!"

"Ah, Callie, thanks for calling. I was just thinking of you. I just got off the phone with Charlie. Were your ears burning?"

"What were you talking about?" I said, a little too anxiously, now feeling jealous.

"Cal, are you mad at me?"

"Maddie, why didn't you tell me that you and Charlie went bowling together?"

"Because of how you are reacting right now. I knew it would upset you. You're funny, Cal. You say you and Charlie are just friends, but I think you really like him, regardless of whether you have a boyfriend or not. Oh, and by the way, the information you said you were going to share, that *thing* you said happened? I had to get the lowdown about the coatroom from Charlie. That was some shit. Are you all right?"

I didn't know whether to be angry that Charlie told her or happy that she was concerned.

"Yeah, I'm fine. He keeps sending me letters of apology. I'm not sure what I'm gonna do."

"Do you still love the guy?"

I had to think about that. "Yeah…yes, I still do. Mad, I'm sorry about before. I shouldn't care who you hang out with. Charlie's your friend, too."

"True, but I knew it would upset you, and I went anyway. I guess we're both just suckers for that spontaneous SOB. I'm glad you called. The warden is pointing to the clock: time to go. See you at school after the holidays."

"You know it. Bye, Schmaddie."

The week after Christmas, I got a letter from Wyatt with updates on Samantha and Brian's marriage. He apologized many times and begged me to write back, but I couldn't bring myself to do it—not yet. He wrote that Samantha and Brian bought a home in Highgate, which was not far from my grandparents' house. Highgate was a great town, and they loved their neighbors. I imagined the front of their house with a wrap-around porch and an American flag flying on the post out front. *I wonder how long it'll take before they have their first baby.* His letter continued:

Sarah continues to take voice lessons and has sung at the occasional Whalers' hockey game. I think she's going places with this singing career. I have some sad news to report: Mr. Silk's dog, Freckles, died over the winter. He was fourteen years old, and one morning Mr. Silk woke up to find Freckles had passed away in his sleep. Mr. Silk mourns for his dog and ended up burying Freckles' ashes on his property. I wouldn't be surprised if Mr. Silk or his daughter, Kitty, get a new dog someday soon. It would be a great comfort to Mr. Silk, not to mention a great companion.

The construction crews are still taking trees down in the Black Forest. I just hope our tree will remain, but I'm not sure it can be saved; only a couple hundred trees remain. I'll make a point of going out to look for our tree soon. Can I still call it our tree? I carved "SW, MW, SW, TW, WW, TW, SW," with the date of 1984 at the bottom. I'm hoping that if someone is cutting the trees down and comes upon this one with all the initials, they'll think twice before cutting it down.

I'm still working a part-time job at Stewart's. Riley's grandmother has hired more help so Megan and Riley don't have to work full-time.

Callie, I miss you so much. I just want to make everything like it used to be. What can I do to make you believe that was not me? I love you, and I need to know that you still care for me. If you have any feelings at all left for me, think about this: I told my roommate that I would help him move back home the first weekend of February. He lives in Connecticut, of all places. I want to see you that weekend, but only if you want me to. I'll stop by your dorm that Saturday around four in the afternoon, and if you're there and want to see me, it's simple—just answer your door. If you don't, well, then I guess I'll know where we stand.

I love you, Cal.

Love,

Wyatt

I had one month to make a decision.

ભ ભ ભ

Christmas break ended and school had resumed in full swing.

"Hey, Cal, what're you doing tonight?" Maddie asked as she popped her head through my door.

"Probably just hanging here to get my psych presentation done. It's due Friday, and I just have to tweak it a little bit. Why, what's going on?"

"I just feel like doing something fun before I have to go back to prison this weekend."

Feeling bad for her, I agreed to go out. "Sure, I'll do something with you. Just give me until around seven. I have a class at three, and then I'll come back to get the rest of this done."

She smiled and left, saying, "Okie dokie." She must have had some big plans, because she was in a great mood. I finished up with my class at four and went to the library, then to the cafeteria for a quick dinner so that I could get back to my room and finish my presentation. By six forty-five, I had finished—just enough time to jump in the shower, change, and be ready to go by seven fifteen. There was a deafening thumping beat coming from Maddie's room. When I knocked, she had to holler, "Come in," over the music.

"Hey, you ready?" I asked, as she sat in her robe, putting on her makeup.

"Almost, gotta finish my war paint." She lit the end of a black eyeliner pencil with her lighter to melt the material, blew on it, and then applied it to her eyelids.

"Where we headed tonight?" I asked, as she finished up.

"I'm not sure. Frankie's coming by to pick us up at seven thirty, after he gets off work."

I had an uneasy feeling about that, but rather than say anything, I went along with the plan. She stood up to get dressed, while I hung out in my room. Frankie showed up at seven forty-five. "You ladies ready?"

We walked to his brown Camaro, and he pulled something from his pocket, saying, "I have a little surprise for you, baby." He handed a little plastic bag to Maddie.

"Ooooh, Frankie, you're the best!" Maddie lunged at Frankie's neck and wrapped her arms around him. We ended up at a college bar called The Library where everyone got in regardless of their age. We thought this name was so clever because if your parents happened to call unexpectedly, your friends could honestly say you were at the library.

Frankie found a spot in the back of the parking lot, away from the other cars, and as soon as we stopped, Maddie brought whatever substance was in that baggy to her nose and snorted loudly. "Oh, yeah," she sniffed. "It's been such a long time. Thank you, baby!" she said, and kissed Frankie.

At that point, I was about to crawl out of my skin. "Maddie, you sure you should be doing this again? I mean"—I looked back and forth from Maddie to Frankie and back again—"you just got out of rehab."

"I'm fine. I can handle this stuff. You wanna try it?"

"No, thanks. I'm going inside to see who's here." I quickly got out of the car and went to the front of the building. The music traveled through the building and out the door while the smell of pizza surrounded me; three slices for a dollar on Wednesdays. I showed my college ID to the bouncer at the door, and with disinterest, he let me in.

Maddie and Frankie stayed back in the car for another twenty minutes or so before I saw them come through the front door. When they reached me, I could see that they were both out of their minds, higher than kites. Maddie's eyes were dilated, and she kept rubbing her nose where the residual white powder was evident. My heart sank. We danced for a while, until Maddie was sweating profusely and became jittery.

"You okay, Mad?"

"Yeah, what? Why? I'm fine." Frankie remained draped over her shoulder, and the scene repulsed me. At that moment, I saw Charlie walk in. I waved him down. I'd never been so happy to see someone.

"Charlie! Am I glad to see you!" I said, hugging him tightly.

Concerned, he asked, "What's wrong?"

I proceeded to tell him what Frankie and Maddie were up to.

"Oh, man. That stinks."

"I know. Can I hang out with you?" No sooner had the words left my mouth than I saw a girl walking toward us.

"Sure. Shannon, this is Callie. She's gonna hang out with us tonight." Shannon looked me up and down, then looked back at Charlie. She was less than thrilled about this new development. We stayed long enough to eat a few slices of pizza and watch Maddie make a complete fool of herself. *Enough.* Walking to the door, I said, "Charlie, I'm heading home. This is too much to watch." I went over to Maddie, "I'm going back to the dorm. You staying here with Frankie?"

Frankie, still wrapped around Maddie like a spider monkey, said, "She's fine. I'll get her home later." Disgusted, I turned to leave.

"Hey, Callie, wait a sec," Charlie called. "You're not just gonna walk home from here alone. Let us give you a ride." Shannon rolled her eyes.

"Nah, Charlie, it's okay, I can…"

"You can what? Get kidnapped or worse? Yeah, no, not on my watch. We'll take you home." I sat in the back of Charlie's car as Shannon territorially took the front seat. An awkward silence fell upon us as Charlie drove past my dorm to the lower quad. He pulled over, put the car in park, and walked Shannon to her dorm, saying goodbye with a hug. I was pretty sure that was the last date they would have.

"I'm sorry. I totally blew that date for you."

"It's not a problem. She wasn't really into me anyway." I didn't feel like going back to the dorm to sit and wait for Maddie, so I offered, "Wanna Toddle?" He started the car, and we drove to our favorite late-night spot. We sat at a booth and talked for hours. I'd missed this; I'd missed my Charlie. I was so comfortable. I felt completely content leaving the restaurant, feeling better than I had all night.

"Thanks, Charlie, for saving me tonight."

"Anytime. You know I'd do anything for you." We drove into the student parking garage and saw three police cars speed by with lights flashing, followed by an ambulance.

Having left Charlie with a hug, I walked up the stairs to my room to find it empty. Thank God. I was hoping to see Maddie back in her room, but knowing Frankie, he'd probably insisted she go back to his place for the night. Too tired to worry, I climbed into bed.

The next morning, Deidra, my RA, came knocking at my door. "Callie, can I come in?" The clock read nine. I had to be at class by ten thirty.

"Sure, hang on a sec." I climbed out of bed and opened the door. Deidra pulled out my desk chair and took a seat.

"So, I have a couple of things to talk to you about. Number one, your roommate and her boyfriend won't be an issue for you anymore. She's moving into off-campus housing with Mark, which will be effective immediately. I really don't care what she does with her boyfriend, she just can't do it in our dorm," she said, smiling. "The second reason for my visit concerns Maddie."

I got that sinking feeling in the pit of my stomach.

"I don't know if you're aware of this, but her mom called last night around ten thirty. She said she couldn't reach Maddie in her dorm room, so she contacted me. Just so you know, I am aware of her past. Her parents came to talk to me before the start of classes. I promised I would keep an eye on her, and we've been in close contact throughout the school year. After I went to check her room and no one was there, I did some investigating. One of my friends is the bouncer down at The Library, and I gave him a call to see if he may have seen her. He told me he had.

"I don't know how else to tell you this, but Maddie relapsed and accidentally overdosed last night. She was taken to Hartford Hospital for observation and to wait for her body to work through the drug she took. According to her mom, it was a rough night: Maddie had several close calls, but the doctors think she's been through the worst of it and should make a full recovery. Needless to say, she won't be back at school for the rest of the school year, and possibly not next year. I'm sorry I have to be the bearer of such bad news," she said this as she stood up and placed a hand on my shoulder. "Do you have any questions? Anything you want to ask me about Maddie?"

"I ... don't know what to say," I admitted, rattled by the news.

"Well, if something comes up and you want to talk about it, don't hesitate to come down to my room. If I hear any more news, I'll let you know." She left the room and closed the door behind her.

I just stood there dumbfounded. Then, another knock on my door; this time it was Liz. "Cal, you there?"

I opened the door, and judging by the look on Liz's face, Deidra had told her the news, as well. She came in, we hugged, then we sat on the floor commiserating.

CHAPTER 47

January's drama left a hole in my heart. Liz did the best she could to fill Maddie's shoes, but it just wasn't the same. I had a chance to speak to Maddie a few times on the phone, just to make sure she was really going to be okay.

"Schmallie, I'll be fine," she said weakly. "I just need time to rest and kick this stupid addiction I have. Now go have fun with Charlie, or get that boyfriend of yours back and bang the shit out of him. Not for nothin', but you've got a life to live; stop worrying about mine."

"I really wish you were here. Do you realize the first weekend of February is this weekend? Wyatt will be here on Saturday. What do I do when he gets here? I'm not sure I'm ready to see him."

"Grab him, throw him on your bed, and have your way with him. No, seriously, all kidding aside, you'll know what to do when you hear the knock."

ଓ   ଓ   ଓ

Knock, knock, knock. At four twenty-five p.m., I sat on my bed listening to Wyatt patiently knock on the door. *Knock, knock, knock.* "Cal? You in there? Ah, man," I heard him utter under his breath.

I dropped the pillow I had been holding and slowly walked to the door. "I'm here," I confessed, as I opened the door. He had his back turned as if he were about to leave. He turned toward me, clutching a bouquet of wildflowers he had tied together with twine. "Are those for me?" I asked, genuinely surprised.

Apprehensively, he said, "Yep, for the pretty lady," and handed them to me. We stood at the door, looking at each other uncomfortably.

"Is it all right if I come in?"

"Sure," I said, as I stepped aside. Closing the door behind me, I turned to him as he sat on my bed.

"Is it okay that I sit here? I can move ..."

I nodded, and sat on my former roommate's bed.

"Okay, I'll just start. I really needed to see you. I don't know how to explain my behavior at the wedding, other than I was drunk. I had no idea the champagne was going to hit me so hard, and then I was looking at you on the dance floor, and I just thought you were so beautiful; I just couldn't control myself," he rambled.

"Wyatt, that's no excuse for the way you treated me in that closet. I told you to stop, and you didn't listen to me." Looking directly in his eyes, I said, "You scared me."

He looked down at his hands. "I'm so sorry. I just got carried away. I knew you were leaving me again, and I was so close to you, and you smelled so good ... I know it's no excuse."

I felt like he was being completely honest with me, and in an instant, I made up my mind. Standing, he walked to the window and looked out at the adjacent dorm. I walked to him and placed a hand on his back. "What if we try to put this behind us and start again, slowly?"

He turned to me, relieved, and gathered me in his arms. "I thought I was going to lose you," he whispered.

When we parted, I looked out at the adjacent dorm and saw Charlie looking back. My stomach turned. *Is it possible to have feelings for two guys at the same time.* Turning from the window, I took Wyatt's hand, and we sat on my bed together. "What are you doing the rest of the weekend?" I asked him.

"I told my buddy I would come by later tonight to see how the move is coming along. I can cancel those plans, though," he said hopefully.

"No, you should stick to that plan. Moving stinks, and I'm sure he could use an extra hand."

Disappointed, he said, "Can I see you tomorrow?"

"Yes, but I was thinking more along the lines of later tonight when you are finished with your friend's move."

Smiling broadly now, he said, "I'm going to make this the fastest move in history. I shouldn't be much later than ten."

"Just meet me at the side door of the building, and I'll let you in."

He gently hugged me and left through that side door. These uneasy feelings kept creeping into my thoughts. *His hugs just don't feel the same. I'm not feeling those familiar butterflies in my belly. What am I doing?*

For the next few hours, I busied myself with homework and a shower. I put a silk scarf over my desk lamp and found an easy-listening station on the radio to prepare for Wyatt's return. *Crack.* That familiar pebble to the window; I knew it well. I raced down to the side door, and to my surprise, found Charlie. *Cue the butterflies.*

CHAPTER 48

"Hey, Callie." He looked nervous. "I know Wyatt was here earlier; I saw him leaving your dorm. I was wondering if we could do something tonight now that he's gone."

Damn it, Charlie, why couldn't you have come into my life sooner? Feeling torn, I confessed, "Oh, geez, Charlie, thanks, but he just went out for a little bit. That's his truck right there, driving into the garage. Can we do something next week sometime?"

Dejected, he said, "Yeah, sure, it's cool, fine, no biggie." Just as Charlie turned to leave, Wyatt walked up.

"Hi," Wyatt said, sizing up Charlie.

"Wyatt, this is my friend, Charlie. Charlie, this is Wyatt."

They shook hands, and Charlie said, "Should I go? Yeah, I should go. Well, you guys have a good night. I'll be next door if you need me," he said, looking in my direction.

"What was that all about?" Wyatt asked suspiciously as Charlie walked away.

"Nothing. Come on inside," I invited, feeling oddly disconnected to Wyatt at the moment.

"Does he always come by like that at night?" he questioned me as we walked into my dorm room. With his questioning, I felt like I needed to defend my friend. Not sure how to respond, I ventured, "Most days I just see him on campus, but sometimes he stops by unexpectedly."

"Hmmm," he said, brooding.

"Wyatt, he's just a friend." Turning to him, I put my arms around his neck and ran my hands down to his chest. He reached over and turned off the overhead light so that there was only a soft glow from the desk lamp.

"Are you sure you want to do this?" he asked, touching my face softly. I nodded my head.

"Or this?" he said, as he ran his hand down my back, kissing my neck.

Breathlessly, I said, "Yes."

He began working his way from my head to my toes with impossible gentleness. His kisses were light as air—a complete 180 from the coatroom—and my head was spinning. Standing in a pile of clothes in the middle of the room, Wyatt picked me up and laid me down on my bed. From the way he was taking his time with me, I could tell he wanted this to take a while. He was patient, and when I began to breathe rapidly, he would slow down and start the process all over again. He was driving me crazy and enjoying the torturous game. Finally, I couldn't take it anymore.

"Please ..."

With a wicked smile, he slowly quickened to a frenzied pace and caused me to whimper. As I was trying to catch my breath, he rolled to my right side.

Slowing his breath, he said, "Wow, what got into you?"

"Me? You started it," I smiled.

Laughing, he admitted, "Yes, I did, and I loved every second of it. Let's do that again."

☙   ☙   ☙

After that visit from Wyatt, we seemed to get back on track. Things were going really well, and I couldn't wait until summer vacation. The school year ended pretty quietly. My presentations were over; my exams were completed. My runs around campus became exercises in contemplation, though the same thought ran through my head each time: *Hurry up and wait ...*

My parents came to campus to help me pack. Charlie was waiting by my parents' car when we were finished. He must have seen us loading the car through his window.

"Hi, Mr. and Mrs. Lamply. I'm Charlie Canfield. It's a pleasure to meet you." My mom and dad shook his hand. Mom's look said, *who is this, and why haven't I heard you mention his name?*

"Charlie lives in the dorm right there," I said, pointing. "We met in October, and we've become really good friends." Turning to Charlie, I said, "Have a great summer. I'll miss you. Thanks for such a great year."

I gave him a huge bear hug that, quite honestly, I didn't want to end, and he said, "You have fun in Vermont. Can't wait to hear all about it." Whispering, he said, "Well, almost all of it." Mom and I said one last goodbye to Charlie and climbed into my mom's Chevrolet. Dad now had to help Jimmy clear out his room and cram his things into the Impala.

ભ ભ ભ

June, 1985

One last sleep and we were headed back to camp for the summer. I was impatient to get out of there. We arrived in Vermont on June 20, on a beautiful summer's day, and had the camp to ourselves. Gramp had told Dad that he and Nanny would join us when they could. Watching my grandparents age was hard, in part because it made me think of my parents aging, which caused me a great deal of anxiety ... *don't go there* ...

With only two bats in the cabin this year, we managed to settle in pretty easily. The windows were all propped open and the breeze flowed through the camp, allowing all the stale air to vacate the premises. Wyatt had stopped in while we were getting our things organized. He said that he and his dad were going on a fishing trip with Tommy up in Canada for two weeks and were leaving Saturday.

Really? "Well, good for you, bad for me," I complained, disappointed and slightly annoyed.

Wyatt said, "I'm so sorry. I know this is terrible timing. It was really the only time my dad had to take my brother and me fishing and do some chest beating." He beat his chest. I couldn't help but smile. "The place Dad's renting has no electricity, so everything will be lit by kerosene lamps, and we'll be grilling from charcoal. Old school."

For the next three days, Wyatt and I hung out a lot on the lake when he wasn't working. He did mention that, because of this vacation, he would have to work extra hours when he returned. Another bummer.

At five thirty in the morning on Saturday, I heard Wyatt's truck crunching down the gravel road. I rolled over, and reluctantly, fell back asleep; there was no one to hang out with today. When I woke hours later, the sky reflected my mood: overcast and gloomy. I looked through my selection of books, and while flipping through one of my mysteries, a slip of paper fluttered to the floor. Picking it up, I read Charlie's address. I'd forgotten that he gave it to me on the day I left, and that I'd haphazardly tucked it away in one of my books. Searching for paper and a pen, I decided to write him.

Dear Charlie,

Surprise! It's me. How'd the transition home go for you? Mine went pretty smoothly, and now I'm in Vermont. My address is on the envelope if you'd like to write back.

Can you believe this? Wyatt is going to be gone fishing for two weeks with his dad and brother, and I'm stuck here with my family, bored. Guess I'm going to get a lot of reading done this summer.

We managed to clear out two bats while opening the camp. Without Freckles around (Mr. Silk's dog) it's really quiet around here. Stubby used to chase Freckles around, barking relentlessly. You would think that they really despised each other, but an odd thing happened when we arrived. Stubby jumped from the car, barking and running to Mr. Silk's cabin like he does every summer. When he kept barking and there was no Freckles around, he didn't know what to do with himself. I watched as he circled and circled the spot that Freckles used to sit in next to Mr. Silk and began whimpering. He looked so sad. I feel like Stubby up here, without a friend.

Well, I guess I should close the letter now. Write when you can.
-Callie

I stuck a stamp on the envelope and walked to the mailbox to deposit the letter. For several days I struggled to keep busy in Wyatt's absence. By day six, though, I got a surprise. Charlie's return letter caught me off guard. Grabbing a drink of water in the kitchen after a run, I noticed his letter sitting on the counter next to Dad's newspaper. Happily, I took it to my room to read.

Dear Callie,

Thanks for the surprise! I didn't think I would be hearing from you this summer, and there you were in my mailbox. Sounds like a great place up there. I'd love to see it for myself sometime. Your poor dog! I kind of feel like Stubby myself; I miss my friend, too.

I'm working this summer with the maintenance crew for parks and recreation in my town. I'm working a ton, and because of all the hours I'm putting in, I'm getting a great tan—but I'm totally overdue for a little vacation time.

Write soon,

Charlie

Really? That's it? That was disappointing to read. First Wyatt left me, now Charlie's leaving me hanging? What a way to start my summer. There were nine more sleeps until Wyatt returned, and a girl could only read so many books. Now what was I going to do? Two days later, my question was answered.

CHAPTER 49

When I got home from my morning run, which frankly, was two miles too long, I slowed as I approached the water pump. I'd started to walk to my tree when I noticed Charlie on the gravel road ahead of me. Unable to process the fact that Charlie was walking toward me, I stopped and stared.

"How…Wha…?" I stammered, confused.

Laughing, Charlie said, "Hi, Cal! Hope you don't mind my unexpected visit. I was thinking about Wyatt going fishing with his dad and brother for two weeks and how bored my friend was going to be; I decided, since I wanted to take a little vacation, what better place than Franklin, Vermont?"

"What a nice surprise!" Genuinely happy to see him, we embraced.

"Where you headed?" he asked, looking in the direction of the Black Forest.

"I was just going to stretch over by my tree. Wanna see it?"

"Lead the way," he said, allowing me to pass.

I felt like I was being watched when we walked past the Wilsons' house. As we passed their yard, Sarah was sitting on the deck, shucking a bag of corn; I waved.

"Who's that?"

"That's Wyatt's little sister, Sarah. So this is it," I said, touching the initials carved into my tree.

"Huh, impressive. All these initials are from your family?"

"Yep. Hey, Charlie, how long are you sticking around?"

"Well, I didn't know if you'd be upset with this surprise or not, so I guess I was just thinking today, why?"

"Because that's a long drive to take twice in one day. Let me check with my folks to see if you can stay until tomorrow. Wait here."

I left him at my tree and ran back to the cabin. When I returned, Sarah stood at the tree talking to Charlie. I didn't really like this development; it could only mean trouble.

"...yeah, I'm just in town to visit the Lamplys for a few days," I overheard Charlie say.

"Hi, Sarah. What's going on?" I asked, sounding a little too friendly.

"Oh, nothing. Wyatt comes home this weekend, ya know," she said with a naughty little grin, just for me.

"Great! All righty, well, it's been great to see you," I replied. "We're gonna head out in the boat now. See you later."

"Yeah, you do that," Sarah bit.

"Why do I get the feeling she's not too happy about this?" Charlie asked, pointing at himself, then at me, and then back at himself.

I sighed deeply. "Because she's not."

We walked to the cabin, and I asked Dad if he could take Charlie and me out in the boat. We spent the remainder of the afternoon zip sledding and skiing on the lake. I could tell Dad liked Charlie from the way he was laughing at all of Charlie's bad jokes. As we rode past Rock Island and slowed to return to the dock, Sarah stood watching us from the rope swing.

Jimmy came whistling into the cabin after seeing Riley at the exact moment Charlie and I walked in. Instantly, his whistling stopped. "Charlie? What are you doing here?"

"Hey, Jimmy! Wait, Jimmy? You and Callie are related?" Charlie asked Jimmy, dumbfounded.

"Yeah. How do you know my sister?" Jimmy asked.

"Hold up. You know each other?" I asked, flabbergasted.

"Callie and I have friends in common at school," Charlie answered Jimmy. Then he looked at me and said, "Yeah, we had speech class together, and he and I were on the same debate team for an assignment."

"Holy cow, it's a small world," I said, amazed.

ଔ   ଔ   ଔ

That evening, while Charlie and I were washing the dinner dishes, Jimmy was sitting at the kitchen counter, talking about school.

"Jimmy, can we not talk about school? It's summer break," Charlie said, smiling.

"Okay. You guys done yet? I'm ready to beat the pants off you guys in cards."

"Can you tell he's a little competitive?" I said to Charlie, nudging his arm with my elbow.

Putting the dish towel down, he said, "Me, too." When I looked at him, I sensed he wasn't talking about cards.

CHAPTER 50

"Charlie, I'm sorry we don't have better accommodations for you. We weren't expecting any houseguests," Mom said, embarrassed.

"Mrs. Lamply, this is perfect. Thank you for letting me crash here tonight. I really wasn't looking forward to driving another seven hours."

"It's our pleasure. Any friend of Callie and Jimmy is a friend of ours," she said, placing a pillow and comforter on the living-room couch. "Kids, it's getting late, and I'm heading to bed. If I stay up any later, I'll turn into a pumpkin. Sleep well," she said, kissing me on the cheek.

"Night, Dad," I called out to Dad in their bedroom.

"Night, kids," Dad called back.

"You tired?" Charlie asked me after Mom left the room.

"Not really, you?" Charlie shook his head.

Out walked Jimmy: "I'm headed to Riley's for a while. See you tomorrow, Charlie?" Jimmy asked as he walked to the door.

"Yeah, but I'll be leaving sometime in the morning." Jimmy smiled and gave a thumbs-up as he left.

We walked out to the front of the cabin and down the dock stairs. We sat on the dock and talked for a while.

"You have a great family, Cal."

"Thanks, I think so, too," I said, smiling. "They seem to like you a lot. How weird is it that you and Jimmy know each other?"

"I didn't know what his last name was all this time; so strange," he said with a laugh. "Your brother and I had a great time in that class. He can be pretty goofy."

"And you aren't?" I laughed. Stretching, I said, "I think I'm gonna hit the hay. I'm so glad you came to visit. It was such a nice surprise." With a hug, Charlie and I walked back to the cabin.

∽ ∽ ∽

Just as I was falling asleep, I felt the weight of someone sitting on the side of my bed. I opened my eyes and could see in the dark that it was Charlie.

"Callie? Cal? You awake?"

"What's wrong? Can't sleep?" I asked, concerned.

"You should know me better than that. I don't sleep much; why else do you think I come to your room at three in the morning at school?" This made me smile. "I know I'm leaving tomorrow and your regularly scheduled life will continue with Wyatt's return. I just wanted the opportunity to tell you … that … I like you."

"I like you, too, Charlie. You're one of my best friends."

"Yeah, but I *like* you like you. I can't help it. I know you have Wyatt, but at school, we have so much fun and get along so well that I guess I just wish I were your Wyatt," he said bashfully.

This touching sentiment caught me off guard, and I didn't know what to say. I sat up next to him on my bed. "Charlie …"

He leaned in slowly with a cautious kiss. I kissed him back, feeling a need surface, one I didn't know I had for him. I pulled my head back. "Charlie, I'm so sorry. I'm so confused. I don't know what I'm doing. I really like you, but it's complicated."

Running his thumb over my lips, he said, "You don't have to say any more. The fact that you have doubts gives me hope. I just wanted to tell you how I felt before I left in the morning. Go back to sleep." He walked out of the room and went back to the couch, leaving my mind reeling. As I rolled over in bed, the moonlight cast a ray of light onto my ring, causing a strange hue of red to climb the wall. For a fleeting moment, my hand seemed to have the weight of the world on it. As quickly as the sensation struck, it was gone.

True to his word, Charlie left after breakfast the next morning. *What have I gotten myself into*? I had four days to stew in my mess before Wyatt rolled back into town.

The Saturday of his return felt like Christmas. I was so excited to see him and willingly tried to put my feelings for Charlie on the back burner. Once I heard that familiar truck coming down the gravel road, I ran out to greet him. Waving, they tooted the horn as they passed. After unloading all the fishing poles and gear, he came over to camp, picked me up in his arms, and swung me around. Something felt different.

"Eesh, Wyatt, I can tell you guys have been roughing it. You need a shower."

"Really? It's that bad?"

I nodded. He put me down and asked if I wanted to have a "shower", too. So, I went inside, put my suit on and met him at his dock—where he was already in and getting lathered up. I floated around him on a raft as he continued to scrub. We had a lazy afternoon of floating on the lake, but all the while, I couldn't shake Charlie from my thoughts.

We talked about his absence and what I did to keep busy. Trying to talk around Charlie's visit, I decided to tell him more about Maddie. He said he'd seen what drugs could do to a person firsthand.

"Samantha's old boyfriend, a few years back, was addicted to coke, which totally messed him up. She wanted to help the guy, but he was so deep into drugs that he didn't think he needed the help. They eventually broke up, and I heard he's been in and out of rehab several times. It's a tough drug to get clean from. I hope, for your sake, your friend can overcome her demons."

Things seemed to be going well, and we were getting back into our summer routine. Charlie slowly stopped interrupting my thoughts ... until mid-July.

CHAPTER 51

I'd just returned from picking blackberries with my mom when I noticed an unhappy Wyatt sitting on a swing on the rusted swing set.

"Hey there," I said, as cheerfully as possible.

"Hey. Hi, Mrs. Lamply," he said flatly.

"Hello, Wyatt. Will you be staying for lunch?"

"No, I don't think so. Thank you," he said, staring at me.

"All right, but you might change your mind when you see what I'm about to whip up with these berries," Mom said, smiling as she went inside.

"Everything all right, Wyatt?" I asked nervously.

"No, I don't think so," he scowled.

"What's going on?" My stomach was turning inside out.

"Sarah was just filling me in about your visitor while I was gone."

I wanted to throw up. "Wyatt ..."

"When were you going to tell me?"

"I didn't think it was worth discussing. He's my friend, and he wanted to surprise me." I tried to sound unimpressed.

"How convenient," he spat. I could see his anger rising. "Is this what it's going to be like? Every time I have to go anywhere, are you going to have your *friend* visit?"

"That's unfair, Wyatt. Besides, I came up this summer looking forward to our time together to find that the first two weeks of summer break, you were going fishing with your dad. How do you think I felt about that? We haven't seen each other for months, and you decide to go on a fishing trip? Plus, I had no idea that Charlie was coming up for a visit," I said, enunciating every word, speaking much louder than I had anticipated.

"Where'd he sleep?" he asked, like he knew the answer.

"On the couch—not that it's any of your business." Now I was getting upset. "What exactly are you insinuating?" I could feel my eyes brimming with tears.

Seething, he spat, "How *friendly* was he?"

"You think we slept together? Boy, you're not giving me a whole lot of credit here," I whispered to him, looking around.

"Well, did you?" Wyatt asked, a little too loudly.

"No. I would hope you'd think more highly of me than that." With angry tears falling, I said, "Happy now? Just leave, Wyatt. It's obvious you think you know what took place while you were gone, so just go home. If you want, we can talk about it when you calm down."

"Oh, I think I'm done talking about it; I have a pretty clear picture of what happened between you and your *friend*, thanks to Sarah." He got off the swing and pushed it so hard it wound around the top of the swing set. I let him storm off.

I thought he would simmer down and come back later that evening, but I didn't see him for the next few weeks. When he did resurface, he wasn't friendly toward me at all. He was at the pump with Sarah as I began my run. Sarah looked at me with a huge grin on her face—very pleased with herself.

"Hi, Wyatt." Glaring in Sarah's direction, I said, "Sarah."

"Hi," Wyatt said in monotone.

"Wyatt, can we talk later?"

"I'm not sure what more we have to talk about," he said abruptly.

"I'll come over after my run," I said over my shoulder as I passed them, running up the hill, leaving before he could reply.

∞   ∞   ∞

"Hi, Mrs. Wilson, is Wyatt home?" I asked when she opened the door.

"It's nice to see you, Callie. It's been a while. No, he's not home at the moment. Can I leave him a message for you?" she said nervously.

"No, thank you," I said, as Mrs. Wilson closed the door. Before it was completely shut, I got a quick glimpse of Wyatt leaving through the back door. I ran around the house just in time to see him walking into the Black Forest; I followed, just paces behind. As he walked to my tree, I saw him pull out a Swiss Army knife, and as I approached, I saw that he was slashing through the WW + CL.

"Is that really how you feel?" I asked, feeling my throat constrict.

Surprised, he turned around to look at me. "Yeah, that's how I feel. This doesn't feel the same anymore. I thought what we had was real. I mean, the real deal, like happily ever after and until-death-do-us-part kinda thing. I gave you my heart, and you just ripped it to pieces. I'm not willing to share you, and you aren't exactly willing to be with only me." As I watched him continue to whittle away at the initials, he said, "After I met Charlie up at your school, I could tell he was attracted to you; I could see it in his eyes. I tried to get past it, and for a while, I did, but then after hearing about his visit, I couldn't pretend it didn't bother me anymore. Something is going on, whether you want to tell me about it or not. I can feel it."

I felt like he had just read my mind, so I couldn't disagree with him. An honest answer was what Wyatt deserved.

"I'm so confused. I don't know how else to say it. It hasn't changed the fact that I love you."

"Don't say that. Don't say you love me and you're confused in the same breath. You need to make up your mind and decide."

This was one decision I wasn't prepared to make on the spot. "I can't do that, and if you can't give me the space to think things through, then I guess … I guess we're done here." Feeling the weight of that ruby, I began to twirl it around my finger. With a heavy heart, I walked back to camp.

CHAPTER 52

During those last few days before we packed up camp to head home, my parents received some news about the memorial for the Marines unit. Mr. and Mrs. Wilson came over to the house one afternoon to discuss the memorial. Apparently, they had been speaking with some of the folks at Camp Lejeune in North Carolina, and it seemed that the work had begun. The Wilsons told my parents that, hopefully, in October of 1986, they would have it completed—just in time for the anniversary of the bombing. They had some of it completed already but were still waiting for approval to get funding for the second part of the memorial.

Jimmy and Riley were in on this conversation, as well, and were equally excited about the prospect. I sat in my room and eavesdropped on their conversation; my heart just wasn't in it enough to walk into the room and discuss the particulars. As important as I knew completing this memorial was, I didn't feel as excited, knowing that Wyatt wasn't going to be standing beside me at the unveiling. I looked at the brittle flowers that were dying on my nightstand and decided what had to be done. My hands were shaking as I wrote my final letter to Wyatt.

Dear Wyatt,

I guess it's no longer bye for now; it's just goodbye. I'm not sure when I'll see you again, and that hurts my heart. I'm sorry that I'm confused. I'm sorry I have feelings for two people. I don't know how else to tell you how I feel. I love you with all my heart, but Charlie is my best friend, and I'm not sure yet how I feel about him. I don't want to hurt you any more than I already have, so I've decided to return your promise ring. How can I promise to be true to only you if I have doubts? This is the hardest thing I've had to figure out in my life, and I just wanted to be honest with you. You don't have faith in me, and that trust is gone. I get that. It doesn't make it any easier to say goodbye.

I'll love you forever,

Callie

With my eyes welling up, I took Wyatt's promise ring and placed it in an envelope with my letter. I sealed the envelope and set out to place it in my tree.

ରେ   ରେ   ରେ

Back at school, starting my sophomore year of college, I pushed Wyatt into the recesses of my mind. I felt numb about the breakup with my first love. Who would have thought it would be this painful? I tried to concentrate on schoolwork and cultivating new friendships, but it was difficult. My one saving grace was Charlie. I told him what happened when Sarah gave an eyewitness account of his visit to Wyatt. He gave me some space to mourn the end of my relationship, and I appreciated that. We hadn't seen each other much since my return. He realized that I was fragile and still a bit confused about my feelings.

One afternoon, while I was walking to class with Liz, I heard his voice from behind us. "Hey, Callie. Hi, Liz," he said, smiling at us both.

"Hi, Charlie. Hey, Cal, I'll catch up with you later. I gotta run to the library," Liz said, squeezing my hand. "We'll chat later."

As I walked with Charlie, he said, "How are you? I haven't seen you around in a few weeks. Everything all right?"

Sarcastically, I said, "Yeah, everything's peachy. Who needs a heart anyway?"

"You're still smarting from your breakup, huh?" he said, putting his hands in his pockets.

"I guess, yeah."

"I'm sorry you're hurting. It sucks to have to go through that." Raising a hand up in front of him, clearing his throat, he said, "I vow to help make your life easier and more fun from here on out."

Smiling, I said, "Thanks, I look forward to it. Being depressed is so exhausting. Bring on the fun!"

ೞ   ೞ   ೞ

That fall continued smoothly because Charlie was a man of his word. We Toddled several times in the wee hours of the morning. On a few occasions, he took me on afternoon excursions through Connecticut. We went to Gillette Castle, the Science Center, and even to Mystic Seaport. He was being a good friend, and I began to think that I'd dreamt up the time we kissed at camp—until one afternoon while we were walking through a local park and he took hold of my hand. I noticed the differences and similarities between his hand and Wyatt's. Charlie's hands were full of rough calluses from building his loft in his dorm room, callused like Wyatt's, yet his rough hand gently stroked mine.

"Cal?" he asked.

"Hmmm?" I murmured, feeling content walking hand in hand.

"Do you ever wonder what would have happened if you had met me before Wyatt?"

Turning to him, I said, "Why do you ask?"

"I was just thinking about that. I think if you'd met me first, I would be in Wyatt's shoes right now. I'm sure glad I'm not."

We stood still under a maple tree that was just transforming from green to red. I said, "Everything happens for a reason; it was all meant to work out the way it did. A lot of the time I don't understand the meaning of it all, but for now, this is beginning to feel right." And, for the first time since his visit to Vermont, he leaned down and kissed me.

CHAPTER 53

Knock, knock, knock. "Callista? You home?" Jimmy asked from behind the closed door.

"Yeah, hang on." I unlocked the door and let Jimmy in. "Hey, stranger, what are you doing here?"

"Can't I visit my little sister?" he asked, smiling. "Guess what I just heard from Riley?"

"What?" I said, not knowing what to expect.

"Samantha and Brian had a baby boy yesterday. He weighed seven pounds, eleven ounces and was twenty-two inches long." As he rattled off the stats, I thought, *I didn't even know she was expecting.*

Smiling, I asked, "What did they name him?"

"Tyler Samuel Doyle."

That warmed my heart.

"Riley also told me that the memorial for the Marines has been completed and the memorial service is going to be Thursday, October 23. The Wilson family will be there, and I've been asked to do a reading. I hope you'll come up with Mom and Dad. I know you're still hurting from the breakup, but you could at least be there for Tyler."

ༀ ༀ ༀ

October 23, 1986

In North Carolina at Camp Lejeune, we stood before the Beirut Memorial on a beautiful fall day. The site was located at the entrance of Camp Geiger, a sub-base within Camp Lejeune. The monument was made by the same man who made the famous statue of the flag rising on Suribachi in Arlington. The statue of a Marine stood on a pedestal between two broken walls that were meant to represent the crumbled walls of the building demolished by the truck-bomb attack many years ago. The memorial was right next to a cemetery on the east side of the road that led to Camp Geiger's entrance gate. There was a wall containing all the names of the Marines, sailors, and government personnel who died that fateful day. Families of those soldiers requested that a poem by Robert A. Gannon be added to the memorial. The words "They Came in Peace" were etched into the stone memorial.

The ceremony was emotional, with Mr. and Mrs. Wilson, Tommy, Sarah, Wyatt, and Samantha standing in remembrance of their son and brother. Brian was holding his one-year-old toddler, Tyler Samuel Doyle, in his arms. My family was on hand to witness the unveiling, and with Riley by his side, my brother read aloud a poem he had written for this occasion to the families that had gathered that day.

As I stood and listened to the reading of the poem, my thoughts were of Wyatt. I couldn't help but mourn the end of our relationship. *This is goodbye,* I thought, as I looked at him standing next to his family. Slowly, he turned to gaze in my direction, not with malice or hatred, but with pain. Our eyes locked and my stomach began to knot. I had to look away, and when I looked back in his direction, he had already turned toward Jimmy to listen as he read:

CINDY LYNCH

"They Came in Peace"

These men who came in peace
To save us all from war
Their weapons may have ceased
But these Marines live on no more

They slept among their brothers
No preparing was in store
Awaiting a return to mothers
An evil spirit changed the score.

No longer are they free
To walk among this land
Or help another human being
To simply take a stand

However not in human form
With flesh and blood and heart
They serve a purpose to remind us all
To be loving from the start

Now heads are bowed in memory
Protectors from that beast
Braved life with its uncertainty
These men, they came in peace.

Thank you. Hearing those two words, I turned, expecting to see Wyatt. It was a familiar voice, but as I turned, there was no one there.

When Jimmy finished, he wiped away a stray tear as Riley approached him. She reached for his hand and gave it a gentle squeeze.

Tyler? The breeze had picked up during the reading, and the rustling of the leaves suggested that the lost soldiers were among us, whispering. I felt their appreciation.

December 14, 2012

The buzzing of my phone snaps me out of my reverie and my heart drops as I answer.

"Jimmy? Is Prue with you?"

"I'm waiting in *our* church to hear something. Can you believe this?" he says, and I can hear the hysteria in his voice rising. "Waiting is agony! What if she isn't coming back, Cal? I can't bear the thought of losing my little girl ..." He stops speaking, and I can hear his labored breath as he tries to remain in control. Through the phone, a squeaky door opens and heavy footsteps enter the room.

"I gotta go: the police just came in to talk to us," he says in a hushed voice.

"Okay, let me ..." being impatient, my brother ends the call.

My heart is hurting, and yes, the uncertainty is torture.

Hurry up and wait.

ACKNOWLEDGMENTS

Where to begin with acknowledgments… First, this book would not have been a story at all had my parents not taken my brother and me to Vermont over the years. They are my biggest cheerleaders, and a simple thank you doesn't seem to be a strong enough sentiment, but thank you none the less.

To my husband, John, thank you for riding this crazy roller coaster of life with me. I can't think of anyone else I would want to take this ride with. You are a great strength and a problem solver, even when I don't think I have anything to solve. Thanks for having my back and being my biggest supporter.

Jack, Ian and Michael Lynch, my three beautiful boys, who asked me weekly if my book was done yet. Thank you for your patience and little nuggets of wisdom. I still can't believe I managed to write this story while drum lessons and piano lessons (and maybe some tough brotherly love) were going on all around me.

Sharisse Coulter, without your gentle nudge on Facebook and encouragement throughout this process, I would still be at that Procrastination Station. I thank you, friend, for asking me to take that *little* writing challenge. I would also like to thank you for being patient during the photo shoot. The photos look professional even if the subject was not.

Stacy Dymalski, I thank you for all the long talks in Utah on book writing and for your guidance in the art of self-publishing. I couldn't have done this without your help. Thank you for giving me Keltin Barney and Katie Mullaly's names and contact information. Keltin, I finally found an editor that *gets* me. And Katie, you worked your magic on the interior design of this book, for this I thank you.

Denise Cronin, thank you for taking the time to read the first draft and for listening to me blather on and on about my book. I can't believe I got you to read the last draft after all this time. You have been encouraging me all along, from the book's infancy straight through to its final draft. You went above and beyond the call of friendship on this one.

Julie Stern, my H.L.P., as promised, I am mentioning you in my acknowledgments, so thank you for the insightful idea of a D.H. scene. You are truly one of a kind, my friend.

Cindy Eckenrode, aren't you glad you said you'd help edit? All kidding aside, you worked really hard on this last edit and I truly appreciate your work.

Ivan Terzic, thank you for taking what I pictured in my head and making it come to life on the cover. That's exactly the feel I was looking for. I look forward to working with you again in the near future.

ABOUT THE AUTHOR

Cindy Lynch lived in many states growing up, but still considers Newtown, Connecticut home. Living in Sandy Hook throughout her high school and college years brought her many great memories; many of which occurred up at "Gramp's camp." She always wanted to write a fictionalized memoir of her time on the lake, but never found the time. The Sandy Hook shootings both devastated and resonated with Cindy in a way she couldn't ignore, and the time to bring forward the stored memories of her youth felt more important than ever. These images of her past were woven into a fictional story that became the fabric for "Bye For Now."

After meeting her husband, John, at Central Connecticut State University, they moved to Missouri to be closer to Cindy's family. They live in Chesterfield, Missouri with their three growing boys; Jack, Ian and Michael. When she's not writing, editing or otherwise engaged in writing activities, she's coming up with plot line and character development while running, biking, swimming and spending time with her family.

56813041R00166

Made in the USA
Middletown, DE
26 July 2019